Under the Banyan Tree

A.E.Haig

Copyright © 2020 A.E.Haig
All rights reserved.
ISBN: 9798682216215

*

To Kathryn, thank you for leaving nothing unsaid.
For all that you are, with all that I am.

*

*

For Beth, my sister,
immeasurably more than I could have
ever asked for or *imagined.*

*

CONTENTS

0	The Awakening	3
1	The Therapist	5
2	The Lake	21
3	The Yearbook	31
4	The News	50
5	The Premiere	69
6	The Airport	83
7	The Therapist Part II	93
8	The Social Worker	101
9	The Three	112
10	The New Kid	124
11	The Scan	133
12	The Twin Towers	139
13	The Headhunt	156
14	The Woods	161
15	The Therapist Part III	179
16	The Scripts	183
17	The Gardener	192
18	The Break In	204
19	The Truth	222

20	The Boy With The Brightest Smile	247
21	The Truth Part II	262
22	The Delivery	265
23	The Test Paper	287
24	The Banyan Tree	291
	Acknowledgements	299
	About The Author	301

*

"Dream big, little one."

*

"For it's not that you can, it's that you will."

*

0

THE AWAKENING

London, England, 2018

Ash grabbed the glass of water on his bedside table that night, as the prickly cold sweat crept over the back of his neck. It engulfed his bones with crippling anxiety. He hadn't screamed this time, and, to his relief, Lola was still sleeping peacefully beside him, a gentle smile painted across her pretty face. Panting heavily, Ash gulped down the water. The nightmare had been as vivid as ever.

Why disturb his girlfriend though? There was nothing she could do. After all, she couldn't reassure him that it was just a nightmare. What had happened all those years ago, had happened. It was *real*. Would it haunt his dreams forever? He'd never shared the secret. And no amount of money, fame or success could make it go away.

Ash ran his hand over his face, as he often did, when he felt anxious or stressed. But as he sat there in the stillness, regaining his composure and pushing down the terrified child that lived deep within, he allowed himself to think back to that day, the day which changed everything. And his mind was deeply troubled. It had been years, yet something still didn't add up. Perhaps he just longed so much for it not to be true, that he was trying to convince himself it hadn't happened the way he remembered it? Could it be, his memory had deceived him somehow, and all was not as it seemed? But the more Ash recalled the small details, and pieced together the bare facts, he reminded himself that he wasn't the only person who knew the whole truth, and, to make sense of it all, he needed to find *the others*.

1

THE THERAPIST

London, England, 2018

"I just don't understand what made you do it" Lola said. Concern washed over her attractive face, once more.

Ash hung his head in shame. He pulled his knees up to his chin, desperate to shield his eyes from the television screen opposite them.

"Can't we just forget about it, babe? Please" he begged, slamming his thumb down on the pause button of the remote control, just in time. He couldn't bear to watch it again.

"Forget about it? Ash, it's on TV! It's in all the headlines! This isn't going to go away quickly, whether you like it or not. People know who you are" his girlfriend insisted, pointing at the freezeframe which had been live on Sky television the previous day.

It showed Ash, dressed in his trim designer suit outside the film studios, holding Lola's hand. She was wearing a sparkly silver dress which reflected the dazzles of the flashing cameras. The paparazzi surrounded the handsome young couple. It had not been an uncommon setting for the film director and his girlfriend. The reveal of Ash's film trailer, together with the cast and director interview panel, had gone so well. But when the night was up, and Ash and Lola had made their way towards the limousine, Ash had done something so unprovoked and out of character, that it deeply disturbed Lola and everyone around.

"I don't want to talk about it anymore. I've said I'm sorry!" Ash contended.

But Lola's angst was unyielding.

"It's not about being sorry, Ash. I need to understand why you did it. You need to understand why you did it. It had to have come from somewhere, it doesn't just happen. Not for no reason! And it's not *you*, which is what scares me most. You're so kind Ash, so generous, so good with people-"

"Of course, it isn't me, Lola. I'm not some maniac! Look, I can't talk about it anymore. I can't explain why I did it. You wouldn't understand"

"Well, if you can't explain it to me, I want you to explain it to a counsellor, Ash. Because it's not *normal*"

In response, the film director got up from the king-sized bed in a rage, and stormed across his huge bedroom, slamming the door behind him. There was a small gap in the curtains where the dusty city lights outside streamed in to highlight the interior of his grand penthouse. The piano, armchairs and elaborate ornaments were now all silhouettes with a silver lining.

Ash cringed at his hall of fame as he passed his office, where Lola had placed every BAFTA award, film festival trophy and prestigious photograph of him, in a large cabinet which was illuminated by the glowing internet light on the ground.

He reached the kitchen and gazed out of its glass walls which looked out on night-time London. Ash ran his hand over his face, as he often did, when he felt anxious or stressed. How could he have made such a mistake?

Meanwhile, Lola was immediately regretting her bluntness and how it had caused her boyfriend to feel. Ash had been mortified after he'd done it, she supposed. It's not like he didn't care. But then, why do it in the first place? It didn't make any sense. She longed to understand. The young woman turned down the volume on the TV remote and hit the play button, discretely. And then, she watched yesterday's events back. She watched her past self, holding onto Ash, as they strolled out of the studios, adoring the fans, the stardom, and each other. They were only a few strides down the carpet, when Ash suddenly let go of her and spun around to grab a middle-aged, ginger-haired reporter by the collar, in relentless fury. Ash pulled the man's torso over the silver barrier, and simultaneously held his fist a few inches from the whimpering reporter's face, ready to punch him. Lola stared at the screen in bewilderment, reliving how she'd thrown her hands over her mouth in shock and reached out for her enraged boyfriend, only to be brushed aside by Ash's bodyguards. For a split-second, Ash stared into the reporter's eyes, and then, released his grip on him as quickly as he had taken it up. The bulky security guards soon lifted the good-looking star away from the situation and whisked him straight into the limousine.

Lola rewound the scene and edged closer to the widescreen, razor thin TV, allowing its white light to flood over her stunning Hispanic face, and twinkle within her dark alluring eyes. She had spotted something. She hastily tapped at the settings button on the remote and selected slow motion. And then, hitting the play button once more, she watched with intense curiosity. She watched the reporter move his lips to *say something* in Ash's ear, just a moment before Ash lunged for him.

"What could he possibly have said?" Lola whispered to herself, utterly bewildered.

She thought back to the limousine ride home the previous day, and how she had quizzed Ash.

"What do you mean, you didn't know him?" She had demanded.

To her astonishment, Ash admitted he had never seen the reporter before in his life. The man was a stranger. Ash had then held his head in his hands the entire journey home, repeating,

"I'm sorry."

"I'm sorry" Ash said softly, poking his head through the bedroom door. Startled, Lola almost fell off the bed in her panic to switch off the TV.

"No, I'm sorry, Ash. Sorry for forcing you to talk about it" She said.

Ash wandered shyly up to the bed.

"You don't really think I'm a nutjob, do you?" He asked, perching on top of the duvet.

Lola sighed, and opened up the covers to him.

"Of course not. I know you. I love you" She said soothingly, "I would like you to speak to somebody, though. Not just about this, but about your nightmares too"

To her surprise, he nodded.

"Okay. Okay, I will. I promise"

*

It took Ash a month to visit the therapist. Since he unexpectedly attacked the stranger in the crowd, his agents had spoken to the press, and luckily the story was now yesterday's news. The journalists had written of how the film director was trialing a new medication to cope with the overwhelming stress of his career, that caused an "irrational and impulsive outburst", of which the young star was sorry, and had since stopped the medication. Of course, none of that had been true.

Ash thought he was finally ready. But as he neared the therapist's home, his thumping heartbeat and sweaty palms were telling him otherwise. Why must his body react like this? There was a sickly feeling in his stomach too, which cropped up any time he felt mildly unsafe. And what could feel more uneasy than being forced to talk about your deepest trauma and best kept secrets to a perfect stranger in a state of complete vulnerability? But, he was the one in control, and he willed himself to remember that. *"You don't have to disclose anything you don't want to",* the secretary had reassured him the previous week, over the telephone.

Being one of the most successful men in Britain within his field, meant that it was rare Ash wasn't in control of any situation. Everybody, and all things, seemed to work beneath him and under his authority. Whatever he didn't like he had the power to change. That was the beauty of his success. Anything he wanted, he could buy. Anyone he disliked he could fire. And anybody he was interested in would almost certainly reciprocate his admiration.

And yet, with millions in his bank account, a renowned reputation, and a girlfriend he adored, Ash was a tormented young man. There was an inescapable darkness which lingered in the pit of his soul. This notorious artist, who exuded confidence and could make almost anybody smile with his charm and talent, suppressed waves of guilt that still haunted him whenever he was alone. This hidden and deep-rooted pain made his every victory taste sour, and every triumph sicken him. No joy could be felt when channels of rage sabotaged each fleeting happy thought and an intense remorse kept him awake at night. And this is what Ash had realised in recent months; though he could control many aspects of his life, there was *nothing* he could do, nor be, nor buy, to control the past. The void in his heart had been stealing from him for so long that it was finally ready to consume him; creeping up, uninvited like a thief in the night. This is what compelled Ash to agree to such an unlikely appointment. It was time to face his demons.

Although Asha Anjani Lakhanpal, more famously known as Ash La-Pal, had a net worth of over two hundred and fifty million, he wasn't going to visit a top London psychiatrist or award-winning counsellor. Ash had sought out a low-key, and ultimately quite average, by the world's standards, therapist to counsel him. Though he'd spent the entirety of his adult life working for it, he now needed to get away from the limelight. More than this, he could not risk the paparazzi finding out about his hidden sessions, especially in the light of recent events. He didn't want anybody to know his secrets. He had seen what media coverage and the power of the rumour had done to his co-workers and friends, and it was brutal. He just needed somebody human who would listen to him, somebody quite ordinary, with no bias and no pecuniary interest in his affairs. Somebody *normal*.

All the way out in Harpenden, in a quiet cul-de-sac, lived Geoff Daughtry. Ash had found Geoff on the seventh page of a Google search for 'experienced psychotherapists in Greater London'. In all his reviews, Geoff was heavily praised.

"His experience and wisdom is truly astonishing. Geoff helped me progress in ways I could have never imagined."

"A truly safe place. I can live freely now."

"Humbling and open minded, I felt like I could speak to Geoff about absolutely anything and his input changed everything."

Ash exhaled deeply and ran his hand over his face. Then, he slowly pulled up outside the address in his shiny Bentley Continental and killed the engine. The house was a simple four-bedroomed detached brick property with a neat front lawn and a huddle of purple foxgloves in full bloom in the centre. Ash contemplated turning back for a moment and escaping what he had been trying to block out for most of his adult life but, quite suddenly, a large, striped bumblebee buzzed past his car window and into a streak of falling sunlight, landing on one of the foxgloves in the therapist's front garden. Thrown into an involuntarily trance, Ash was compelled to think back to another *garden*, a garden he once knew only too well but didn't allow himself to think of often. That was why he needed to get out of the car.

Ash La-Pal had released unparalleled stories through motion picture in the past ten years, throughout the UK and beyond. But now it was time, to tell *his* story.

Although he'd tried so hard to forget, it was time for him to *remember*.

Ash left his Hugo Boss suit jacket in a slump on the passenger seat of his car and loosened his tie as he pensively made his way down the driveway, his eyes darting around the silent neighbourhood from behind his Ray-Bans. He passed the bumblebee as it crawled into a foxglove trumpet and gulped. He wished he could crawl into a safe haven right now. But, shielding his nerves, he knocked sharply on the front door using the heavy gold-plated letter box. Not long after, there was a shuffling of footsteps and the twisting of a door handle. A well-kept, short and stocky man in his late fifties answered the door. Ash didn't know what it was about a person that made them look wise but Geoff Daughtry certainly accomplished just this. Was it his neatly combed soft grey hair circling his bald patch? Or his deeply wrinkled forehead, representing one thousand different thoughts? Or his rare emerald eyes, peering through his thick-rimmed round glasses which reflected those of every lost soul who had come his way? Geoff wore a smart white collar which poked out from underneath his cashmere vest jumper and his dark tanned skin hinted that he had travelled to many a foreign land underneath hundreds of baking suns. His face was kind and easy, and his voice carried a quiet confidence.

Ash had made his booking under a false surname, but as he tilted his shades and revealed his telling eyes, Geoff didn't look at all surprised that a famous person was on his doorstep. Could it be that he did not recognise the young star? Utterly unfazed, Geoff greeted Ash with the same humility and dignity as he would have any stranger on the street.

"Hello, you must be Ash", he said warmly, reaching out his hand. "Please do come in."

Somewhere between pleasantly surprised and mildly offended, Ash smiled and shook the man's hand firmly. "Thank you", he responded, before stepping into the therapist's abode.
"Did you find it okay?" Geoff asked, leading Ash down a hallway which was decorated with tasteful countrified wallpaper and an oil painting of a watering can bursting with pastel flowers.

"Yes, I used my Sat Nav thanks", Ash replied as he inspected the man's house up and down.

The small talk put him instantly at ease, blanketing him with a feeling of safety and relief.

As Ash followed Geoff past the dark plum living room, with the pinstriped green and cream armchairs and the mahogany fireplace, he could see that the therapist and his wife were humble people who had worked to make their home rather beautiful. Regardless of what type of house Ash entered as an adult, whether it be a high-rise he was visiting on one of his charity visits to Peckham, or somewhere more similar to one of his own grand London properties, such as a film star's mansion in East Grinstead, Chelsea or Los Angeles, he felt appreciation for a home only for one reason; whether he felt safe there or not. After all, Ash had been no stranger to fearing his own home in the past.

Ash followed Geoff to the end of the hallway, past the staircase and down some steps into a small study.

The square room had a superbly shiny wooden floor and a traditional double bookcase filled with dozens upon dozens of old bound books. Ash caught the titles of "How the Mind Plays its Tricks" and "The Psychology of Fear" upon two of their bindings. There was a large golden ornamental mapped globe on Geoff's desk and a framed photograph with three beaming blonde children pictured. The walls were plastered with framed certificates and a family portrait in which Geoff was joined by a beautiful wife and the three blonde children as adults. There were also some other photographs mounted on the wall of a younger, slimmer Geoff, fishing with his son, and in the Savannahs of Africa with his wife. The photograph which caught Ash's eye however, was the largest of all, sitting on the bookshelf in a carefully set aside space. It was a black and white photograph of a strong jawed, emerald-eyed man in a captain's uniform. As Geoff unlocked a concealed door in the corner of the study, Ash stopped and looked at the picture discretely, or so he thought.

"That's my father", Geoff remarked, although his back was turned to Ash. He spun around and the creases by the sides of his perceptive eyes deepened as he smiled. Then, Geoff opened the door and both men stepped into the light.

It was a garden-room, with each wall made of glass. Ash had not been expecting it. The sun flooded through each pane bringing a comforting warmth. The sweet aroma of the abundant tropical plants, which were dotted around the conservatory perimeter, filled the air. Ash peered over their splayed out leaves and twisted stalks reaching out from their pots, to view the perfectly kept lawn and flower beds in the garden outside. There were two cushioned wicker seats opposite each other in the middle of the foliage, a glass coffee table in between them, and a large rustic dresser, on which a jug of water and a tea tray sat.

"This is our room where we'll be having our session today, if that's okay with you?" Geoff asked. "There's tea and coffee or water or-"

"Water would be great, thanks."

Ash then waited for the welcoming man to gesture him to a seat before sinking into its comfort and admiring the room.

Geoff poured two glasses of water at the dresser and handed one to Ash.

"So, Ash La-Pal, welcome. A very warm welcome. What is it that brings you here today?" the therapist asked, with an intense confidence, as he rested in his chair.

Ash hesitated for a moment. *There should be no confusion and no miscommunication if this is going to work*, he thought, remembering back to his preliminary phone call with Geoff's secretary.

"Wait, sorry, you *do* know who I am?" he asked, putting his glass of water down before he had even taken a sip.

"From the moment you walked in", Geoff beamed, leaping to his feet, and pulling at a drawer from within the dresser. He rummaged inside it before lifting out a slim DVD and, grinning, he explained, "My wife and I watched this only last week. If I may say so, you are exceptionally talented. It was a masterpiece!"

Ash stared at the DVD cover he had seen so many times before; in his own DVD collection, on shop shelves, on the television, among the adverts, in the magazines, at the premier.

"A Coward's War", read the DVD case in bold white letters. The title stood above an image of a bloodied young soldier in green camouflage, holding a small Vietnamese child amid fire and explosions.

"Written and Directed by Ash La-Pal"

Despite the exulting praise of his family, friends and fans, Ash had never felt the expected bursts of pride and satisfaction when he watched his films in motion or on the big screen. But listening to the perfect stranger marvel at his work, made him feel a rush of shame far greater than that which accompanied any congratulations which had gone before. He spun the wise man a weak smile. Deep down, Ash knew these sessions were going to lead to the truth. But for now, only he knew that this film was not *his* masterpiece.

"Thank you. Thank you, that's very kind. It's strange, I don't always expect people to recognise me outside of my work", he stammered, grabbing at the water.

"Well, I'm a bit of a movie buff if I'm honest. My daughter's a drama teacher and …and I don't know why I'm telling you this. Perhaps for the first time in my career, Ash La-Pal, I feel a little star struck!"

"By me?" Ash giggled, relaxing in his chair more comfortably. "Your reviews were good too, you know."

"And so they should be, I did write them myself!" Geoff chuckled, and they both laughed.

"You know, I think most professionals of my kind would have acted as if they'd no idea who you were,

Ash, even if they did know you."

"Why's that?" asked Ash, intrigued.

"Well, since you went to the trouble of booking under a different name, I suppose they would have wanted to respect that anonymity."

Ash raised his eyebrows curiously. "I'm guessing you have a different idea?"

"You'd be right. I don't want you to think I have disregarded any discretion. Forgive me if I have come across as unprofessional, but in my career, I believe real-life experience is more valuable than by-the-book standards. And in my experience, for me to be able to help you, there should be complete honesty between us. I hope that's okay?"

Ash looked at the stranger gratefully. "It's okay", he said softly.

"So tell me, Ash, what brings you here? And what would you like to get out of these sessions?"

Ash took a gulp of water, and his leg began to tremble unwillingly. He sighed, uncomfortably.

"I'm tired of feeling angry."

"Angry? How often do you feel angry?" Geoff asked, leaning forward in his seat and holding his hands together.

Ash paused.

"All the time. Every day."

"That must be exhausting", Geoff exclaimed. "Can you explain why you feel this anger?"

Ash wanted to be ready for this but no words would come. His mouth felt dry suddenly. Another cold sweat crept over the back of his neck. His palms were sticky again.

Geoff could recognise the unfathomable heaviness

which burdened this picture-perfect young man. But what could possibly be so troubling that it robbed him of the words to explain it? Geoff knew from the offset that it was rooted in far more than a stressful career or a sudden relationship crisis. He stared at the young man before him. Ash's clothes were immaculate. His body fit and trim. His square jawline was clean-shaven and he boasted a smooth luscious complexion. His stylish black curls danced around his artistic quiff and his handsome features could make any girl giddy. But it was his dark arresting eyes which carried an anguish that only a man of Geoff's wisdom and expertise could see through. They intrigued the therapist, for it was Ash's eyes that held a thousand secrets of what they had seen.

"We can start at the very beginning if you like", Geoff suggested, "or, we can work backwards, and you can tell me about where you are now in your life and we can look at the feelings you are experiencing more closely. You don't need to tell me any of the who's and the why's just yet. This is a safe place, Ash. Nothing leaves these walls."

Ash exhaled again. How could he possibly begin? Where was he to start? *Just say something you moron,* he begged himself.

"Why don't we start with where you were born and grew up, and who your family are? What did you want to be growing up? Had you always wanted to be a film director?" Geoff asked patiently, taking out a small black notebook from beneath the cushion on his seat.

Ash found his voice.

"Well, I was born in Kashmir, in India", he sighed, filled with regret.

He stared at the ground uncomfortably. It was

impossible not to envision Kashmir when he said it aloud. He could see the trees in his mind - thousands upon thousands of them, covered in vibrant green moss and windy vines. He reminisced over the sun on his face, as it set on the mountain tops, expelling strokes of pink, orange and yellow in the sky. He could hear the orchestra of crickets chirping in his ears, and the touch of the long grass brush against his bare legs. He could almost feel the excitement again, smell the scent of the flowers, and taste the brink of a new adventure waiting to be lived in the air. But these were fleeting feelings, held captive in his memory. They were feelings he could not imagine having back. That blissful life was all too far away now. All that was left of those memories was a cloud of rage and a deep longing and emptiness, buried beneath the dissatisfying materialisms he had tried to fill his life with.

"India. What a spectacular country. Why don't you tell me about India, and your earliest memories there? Were they happy?" Geoff pressed, gently.

"The *happiest*", Ash exclaimed, forcing himself to remember. "Um, my father was a shoemaker. I don't know if you've heard of them, but he created Lakhan shoes. Everyone in India wore them. He owned quite a few factories in New Delhi, so we grew up in a huge mansion in Kashmir, right by Dal Lake and close to the border of Pakistan."

"That must have been a wonderful place to grow up, no? Please, go on", Geoff urged.

"My mum stopped working once she met my dad. So, I guess she had a lot of time to spend with us kids. She came from a poor family in Madha Pradesh. She met my dad when she was a shoe shiner in Delhi and he had been promoted to the manager of a private shoe shop where he had worked behind the counter. By the time they married, the shop was left to my father in the owner's will, and he built his first prototype of a Lakhan shoe with the profits from the shop. Three years later, he owned four factories in India, and they bought and restored an old crumbling palace in the Kashmir forest, away from the cities. That's where I was born, that's where I grew up. I was the middle child."

"Wow, incredible. So, you were happy as a child, Ash?"

"In India, most definitely", Ash remarked. "Every day was an adventure. We lived like princes. I was lucky. Well, so I thought."

Ash closed his eyes for the briefest of moments, and it was almost as if he was back in that place once again. For so long, he had blocked out the mansion because it filled him with rage. He had pushed away the green garden because he only saw red. He had drowned out the lake because it made him clench his fists. But as he listened to Geoff's soothing voice, leading him back in time, and willing him to remember, he began to see his nine-year-old reflection glimmering in the waters of Dal Lake, and he could even hear his brother's voice beckoning him.

2

THE LAKE

Kashmir, India, 1998

"Come on, Asha! You're paddling like a girl!" Daruk laughed, showing off as he drove his muscular arms backwards and forwards, pulling on the paddles which cut through the mirror-like water. Daruk, was the boy with the brightest smile.

"Shhhh! You're going to disturb the snakes, splashing like that, brother!" Ash begged, poking his older brother in the back of the ribs with his big toe. The little boat edged forward through the long reeds, which were much taller than either of the boys.

"I'm not scared of the snakes. It's the missionaries we need to be wary of!" Daruk whispered, and both brothers fell into a fit of giggles, so much so, that their wooden canoe wobbled on the glassy surface of Dal Lake.

A thick white mist circulated the bases of the blue snow-capped mountains surrounding the great body of water, as they headed for the outskirts of the shanty village.

"They thought we needed saving", Ash squawked, picturing the white people in his mind, who had rushed over with free bibles on the boy's journey home from school the previous week.

"Well, it's no wonder, after they saw the state of you!" Daruk grinned, swivelling his athletic body around and ruffling his little brother's messy hair. "They probably thought we were off the streets!"

Daruk had the cheekiest and most charming way about him. Ash could always tell when his brother was about to insult him and make him howl with laughter. And he could not help but laugh, even if he were the subject of the joke. He admired his brother's quick wit and felt joy amid his humour. In fact, there was nothing he loved more than when Daruk turned down all of his many friends to spend the day with him.

"*You'll* need saving in a minute!" Ash responded excitedly, swaying his little body from side to side and rocking the boat. The water lapped the sides of the canoe, sending refreshing droplets flying all over their baked skin. The sun had been unforgiving all day and they had been paddling hard, but with no fish to show for themselves, it had been a day for endless fun.

"Come on, then!" hyped Daruk, standing up on the canoe with a huge smile painted across his bright-eyed face. His legs shook as he gained his balance and held out his arms.

"Dar, no! The snakes! The eels!" Ash screamed, adopting a crouching position and hanging onto the boat's edges. Neither of the boys had any shoes on and the wood felt hot beneath their feet. They received a few disapproving looks from the fishermen and fruit boats wading through the green heart-shaped lilies which gathered sporadically in congregations on the lake at this time of year.

Although Ash was genuinely afraid of snakes, he always felt an overarching safety when he was in the presence of his big brother. Daruk was extraordinarily smart, and he always seemed to know what to do in any situation they found themselves in. He knew how to outsmart his peers, and even his teachers. He knew how to outrun the wild animals, and even sometimes trap them. He wasn't scared of the arguments their parents had, or even of their father's sharp hand. In fact, Daruk didn't seem to be afraid of anything in the whole world. Ash was frightened of almost everything.

Ash found himself in a headlock, captured by the steel grip of Daruk's bicep. He knew the tickling would follow, which infuriated him because he *hated* the torture of the tickling but was powerless not to laugh, and the laughter jiggling his body caused every muscle to weaken.

One wobble too far and both boys found themselves toppling over, flailing their arms and legs in the air before being swallowed by the deep saturation of the lake. It was exhilarating! They were suddenly surrounded by the overwhelming heaviness of cold, swamp water, which dragged at their limbs. Ash felt something soft brush against his arm. He let out a huge scream, and both brothers gasped for breath as they fought to stay afloat. They rose to see their upside-down boat, bobbing up and down in a tease.

"You idiot!" Ash screeched. "Turn it over! Turn it over!"

He flapped his small arms around, causing quite the disturbance.

"It was an accident! I'm trying! I'm trying!" Daruk yelped, though his eyes widened in excitement. He mopped his sodden black fringe away from his forehead and it spiked upwards in a tall quiff reaching for the sky above.

"Push it", he gasped, reaching for the side of the canoe, but their attempts to touch it just pushed the boat further away from them.

"We're going to get eaten because of you!" Ash spluttered, though his uncontrollable cackle soon echoed.

The boys splashed around in hysterics, to the backdrop of the great mountains, the endless expanse of the shimmering lake and the scattered village within the valley of flowers. The sun sat on the horizon as if she were amused and had all the time in the world, beaming her rays down on their illuminated skin.

A couple of women from the village who were chatting on the jetty caught sight of the frenzied boys. Their brightly coloured saris, covered in shiny jewels, reflected the sunlight down onto the lake to display a dance of a thousand diamonds sparkling on its ripples. One of the women shook her covered head in disapproval but the other tried hard not to chuckle, as both carried on with their gossiping. Others looked at the children from the comfort of their large, elaborate houseboats, but continued with their afternoon supper.

"We're going to have to swim it to the shore", Ash panted, spitting filthy water out of his mouth and using a questionable, frantic swim technique to propel himself through the water as he pushed the boat deeper towards the reeds on the bank.

"Sorry, where did you learn to swim?" Daruk laughed, poking his tongue out.

"It's the *butterfly*!" Ash insisted.

"More like the drowning albatross!"

Then, Daruk reached his arm out and towed his little brother towards him.

Ash clung to Daruk's shoulders like a baby koala on its mother's back, and as the laden boy swam, they began to make progress until the wooden boat was finally wedged deeply in the reeds and they could feel the squishy mud seep between their toes on the waterbed. They had reached the shallows.

Ash clenched the thick reeds in his small hands and hauled himself up out of the water and onto the marshland. Gasping for breath, Daruk did the same and the two boys worked together to pull the boat. It slid over the marshland effortlessly, and they clambered onto the jetty. The wood beneath their sopping bodies was still warm, and while Ash collapsed onto its sweet relief, his brother quickly tied the sodden rope, which was attached to the front of the canoe, in a tight bind to the post. Other children who were playing outside of their shabby wooden houses stared at the brothers, in delight.

"You've been *swimming*!" a little girl called excitedly, pointing at the pair.

Ash waved at her in embarrassment. "Let's go home", he remarked, shaking his flustered head.

The journey home saw the boy's bodies as silhouettes against the setting sun. Their figures trailed over the grassy hills and into the dense mossy forest, where they listened to a soundtrack of kingfishers and grasshoppers, following the dusty path carved out by only feet.

By the time they reached the garden, their dirty clothes were almost dry. The garden was nestled deep within the lush green forest. Helping each other up, the brothers scrambled over the ancient chalky wall which encased it. They were home.

Both boys fell with a thud onto the spongy grass beneath them which blanketed the acre. Rosewood trees were dotted around them, rich in dark emerald leaves and busy with small rose-ringed parakeets which chirped in the light of dusk. As if designed by an artist's paintbrush, the garden was laced with purple and orange frangipanis and chrysanthemums, on which the bees and bugs found rest. Cutting through the grounds, on the far side of the garden, towards the ancient mansion was a dark blue stream, teaming with tropical Koi. The jungle trees outside peered over the walls of the perfect garden, envying its paradise.

The remains of ancient ruins, which dated back to the golden kingdom, were scattered throughout the wild grass, within the walls, in the form of chalky coral pillar stumps or broken steps. These forgotten foundations always proved exciting when the boys were playing pirates, or treasure hunts, or "Raiders of the Lost Ark". Indiana Jones was Ash's favourite hero of all time, and Daruk entertained his brother's games, though they were far too young for him.

Ash's favourite part of the garden had always been the waterfall, which stood about halfway between the mansion veranda and the very end of the garden wall, where the stream spilled out into the pond, stirring the waterlilies in a frenzy. The rocky waterfall gushed from further upstream and outside the garden walls, from the mountains in the forest. When Ash was only four, he had slipped off an overhanging branch into the pond, whilst pretending to be a gladiator. If it had not been for Daruk diving in after him and pulling him to the safety of the bank, then Ash would have drowned. Their mother had given them both a smack on the hand that day, as they knew the pond area and waterfall was out of bounds until Ash could swim. Her heart had softened at the sight of her two sons though, dripping wet and fuelled with adrenaline. She had wrapped them both in thick blankets and sat them in front of their favourite bowl of dhal, cursing them for worrying her so.

Daruk's favourite part of the garden, however, was difficult to miss. Towering, mystical and covered in moss, *The Banyan Tree* stood at the very bottom of the garden. It had grown so large and so obscurely that its roots and winding branches had obstructed the garden wall, spreading out from beneath its crumbling foundations and hanging over the top of it like a wild contortionist. The great twisted branches of the banyan acted as the very gateway into the forest, marking the end of the boy's territory, and the beginning of the wild. The boys would so often climb into the arms of the banyan, nestling beneath its abundant canopy, and looking out to the world beyond. They watched the creeping vines sway, wondering what beasts and creepy crawlies caused them to move. They listened to the crunching of leaves, whilst Daruk hoped it would be the day the tiger they had spotted only once, had returned. And they fixated upon the creatures of the forest, each of which filled Daruk's dreams, and Ash's nightmares. This evening would be no different.

Ash straddled the aged branch of the banyan, as he felt most secure this way. He swung his legs either side of it, as if riding a warrior horse, holding on with both hands. Daruk stretched his legs out over the branch, relaxing, as if it were a deck chair and leant against the great trunk of the tree where both their names were carved.

Daruk and Asha's Tree

They stared up the garden to the great mansion which they called home. Their mother, Roshni, covered by her sari, was just a small purple dot on the veranda, cradling their baby sister, Jayminee.

"This was the best day", Ash exhaled. "I hope we live here forever."

Daruk smiled in agreement, though he doubted this would be the case. He'd heard some of his father's phone calls late at night.

"Brother? Do you think we *will* live here forever?" Ash worried, reading into his brother's silence perceptively. The insecurities of life could flood the young boy's mind so quickly. Ash could never just let something be. He lived in a world of fear and questions, but, fortunately, Daruk never got tired of reassuring him.

"I hope so", Daruk said. "But no matter what happens, you and I will always be together. So it doesn't matter where we are."

"How will you make sure of it?" Ash persisted. "It will be like you always said won't it? We'll inherit the house one day and I will have the biggest bedroom and you can have the room next door, but I'll let you sleepover with me when it thunders, and Jayminee can have the pink room and Mama will be in the blue room, and we'll give all our friends at school the other rooms, Jai, and Sandeep, and Rajan, and Raksha."

"You didn't mention Father", Daruk said, glancing down at his brother, who gulped.

"Oh…yes well, I suppose he'll have to be here too", Ash exclaimed.

There was a sadness in their silence.

"Does it still hurt?" Daruk asked.

Ash pulled at the neck of his t-shirt, gently pressing the tender bruise on his shoulder.

"Not so much", he said. "Does yours?"

Daruk shook his head, though the lashes to his back were still healing. He didn't want his younger brother to know that when he'd stood up to his father and Mr Lakhanpal had let Ash go, he'd saved the rest of his anger for his older son.

A songbird filled the air, and they heard the distant call of their mother shouting.

Daruk turned to move, but Ash's mind hadn't finished wondering yet.

"Will you *always* be here? Even if the world was to stop?"

"I'll always be here, Ash."

"Will you always love me? Even if everyone else was to stop?" Ash pressed.

Daruk smiled.

"*For as long as this tree is standing*", he said, tapping the banyan tree.

But Ash's expression was troubled still. "*What?* What if someone were to cut it down?" he worried.

Daruk sighed and ran his hand over his face before

running his fingers over the etched carving on the tree trunk:

Daruk and Asha's Tree

"Brother, this tree isn't just the branches. It's not even just the trunk. This tree has roots that nobody can lift… they run too deep."

And with that, Ash was finally reassured enough to swing his legs over the branch and slip onto his brother's back.

"For as long as this tree is standing, then", he repeated happily.

"Coming, Mama!" Daruk called, as he carried Ash up the garden and all the way home.

3

THE YEAR BOOK

Essex, England, 2018

It had been years since Ash had allowed himself to remember the *garden*.

It was too painful to recall such gloriously joyful times in the bitter knowledge that life could never look like that again. And so, it had been easier to block out the past entirely. The guilt was crippling. It sickened him just as it had done all those sleepless nights in his teenage years, before he had embarked on the journey of great distraction at film school. But Ash could not live this way, anymore. Life was not meant to be merely existed, but rather, *lived*. And lived in all its fullness. In ignoring the sorrow, he'd also shut out the joy. In escaping the disappointment, he could never find the trust. And, in forgetting the heartbreak, he had barely remembered the love. Ash wasn't an empty shell, though his lavish lifestyle and materialistic nature implied just this. He had a heart, arguably with a capacity far greater than most. But, up until now, it was almost as if he wanted to live in the pain and punish himself forever. He couldn't move past what happened all those years ago, on that dreadful day.

And yet, in meeting with Geoff, he had been forced to recall the roots which ran too deep. He had finally begun to unlock the pathway to the past, and the emotions that had helped bury his memories were surfacing like a rising tide as he left the therapist's house. In the moment he shook Geoff's hand goodbye, the rage and the anger propelled him into a decision. He was tired of punishing himself. He was a powerful man now, not a cowardly child. He was not the only one punishable, and it was time for accountability.

Ash put on his shades and strode out of the door, quite casually. He fobbed open his car as he usually would. But then, he pushed down on the accelerator in relentless haste and began driving in a direction he hadn't ventured to go in, in almost twenty years. This had been the push he needed; he was finally ready to face his demons.

Racing through the residential streets, Ash threw his phone into its holder and smacked at the loudspeaker button, as it began to ring out.

"Ash, long time! Alright, man?" answered a deep, young man's voice on the other end.

"Hey bro'. Listen, I need your help…don't ask me why, but I'm headed to Essex, to a…place and… and I need you to help me hack their database. Can you do it? I'll ping you the location. I'll pay you good money." Ash gripped the steering wheel fiercely as he sped through the changing lights.

"Woah… Ash, man, what's going on? You sound angry. What's happened?"

"Look, nothing's happened, just, can you do it or not?" he snapped, flicking open the tub of chewing gum fixed to his dashboard and throwing three strips in his mouth. He chewed savagely.

"Well…I'd need to know more. I mean I could use a bit of money, but I don't really do that kind of work these days. Not since Nina had Karla. What is this place? Do you have access inside?"

Ash ran his hand over his face, as he often did, when he felt anxious or stressed. He slapped down his indicator to join the motorway, and sped into the fast lane within seconds.

"I haven't been there in years, but yeah I'm pretty sure I can get us in with all your stuff, that is."

"*Pretty* sure? That's-"

"Look, it's a school alright." Ash snapped, impatiently. "A secondary one, private. I can get us in. I just need you to find somebody's details for me on their system. I'll pay you three grand, straight away, tonight."

"Three *grand*?" responded the voice eagerly. "Okay, okay, I can do it!"

"Thank you, Kenny."

There was a brief pause.

"Ash… it's nothing dark is it? It's just… you say it's a school. It's not, like, a kid's details or nothin'? Because I can't be part of anything like that… I got kids at home, y'know."

"What? Kenny! Who do you think I am?! Of *course,* it's not a kid's details! It's nothing like that. I'm looking for a grown man."

"Sorry, no, of course, mate. I knew it wouldn't be. I just had to ask. No more questions, I know. I'll get my kit together and see you there. I'll tell Nina I'm coming round yours to help with a trailer or something."

"Good. See you." Ash said irritably, thumping his thumb on the end call symbol.

He slammed down harder on the accelerator and undertook all the drivers going below ninety in the fast lane, which he ducked in and out of for the duration of the motorway, breathing heavily. He had been calculating this journey for most of his adult life. Though it had just been a sick fantasy, until now.

It was getting dark when Ash crossed the border into Essex. He didn't recognise anywhere yet, which he was glad about. He cut through a residential town. The streets were lifeless, with the exception of a few youths gathered around a lamppost in hoodies, and an old man walking his dog. His built-in GPS showed that he would arrive at Beacon Cliffe High School in forty-two minutes. His journey carried him through a busier upmarket high street with lit up restaurants, and a large green where a couple held hands on their evening stroll.

He turned a corner, and suddenly, his heart began to race. His sticky palms gripped the wheel and his stomach felt queasy as he pulled away from the town and entered an impoverished and run-down estate. Nothing had changed since he had lived there. Dunwell Reens was a bleak and merciless area, comprised of grey streets, smashed up lampposts, graffiti covered bus stops and boarded up corner shops. Pubs, which were just scraping by on minimal income from the larey locals, were a haven for drug dealers and red-faced drunks.

The hum of distant sirens filled the air, murmuring from among the rows of cloned buildings, which housed prostitutes, those on benefits, or those seeking asylum. Ash had never met anybody outside of these realities who lived in this grave place. How bleak it remained after all these years. Ash's car was preyed on by two thugs talking outside a high-rise block of concrete flats. He looked down on them with superior eyes, from the comfort of his air conditioned, leather seated Continental. But internally, he felt the familiar intimidation he had experienced living here as a child.

He recognised more than he wanted to now. Uncomfortably more. The woods were approaching. The dark spindly trees and the never-ending path. The mud which had sunk underneath his fingernails and the bark which he'd clawed at, still lurked within the forest that had listened to his screaming that doom-filled day. It appeared almost as terrorising as it did in his flashbacks. He pushed harder on the accelerator and sped past the woods, blasting out the air conditioning and flicking on the radio. Anything in the charts would have been his usual listen, but right now, he felt the need to blare out Classic FM. Anything to take his mind away from the woods. Anything to calm his racing heart. He felt his eyes well up with stinging tears, and a hard lump filled his throat.

Just keep driving. You're almost there. You can do this. He willed himself to continue, just as he'd willed his trembling, eleven-year-old body to continue through the woods, back then.

Eternity seemed to have passed in the space of a few minutes, and he'd finally cleared the woods. Another dead high street brought him into a high-end neighbourhood, where the pubs were quaint and idyllic, the square was decorated with hanging baskets, the greens neat and clean, and the jewellery shops lit up the pavements. The rolling hills came into view in the distance and he turned down a narrow country path, which lead him up to the private estate. Once he could see the gates of the grand building drawing closer, he pulled over into a small lay-by which cut into the hedge, avoiding the inevitable CCTV cameras that guarded the school.

Exhaling deeply, Ash climbed out of his car and with shaking hands, opened his boot. There, he reached for his soft black hoody and threw it over the top of his smart shirt. He knew he had a baseball cap in the mess of his boot somewhere too, from his day out at the beach with Lola. He found the black cap, flipped it over his head and slammed the boot shut. Slipping back into the driver's seat, he checked his phone to see the location of Kenny. The flashing blue dot was half an hour away. Then, he flicked onto a new incognito tab on his phone and began the routine search of Facebook, then Twitter, then LinkedIn, then Myspace. But the search results never gave him what he wanted. He typed the name in again and again, but no profile picture matched the face which haunted his memories.

His search history on Google showed one thousand two hundred and forty-two searches for the same name.

Charles Wincott

He had searched the name *Charlie Wincott* too, because that's what they called him back then, but he could never find the face he was looking for. Ash never grew tired of the searching, however many failed attempts there were. It had become an obsessive part of his private routine, usually just before bedtime, when his thoughts were at their darkest. There was a time when Lola had found his open laptop in his penthouse in London and questioned the endless searches for a man she'd never heard of. She had even worried he might be gay and looking for a long-lost lover. But Ash had spun her a lie that he was looking for a guy who *owed him money*, which his girlfriend had never quite believed. It was unconvincing when Ash had more money than was necessary and was usually very relaxed and generous with it.

Ash scrolled through his text notifications, the first was from Lola.

"*Where are you baby? How was counselling? I'm worried about-*"

He scrolled down further.

"*Got the kit. On my way mate, Ken*"

"*Ash! Just seen first draft of the trailer for your new film "Dragon Train"-*"

"*Asha, congratulations on securing Ricky for Friday's audition, it's-*"

"*Bro', please get me on that guest list for the celebs only Sky Lounge party on Saturday night!!*"

"*Las Vegas or Paris for Smarties stag, what ya reckon????*"

"*'Ash La-Pal will attend premiere of "Dragon Train" on Saturday' *LINK* You got two tickets for your baby sister Ash?! Jay xx*"

"*Can't wait for your premiere*"

"*So proud of you, son*"

"*Smashed it again I see. When you gon' give someone else a chance!?-*"

There were a dozen more messages, but Ash silenced his phone and slipped it into his jean pocket. He couldn't bring himself to reply to any of it right now. He tapped his fingers over the steering wheel anxiously, whilst peering up at the old building, sitting in all its greatness behind the tall gates.

Finally, the hum of an engine slowed behind his car, and the headlights flashed at his rear-view mirror in a blinding dazzle. It was Kenny.

Kenny was a small and skinny Pakistani with a bristly beard and eyes too big for his face. He upheld a strong southern accent and had become a friend of Ash's during their early twenties when Kenny had lived in the room next door to Ash in their student accommodation. Kenny had studied computer software development at Arden University, London and Ash had attended Ealing Film School, specialising in directing features. Sharing halls of residence, it wasn't long before Ash became aware of Kenny's hacking abilities, and by the second year they were both making money selling university exam papers which Kenny had been able to get hold of illegally.

Ash waved Kenny over and shook him by the hand, slapping him on the back. When he looked at the black briefcase, cables and rucksack Kenny had brought with him, he felt bad for snapping at him on the phone and flattered by the reliability of his old friend.

"I told the missus we were down the pub having a drink, so I can't be too late", Kenny whispered, staring at Ash in his shady outfit.

Ash raised his eyebrows. "Well, it doesn't have to be a complete lie", he said quietly, pulling a hip flask out of his car glove compartment and knocking back a swig of straight whiskey. He grimaced as he swallowed the intoxicating drink.

"Want some?"

"Nah, you're okay. I brought you one of these, 'cause there's gonna be CCTV here, Ash, I can tell. I can't afford to get caught, y'know."

Ash scoffed at the black balaclava held out to him, but soon slipped it snugly over his face, peering out through the eye slits. Then he placed the black cap back over his head.

"We look ridiculous", he remarked, staring at his friend who mirrored his disguise.

Then, he locked his car with a bleep, and they began making their way up the path, past a large sign:

Beacon Cliffe High School for Boys and Girls

As the hill inclined, Kenny quickly grew out of breath and Ash's pensive silence fuelled his curiosity.

"So, what's the deal, Ash? I know I said I wouldn't ask, but I just gotta' know what I'm gettin' myself into. You know I had to do time for hacking that cruise ship."

"The cocaine case?"

"Yeah, it was grim, man. That's three months of my life I'll never get back. Nina only took me back because she was pregnant."

"It's not going to be like that, I promise. We'll be in and out within an hour. A minor school break-in isn't exactly going to make the headlines. We'll take a laptop or some cash from the reception and they'll put it down to kids robbing the place, that's all."

There was a brief silence, as they drew closer towards the impressive academy. Its turrets were darkened silhouettes against the moonlit sky, and its stained-glass windows were lit up by the floodlights on the cricket lawn in front of the eerie institution.

"It's not a teacher that used to abuse you, or

something ugly like that is it?" Kenny asked breathlessly, jogging to keep up with Ash's determined pace.

"No", Ash insisted. "I never even went to this school. Now, no more questions, unless you want that three grand to become two..."

"Okay fine, but if I go down for this-"

"Kenny, what's got into you? I thought you were my guy!"

"No, I'm sorry, mate, I am... it's just, I've got a wife and kids to think about now. It's not like when we were younger and it was just us."

"You and me against the world, wasn't it?" Ash reminisced, sighing weakly.

Ash stopped in his tracks and placed his hands firmly on Kenny's shoulders.

"Look, an hour tops, okay? I just need the details of somebody that used to go to this school. I can't think of any other way to find him. It's been years."

"He's not on social media?"

"No, I've searched a million times. It's like he disappeared off the face of the earth or something. But they will still have his details stored in the school database. It's my only connection to him", Ash urged, "and you and I both know that if you go down for this, I've got more than enough money to get you out of trouble just as quick as I get you into it, got it?"

Kenny nodded uneasily, "So, you got this person's name? And that's it? Why do you need to find him so bad?"

Ash's face changed within an instant, scrunching into an unyielding frown. He clenched his fists in anger as they approached the towering gates.

"Because, I need to find out the truth, alright? He took something of mine, and it's about time he paid for it. Now, no more questions, I mean it. Your money includes you keeping quiet after this is over."

"Clearly, I'm not planning on telling anybody, mate", Kenny said sarcastically, tapping the balaclava on his head.

The pointy black gates were triple the height of the men, so they headed over the shorter railings surrounding the school grounds and helped each other over the spikes.

"Careful! That's the laptop", Kenny insisted, as Ash tossed the black bag over the fence, casually. Kenny leapt to catch it as if it were his own child.

Once Ash had climbed up onto the pointed tops of the railings, he crouched uncomfortably and then leapt through the darkness, landing softly on the mowed pitch.

They hurried up to the grand Victorian building, surrounded by the immaculate front lawn with white rugby posts. The building had huge bay windows and was just as pretentious as Ash had remembered it. A big gold sign, reading '1809' hung above the archway door.

"We'll go around the back", Ash whispered, and Kenny continued to tiptoe behind him as they snuck around the side of the school, over the stripy lawn, under stone archways and through a cobbled courtyard with a fountain.

"Bloody 'ell, this is posh", Kenny whispered. "It looks like Hogwarts!"

"That's what Daruk said", Ash muttered under his breath.

"What?"

"Nothing. It's this way. We'll go through the pool house."

Both of their hearts pounded with adrenaline, though Kenny's motives were fuelled by money and Ash's by anger.

They peered through the glass walls of the pool house, at the huge rectangle cut into the ground which was covered over with a silver sheet. Streaks of white moonlight reflected off the pool cover's surface. The flimsy, single glazed glass walls looked as though the place hadn't been refurbished since the school was first built. Kenny hastily lay his black briefcase on the cobbled ground and twisted the combination lock. He pulled out a glass cutter tool, which he stuck onto the pool house door, and wound around like a tin opener, cutting a quiet tidy circle in the glass. He then pressed the circle of glass gently, and it fell through to the other side, breaking quietly in two clean pieces on the floor. Carefully, he reached his hand through the hole in the glass and untwisted the lock from the inside. It was surprisingly easy.

"As *if*", Kenny remarked, baffled. "My kids school has better security than that and we pay nothin' to send 'em there!"

"Shh", Ash ordered, stepping into the pool house, which was deceptively humid.

Ash carried the rucksack for his friend and the young men made their way across the darkened room, past the huge pool. They slipped through one of the doors which lead them through some basic changing rooms, and out into a spooky sports corridor. The ceilings were high, and the walls were plastered with medals and old photographs of sporting events. Glass cabinets with trophies decorated both sides of the long corridor. At the end of the corridor, through the heavy double doors, they descended into a colossal indoor sports hall. Their tiptoes echoed throughout the arena as they quickly left it via one of the exit doors, where they carried on down another narrow hallway which cascaded into a huge hexagonal marble lobby. Here the ceilings reached towards the sky. The walls were complete with oil paintings of Victorian Kings and Queens, and green marble statues, of men on horseback, guarded the gateway to the staircase. The carpeted stairs split into opposite directions, wandering around the balcony. The walls were covered with leader boards, gold plated name plaques, dates, and photographs.

There were six different archways cutting out of the foyer. Ash squinted to make out the gold-plated signs hanging above each archway, *Library, Globe Theatre, Arena, Sports Quarter, Humanities* and *Science Quad*. He searched the lobby for the reception, but it was enclosed behind silver shutters in the far corner by the theatre archway.

"That's where the database will be", he exclaimed.

Though Kenny was far more familiar with break-ins than Ash, Kenny felt uneasy in the grand establishment. Ash, however, was more determined than ever before.

Kenny searched the lobby for cameras and could see only one, dangling from the ceiling about halfway up the left stairway. He took a bottle of silly putty from his rucksack and darted up the stairs. Then, Ash watched his friend, like a ninja, bounce up onto the wide, hand-carved bannister, and reach up to spray the camera lens, after shaking the bottle of foam.

Meanwhile, Ash picked at the lock of the silver shutter to the reception, though he didn't really know what he was doing. He used his car key to scrape the small round lock unknowingly. Kenny returned and shook his head.

"Not like that, mate", he hissed, shimmying Ash out of his way and pulling out a small silver pin from his rucksack. "Why don't you leave me to get this done and you go keep lookout and search for cameras?" Kenny suggested, handing his friend the bottle of silly putty.

The flimsy lock snapped beneath his hand, and he rolled the shutter up to reveal a surprisingly small reception, full of filing cabinets and two large desks with computers. Then, Kenny jumped into the office and fired a computer up, laying the contents of his briefcase out on the desk, complete with cables and a laptop. There were two more cameras with little red beaming lights, in two corners of the office ceiling.

"Spray those out, Ash", he pointed.

Ash used a swivel chair to balance on, as he reached to spray the lenses of both cameras. Their laser beams soon dulled.

"I didn't know you were such a ninja", Kenny remarked.

"I was thinking the same about you!"

Kenny fell onto his knees and began shuffling his cables around underneath the desk, attaching them to the computer which was now on and blaring out a welcome screen with a password lock. The desktop background was the school's gold-plated shield logo, with the words: Beacon Cliffe High School for Boys and Girls; Excelling in Excellence, etched onto it.

Ash took a piece of paper from one of the paper

trays on the desk and helped himself to a pen from the pen pot.

He scribbled on the paper.

Charles Wincott, 1998-2002

Then he slid the piece of paper towards Kenny.

"I need you to find out whatever you can about this student. These are the dates he was here. Find his parents' address, a home contact number, any siblings, what clubs he was in, anything you can."

And with that, Ash slipped over the office counter and back into the lobby, where he headed for the staircase. He held the torch he had poached from Kenny's bag out in front of him, and shone the light over the walls. The gold-plated plaques glinted before his eyes. They were the names of every student who had ever come through the gates of the school, dating back to the 1800's. Ash scanned the first few closely, before realising they were not in alphabetical nor chronological order.

Geoffrey Andrew Bates, class of 1978, Innsbrook House
Brian Chase, class of 1901, Innsbrook House
Paul Peter St-Matthias, class of 1993, Innsbrook House

There were thousands of names stretching all the way up the staircase and over the walls throughout the balcony. Ash shone the light up to the spooky oil portrait of a young, pale man in an elaborate school uniform. He hung proudly above the section of gold-plated names.

George Reginald Innsbrook, House Captain, 1809

"They're sorted into houses. It really *is* Hogwarts", Ash whispered to himself, climbing further up the stairs and shining his light up to the next grand portrait.

James Nicolas Ridgemoor, House Captain, 1809

Below, all the names were engraved with Ridgemoor House.

Ash ran his hand over his mobile phone in his jeans pocket.

"Which house were you in, Daruk?" he asked himself softly, but he decided to leave his phone alone, as he caught sight of the other two portraits hanging the other side of the stairway. He raced down the stairs and up the other set, shining the light at all the names in Sidestroke House.

"No, that wasn't it", he muttered frustratingly.

And then there he was; the portrait of a round faced, broad shouldered boy with piercing eyes.

Jonathon Christopher Joseph, House Captain, 1809

"*Joseph* House, that was it", Ash said quietly.

But, he could not find his brother's name, nor Charles Wincott's for that matter. He scanned over the names impatiently, but had no idea which house Charles would have been in. *Seymour Jones, Owen Hughes, Grant Harlow, Samuel, Simon, John, Arthur, Peter, George… Andrews, Taylor, Norman, Stephens, Carpenter, Cartwright…* so many names. It was hopeless. But Ash trusted Kenny would have been more successful in his search, and it filled him with anxious anticipation. He darted down the staircase and headed for the library, realising his fear didn't lie in being here, but in walking away empty handed.

Ash passed Kenny, whose face was lit-up by the computer screen as he tapped cryptic codes into his own laptop. Within seconds, he had broken through the initial password screen on the school's computer. He then brought up different search bars on his own laptop and tapped in *Wincott.*

Ash soon found his way to the library, which was a gigantic semi-circle room, surrounded by books on bookshelves that reached up to the ceiling. Grand throne-like chairs were dotted around the tables. Ash flicked the main light switch on, as the room spooked him a little, with its darkness and echoing silence.

He wandered straight over to the glass cabinet by the bay window, which reflected his manic expression hovering over a huge cricket lawn outside. It was exactly as he had remembered the regal cabinet. It contained every yearbook in chronological order, dating back to the early 1900's. He slid the glass protector open and ran his fingers along the thick bindings of each book until he reached "Class of 2002".

Taking it for himself, he flung open the double page spread at the front of the book, which showed photographs and names of every student in the year group.

Aaron, James Salcombe
Albert, Felix Lewis
Alice, Elizabeth Stone

Ash scrolled down to 'C', but to his frustration, there was no sign of a *Charles Wincott*. He let out an embittered sigh. *He was definitely in this year group,* Ash thought to himself, angrily. He slipped the yearbook under his arm and forced the 2001 and 2003 yearbooks next to each other to seal the gap he had left in the display, and then he closed the cabinet gently and stole away from the enormous library.

By the time Ash had arrived back at the lobby, Kenny was packing up.

"Well? Tell me you found something?" Ash begged.

Kenny leapt out of the office and pulled the shutters

back down, joining his friend.

"I did. I found everything you wanted, but let's get out of here first."

"Okay", Ash agreed in quiet satisfaction, though the anticipation was unbearable. "Let's get the hell out of here."

The pair dashed back through the premises, out of the pool house and into the night. Kenny brushed down the door handle as they left.

It wasn't until they reached their cars and ripped off their balaclavas, that they spoke again.

"Congratulations, Shawshank", Kenny panted. "I'm so glad that's over!"

Ash was too troubled by his own dark thoughts to have even heard his friend. But he soon snapped back into reality,

"Listen, thanks, man. So, what did you find?"

Kenny handed him a sheet of paper.

"It's all on here. They list the students by their middle name's first on the system, that's why he appears as *F.C. Wincott* on the sheet. You know, Harvard style like that dumbass referencing we had to do at uni. But your guy's full name is *Charles Frances Wincott* and he graduated here in 2002. I got his family address and number. He was captain of the cricket team. I downloaded his picture and there's an account of every time he visited the school nurse too, under his school medical record."

Charles Frances Wincott. Ash seethed as he heard the name out loud, fixating on the image of the boy from his memory.

Ash slipped the paper into his pocket and shook his friend's hand.

"I'll wire you the money into your account tonight. Remember, not a word about this to anyone though?"

Kenny nodded and his eyes widened in excitement at the thought of the cash. The possibilities for how he would spend it were already whizzing through his mind.

"I promise, Ash. Don't do anythin' silly now, bro'. I'll see you."

And with that, Kenny slipped his friend a wink and got into his car, rolling away into the night, towards London.

Ash sped away shortly afterwards, but as soon as he reached the deserted upmarket high street, he pulled over by a row of closed shops, and flung the 2002 yearbook open in eager anticipation. His heart was racing again, this time, in fury. He looked through the photographs of the students under 'F', and finally, there he was again, after all these years, staring him smugly in the face, just like he had done that day.

Frances, Charles Wincott

Ash scratched over the all too familiar face, digging his fingernail across the boy's eyes, enraged. He had no excuse now. He had found him.

Ash then flicked the pages back to the front and scrolled through the list of 'A's.

His face outshone all the others.

Anjani, Daruk Lakhanpal

Ash felt sick again.

4

THE NEWS

Kashmir, India, 1999

"So, when Mamma asks you how school was… what are you going to say, brother?" Daruk grinned, as the two boys began their long walk home, out of the valley and over the sun kissed hilltops.

"It wasn't *my* fault", Ash insisted, dragging a stick along the dirt trail sulkily.

"Ash, you made your teacher cry, said that a *tiger* ate your homework, and now you're wearing a dress! It doesn't get worse than this."

Daruk's laugh echoed throughout the valley of flowers, causing the birds to flutter up into the clear blue sky. Ash lobbed his stick down the hill, watching it tumble towards the silver lake and disappear into the plants. They made their way through the outskirts of the village, and Daruk stared tenderly at the group of small children who were dressed in filthy rags and rummaging through the mountain of litter which sat at the back of a lake house. He unzipped his school bag and approached the children with the banana bread he hadn't eaten that day.

"What are you doing?" Ash whispered, as Daruk crouched down before the small group of boys and girls and handed the food to the oldest girl in the group, who looked about eight. A timid smile spread across her dirty face, stretching the white scar on her cheek. She took the bread slowly, breaking it into pieces and sharing it with the others.

"Did you know them?" Ash asked, as the brothers began to walk away.

"No, they're from the city, I think."

"Dad says street kids can be dangerous", Ash urged, looking back at the children who were licking their hands of crumbs.

"Not those ones", Daruk sighed. "If I had as much money as Father, I'd give them all a place to live."

Ash stopped in his tracks.

"But maybe they choose to live like that?" Ash argued. The thought of the unknown scared him greatly, and he continued to stare at the children, whose lives appeared so foreign to his own.

Daruk placed his hand on his brother's shoulder, empathising with his anxious mind. Then, he stared at him and said kindly, "Nobody chooses to search for food, brother. They didn't choose their life any more than we chose ours. It was the hand we were dealt."

"Like in cards? It's just luck? That doesn't seem fair", Ash observed.

"It's never fair. But luck can change, Ash. It's what

you do with your cards that can change the game, you know that. Your reality doesn't have to be your destiny, *if* you're brave enough to play the game."

Ash stared at the ground, confused. He absorbed his brother's words which were wise beyond his years. Although he did not fully understand, he felt his moral compass turn inside of him. Compelled, Ash willingly swung his school bag off of his shoulder and reached for the leftovers he had inside. After all, he'd much sooner trust his brother's advice over his father's. There was an orange and a pot of dhal which he hadn't touched inside his bag. He held the food out to Daruk, willing him to return to the children.

"You do it", Daruk said, "it will make you feel good."

Unsure, Ash jogged back up to the children and was glad when the scarred girl acknowledged him, as the others scurried around in the garbage. He stared deeply into the little girl's eyes and placed the food gently on the ground before her. He gulped nervously. The little girl looked up at him, and smiled again.

"Thank you", she whispered. She didn't laugh at his dress. She didn't even stare.

Ash nodded and smiled back.

Daruk was right, it did feel good.

*

It had been an eventful day for Ash at The John Harper International School. The boys had arrived late after picking up Raksha on their way, as they did every morning. Raksha was in Ash's class and lived in a big house on the outskirts of Srinagar, opposite the great lake. The three of them had found a hissing Himalayan pit viper preying in their pathway on the final leg of their journey to school, and Raksha had teased Ash, accusing him of squealing like a little girl at the sight of the snake. Daruk however, had excitedly pranced over to the intimidating reptile, reciting to the two younger children that it was one of the most fatally venomous creatures in all of Kashmir. He had stared at it eagerly, admiring the black patterns on its scaly skin and his eyes had widened in intrigue. He then used a stick and Ash's schoolbag to create a pincer, scooping up the snake and flinging it into the bulrushes. Unfortunately, in the process, a few sheets of Ash's maths homework had flown out of the schoolbag and been blown away into the angry creature's territory.

When Mrs Sharma demanded Ash explain his missing homework in front of his wide-eyed class, he could hear Raksha sniggering with her girlfriends on the back row of dalbergia desks.

Ash stared at the immaculate sandstone floor, in humiliation.

"I'm sorry, Miss. I did do it, honestly I did it", he urged.

"Then where is it? It's a simple question", Mrs Sharma snapped, slamming the blackboard eraser down on her mahogany desk so hard that the chalky dust whirled around her chubby hand in a frenzy.

"Well, on my way to school, there was a very dangerous animal, Miss."

The whole class broke out into giggles, whispering jovially.

"And what animal was this Mr Lakhanpal?" the unamused teacher asked, brushing down her gaudy flowery skirt and shirt jacket.

Ash's ears burnt with rage as he listened to Raksha's taunting whispers from behind him, "it was a tiny little snake, the size of a *grasshopper!*"

"It was a... *tiger,* Miss!" Ash insisted, throwing his small hands down on his desk. To his relief, there was a brief silence in which he regained his pride and gallantry. And then, the entire class, including Mrs Sharma, began to bellow with laughter.

"A tiger!" his teacher yelped, revealing her huge sparkly grin. "Never mind maths; you need a lesson in lying my child!"

Mrs Sharma rarely laughed, but when she did, she guffawed. She took out her handkerchief from the gap between the buttons covering her full chest and wiped away a tear from underneath her eye. Her unexpected outburst hyped the children up eagerly.

"What did the tiger say to you Ash? Did he ask you for a pencil, too?" Joshy howled.

"Tigers love the taste of paper over meat", Anil teased from the front of the echoing classroom.

The remarks continued until Mr Patel, the class six teacher, as well as Head of School, charged into the room. He had been teaching in the science laboratory next door and could hear the ruckus through the glass doors that separated the two rooms.

"Mrs Sharma, a word please", he said sourly, beckoning the woman with his bony finger.

Immediately the class was silenced, and Ash slipped down into his seat, embarrassed. He glared at Raksha, who had begun to look somewhat apologetic. Mr Patel was a stern and regimented man, with a tall, bony frame and sharp eyes. The children knew he had no sense of humour, at all.

Mr Patel lead Mrs Sharma outside onto the huge school pitch, where the grass was lush and bright, like the neon skin of a chameleon. The juicy blades of green made playing football delightful on bare soles. There were two sets of white pillars opposite each other, poking out of the ground, acting as goal posts, and the pitch was encased by tropical trees, separating the resplendent school grounds from the lake outside. There were also neatly kept gardens directly outside the school pool house, which was attached to the west side of the majestic school building; the building which had stood for over three-hundred years. The gardens boasted sandstone statues, fountains, and flowers. But, it was the playing field where every boy liked to play at lunch time, including the Lakhanpal brothers.

Ash's classmates peered outside to the pitch they so frequently enjoyed, but now the place their teacher was being belittled by their merciless headteacher. Ash began to feel guilty in his stomach. It wasn't funny anymore. He knew what Mr Patel was like. He had never forgotten the day that he had caned Daruk's palm so hard (simply for jumping over the digging site of the two new school latrines), that it had made even their father furious. Anjani Lakhanpal did not shy away from hitting his sons, but for some reason it enraged him when somebody else had done so. The boys never knew what had happened when their father visited the headteacher that time, but Daruk had never been caned since.

Ash stared out at the abundant trees encompassing the school field, and at how their vibrant colours danced and wobbled in the heat wave. He hoped the tongue lashing would end soon.

"He's brutal", whispered Ruby, who was a British-born missionary child, and boarded at the school. She knelt up on her chair, to get a better view.

"All she did was laugh", agreed Miriam, whilst adjusting her pigtails.

"It's Asha's fault. You shouldn't have told that stupid lie", Deepak remarked, swivelling round to glare Ash directly in the face.

"Shut up Deep, you found it funny until *he* came in", Ash spat, scowling. Then, he leant forwards and banged his head down on his desk despairingly.

When Mrs Sharma re-entered the classroom, she used her handkerchief again, this time, to wipe away a different kind of tear. Ash had certainly never seen his teacher cry before, and it softened his heart towards her, even though she had never been his favourite teacher.

"Please open your math's books to page 86", she croaked, and the whole class obeyed without hesitation. "Asha, come and write lines on the board."

Ash turned around and scowled at Raksha, who mouthed "sorry" earnestly. The sight of her innocent round face and huge dark-chocolate eyes eased his anger somewhat, though he still felt humiliated. He had screamed like a little girl at the sight of the snake, he supposed. She'd been right.

Ash took the piece of chalk out of Mrs Sharma's hand regretfully, but to his surprise, she slipped him a wink, wishing away his guilt. And so, as he wrote out 'the tiger did not eat my homework' fifty times on the blackboard, until the white chalk in his fingers was the size of a pea, he did so, smiling. It was as if he finally understood the joke.

At lunch time, Ash sat on the steps outside the classroom longingly, watching as the boys in his class formed a football team on the pitch.

"You can't play with us today, dummy. You made Mrs Sharma cry", Anil had announced as he dashed outside. Ash picked at the grass bitterly, squinting in the sun.

Raksha came to sit beside him, wondering what to say. Her friends were holding hands and spinning around in circles over by the poplar trees, collecting flowers and putting them in each other's hair.

"You can play with us, if you like", she said softly.

Ash picked her a small yellow flower from the grass and placed it in her hand. He wondered how he could have ever been so angry with her in the first place.

"It's okay", he said. "Thanks anyway."

The class six boys exited their lesson in a stampede, jumping on each other's backs and hollering as they took over the football pitch. Ash's classmates moved to one side. Daruk was always the captain of the class six team. And everybody wanted to be on his team. It was not only because Daruk always made the rules and you had to ask his permission to join the football game, but because everybody wanted to be the boy's friend. He was the most popular in the whole school, and for good reason. Daruk was smart and funny and excelled in sports, but as well as this, he lived in a mansion where he had the best birthday party of the year, and the whole school was always invited.

Ash watched as his class three and four peers eventually streamed their way into the class five and six crowd.

"Both teams are allowed some class five and sixes,

but have to have an equal amount of class threes and four's as well, so that it's fair", Daruk said bossily, sifting and shoving children as if they were pawns on a chess board. "I'm the captain and I'll pick first, then Boaz will choose for the other team", he continued confidently, spinning the football on his finger.

"Pick me!"

"Pick me!"

"Over here, Daruk!"

The desperate pleas from the crowd of children swarmed around Daruk's athletic body. Daruk glanced past the crowd of jumping children and across the field to the school steps in the distance.

"Ash! Asha!" he called, "you're on my team. First pick!"

Ash hopped to his feet, absolutely beaming, and raced across the pitch to join his brother. He knew that none of his peers could argue or refuse him, not when Daruk was there. He felt elated.

When the teams were roughly even, and there was a mix of fifteen either side, Daruk threw the ball into the air and declared play. The boys screamed for passes, dribbled the ball energetically and never seemed to tire of the game, even under the blazing orange sun. Arrogantly, Daruk tackled three of his own classmates in a row, circling one with the ball, kicking it through another's legs, and kneeing it over another's head, until his route was clear and he booted it straight between the two posts.

"He's done it again!" Daruk cheered, holding his arms out like a bird's wings and pretending to soar across the pitch.

"Yes!" Ash exclaimed, throwing his fist in the air and

feeling proud to even be playing on the same team as Daruk. He poked his tongue out at Anil gloatingly, who was on the opposing team and panting under the shade of a lime tree.

Mr Vaughan and Mr Lee, who had been supervising the children from the gardens, caught sight of the goal.

"That boy could play for India, you know", Mr Vaughan exclaimed.

"You should see him in cricket. He's highly skilled", Mr Lee agreed.

Ash's revelling didn't last for long. The football had slowly deflated not far into the game, and it was like kicking a rock around.

"Someone go and see if we can borrow that one from the village", Daruk ordered, eyeing up the breathless boys. The children had been forbidden to use any sports equipment owned by the school for play time, due to so much damaged property in the past.

Ash lifted his head. A heroic redemption would work in his favour.

"I'll go and find it", he volunteered.

The village was only a five-minute jog away, through a foot-carved path in the trees, down an open hill, and into the houses on one edge of Dal Lake.

Ash skipped down the hill, panting in the hot sun, and occasionally stopping to catch his breath. The village was quiet in the daytime as all the children were at school, the men were out on boats, fishing, and the women might be planting or picking in nearby fields.

The football caught Ash's eye instantly. It was plump and inviting, glinting in the sunlight. Its round body was wedged underneath the wooden jetty. Ash checked his surroundings and couldn't see anybody except a woman wading in the shallows of the lake about one hundred yards away, with a bucket on a string bobbing up and down behind her. She was too far away to call. He was fairly sure the ball belonged to Anand in class three anyway, who lived in this village. Nobody would mind him taking it. And he would be the school hero once again. The small boy crept over the hot wooden planks shadily, and crouched down, reaching his hand underneath the jetty until he felt the firm plastic football tease his fingers. It was jammed between the two halves of the split jetty post. Shards of the splintered post towered over the ball like daggers ready to stab a frightened victim. Careful not to burst the ball, Ash gave it a gentle push, steadying himself with his free hand. It wouldn't budge, so he jiggled and wiggled it and pushed it a little harder, until *voila!* The ball gave way and pinged out of its fixed position, flying through the air and throwing the child off balance. Ash hurtled forwards and toppled head-first into the water with a huge splash.

He tread the cold water urgently, gasping for breath as he surfaced. Then, as he reached for the ball, each time he brushed it with his fingertips it bobbed a little further away, tauntingly. Ash spun around in humiliation, and flapped his way back to the jetty, hoisting his sodden body onto its frame like an ungraceful fish.

The walk of shame back to school was not only hugely embarrassing but also uncomfortable, as his heavy clothes clung to him, dripping wet. He hadn't even got the football.

Hanging his head sheepishly as he re-approached the school pitch, Ash saw that all the children were back inside their classrooms, staring out of the linear windows as they caught sight of him.

His appearance stirred up class six in a flurry of laughter and whispers, as they pointed and cheered. Emerging from the sea of faces and matching blue uniforms, Daruk stood to his feet and his eyes widened in bewilderment. Ash had never seen his brother try so hard to hide his laughter. He puffed out his cheeks trying to keep the air in, but his eyes beamed with delight. *What on earth?*

Mr Patel was infuriated, and Ash's heart sank at the sight of the man marching out of class six and approaching him on the field. Without saying anything, Mr Patel grabbed the small boy fiercely by the ear. He pulled him over the grass as Ash clenched his fists in pain at the pinching, standing on his tiptoes to ease the pressure of the pulling. Once in his own classroom, Mr Patel let go of him, and Ash stood in the puddle of dripping lake water quivering, facing his classmates who didn't know whether to laugh or cry.

Mrs Sharma shook her head in anguish, empathising with the sorry child. Mr Patel prided the school on their neat uniform and had been known to send children home if they had a white collar missing, or a stained shirt.

"You disrupt your class *and* you come in late from break time looking like this! Do you think this is funny?" Mr Patel bellowed, sending spit globules onto Ash's scrunched up face.

The boy wiped at his cheek subtly. "No, Sir…I-"

"Enough! I'm sending you home. But I'm not having you walk through the village like that, it's a disgrace. Just because your father sponsors this school does not mean you and your brother can walk around like you own the place. You will take off your clothes and change into something from lost property, immediately!" he ordered.

Then, the incensed man charged over to the cupboard in the corner of the room. On the top shelf was a fresh blue and white uniform.

"Go and get changed, right away!" he screamed, throwing the uniform at the boy.

Ash squelched across the classroom and tiptoed out of the doorway, onto the concrete veranda outside, where he began unbuttoning his shirt. He listened to the fierce sound of Mr Patel addressing the whole class inside.

"You have *disgraced* me today! Do you know how many children in India cannot afford to go to school? And here you all are, blessed with the gift of an education in one of the best schools in all of India, and you're messing around, talking over your teacher, not doing your homework, thinking it's funny..."

Ash groaned under his breath as he willed himself to poke his head back into the classroom, shielding his skinny chest from his class.

"Sir... Sir, I can't wear this", he insisted.

Mr Patel's eyes widened in rage. He hated being disrespected but moreover, *hated* being interrupted.

"You will put that clean uniform on at once boy, *if* you want to maintain your place in this school!"

He pointed his finger at the distressed child, glaring at him with such rage. Ash opened his mouth to argue once more, but quickly edged back through the doorway as the teacher eyed up the cane in the corner.

Mortified, Ash peeled off his sopping wet trousers and rolled them down his legs, slipping into the blue and white school *dress*.

It was probably Rita's. Ash knew that Rita was different to the other children in his class, through no fault of her own. Her iris's moved in different directions inside her bloodshot eyeballs and she often dribbled. She sat at the front of the class, and her parents always packed her a spare school uniform because she was prone to having what Mrs Sharma described as "*accidents*".

Shuddering, Ash buttoned up the dress. He had never wanted the ground to swallow him up more now, than in his *entire* life. It was even more unbearable than being called into his father's study alongside Daruk, after Mr Lakhanpal had discovered their carving of "RIP Elephant" in the bottom of his ivory desk. That had not been a good day.

Ash re-entered the classroom and allowed the whole class to gawp at him, their jaws dropping to the floor. Some of the children sniggered, some of them howled, and some of them were simply lost for words. But his brother, who was watching through the conjoining doorway, appeared elated. This was possibly the most embarrassing thing that could ever happen to a class three boy, and the fact it was happening to his brother Ash, was hilarious. Mr Patel, darted across the room and reached for the cane. Ash's heart sank, and even Mrs Sharma tried to stop the man.

"Please, Sir, the child only did as you asked", she begged, rushing to intercept the cane. But it was too late, the headteachers fingers were already wrapped around the fierce instrument.

"Get outside", the infuriated man spat, pointing the cane at Ash.

Ash ran out onto the veranda, quivering. He scrunched his eyes shut, waiting for the inevitable lashes which filled him with anticipating fear.

But it was not Mrs Sharma who stopped the beating just in time, it was Daruk. Ash and Mr Patel looked up in shock as Daruk stood on the veranda.

"You're not allowed to hit him…. by my father's orders." Daruk said firmly, slowly walking up to the unreasonable man. Ash noticed that Daruk's voice was shaking a little when he spoke, but his eye gaze remained calm and strong.

To all of their surprise, Mrs Sharma, who was standing in the doorway; Ash, who's feet were fixed to the floor; Daruk, who seemed fearless; and Mr Patel, who seemed in a state beyond reason, released his grip on the small boy's dress collar, and dropped the cane to the ground.

"Both of you, you are dismissed for the day. Leave the school premises, at once", he said quietly.

*

When the Lakhanpal brothers arrived back home in the early dusk, they found some of the household staff gathered underneath the veranda pillars. Ash was still wearing the dress. They were surprised to see that their father's blacked-out convertible was parked in the front garden, as he was never usually home on a weeknight, certainly not this early. His schedule usually meant that he'd be away on business in Delhi, Jaipur or Mumbai during the week and he'd come home late on a Friday night, reeking of alcohol and tobacco, and use the weekend to recover. He was a very unpredictable man, and this troubled Ash. It's not that he was a monster, he just had the most unbearable mood swings. The boys never knew whether to expect the father who took interest in their school work and occasionally wrestled them in the garden when he was feeling playful, or the father who would be snappy, impatient, and beat them for saying or doing anything that was apparently irritating.

"Oh, no! Mr Patel must have called him", Ash stressed, staring at his father's car in front of their palace home. He hastily began tugging at the dress. Daruk then hurriedly pushed his brother behind the large Rosewood tree in the front garden, and all that could be heard by the household staff was the sound of the brother's shuffling, unbuttoning, and desperate whispers and giggles.

When Daruk finally pushed Ash out from behind the tree, he came face to face with his father, who caught sight of them instantly, from his phone call on the veranda. He snapped his cell phone shut and beckoned his sons towards him, sharply. Ash was now wearing his brother's uniform, which was far too big for him.

Daruk gulped.

"It'll be okay", he whispered, as they made their way across the lawn. They nervously jogged up to the veranda, where Jayminee was lying on her back on a cashmere blanket, wriggling her chubby legs in the air and being cooed over by Gloria, one of the housemaids. Shivani and Manvik, the household help, were packing Mr Lakhanpal's trunk with his suitcases. The setting sun illuminated their white uniforms.

"Boys, your mother and I need to talk to you. Come, sit." Mr Lakhanpal ordered, though his tone was surprisingly soft. He only spoke in Urdu when Roshni was present, as he liked practicing his English with his sons. He'd once before even asked Daruk to help him translate a call with an English business man.

Ash sat down on the rocking chair, gently stroking Jayminee's head, and Daruk knelt beside her. They adored their baby sister, and often fought over who got to hold her first on their return home from school. Gloria was a practical housemaid, who sometimes lacked emotion, but on this day, she gave the boys an especially warm smile, although she appeared somewhat dismayed. Then, the middle-aged woman took her leave and headed into the house.

"*They're home, Mrs Lakhanpal*", she called through the lobby.

Anjani Lakhanpal was wearing his usual smart trousers, a crisp white shirt, which he'd unbuttoned at the collar, and of course, a dazzling shiny pair of black Lakhan shoes.

Roshni joined her family on the veranda, shooting the boys a pain-stricken smile. Something was not right. Ash's eyes wandered to his father's car which had been packed to the brim with various belongings. Could it be they were getting a divorce? Could it be his father was leaving for good? Strangely, Ash did not feel sad about this.

"*What is it, Father?*" Daruk urged, a concerned look replacing his almost permanent smile. His father ran his hand over his face. "*Boys, an opportunity has arisen for us, as a family. An exciting opportunity*", he explained, looking to his wife and putting his arm around her, though she winced uncomfortably.

Anjani rarely showed affection to his wife, in fact,

Ash had only ever witnessed him kiss her once, when they were on a family vacation in Goa.

"*Are we changing schools?*" Ash hoped, still mortified by his day.

Daruk shot him daggers. They both loved their school and deep down, Ash would be sad to leave.

Mr Lakhanpal let out a sigh. His face looked pale and gaunt. The dark circular pads under his black eyes made him look more tired than usual. They often appeared on one of his hangovers, but today, even his facial hair was unkempt.

"*Actually, yes*", he breathed. "*I'm selling the house and we're moving. There will be no tears and no arguing about it. I'm doing this for you. For us. I've had the all clear for setting up two new factories. This will be our biggest success yet.*"

There was a tense silence, as the boys processed the news. Ash's mind began to team with insecurities and worries. *But I love this house, I feel safe in this house. Does the new house have a garden? And a waterfall? And a banyan? Where is this new school? What if the children don't like me? Or tease me? What if I have no friends? What if Daruk and I are split up? What if he can't protect me? Will I still see him every day? Did Mother already know about this? Why didn't she tell us? Why does she want to leave? Have I been bad at school?*

Daruk's silence was fuelled by his own thoughts. *Moving. How exciting! I hope the new house has a tennis court, or maybe a pool. Father's surely upgraded! We'll make new friends, and then at my birthday party, all the friends from our school now and all the friends from the new school will be there. There'll be new girls, too. I'll get double as many presents. Ash and I can share a room again, and explore the new garden, and-*

"*We're moving to England*", Mr Lakhanpal announced.

England.

And with that, even Roshni could not hide her angst anymore at the sudden decision which clearly had not been agreed, or even jointly made. She gulped bitterly, though she did not say a word as her husband squeezed her shoulder controllingly.

Ash knew barely anything of the strange and far away country. Only that the Queen lived there. He couldn't even begin to imagine living there. Daruk frowned, imagining in his head that his mother had probably only just been told the news a few hours earlier. But he knew better than to argue.

Mr Lakhanpal didn't even bother to give his sons time to respond, when his cell phone rang. He flung it open in front of them, letting go of his wife and standing to his feet. Daruk, Roshni and Ash all exchanged concerned glances, which comforted Ash in the moment. Perhaps they were as scared as he was, for once. Mr Lakhanpal spoke in Kashmiri to the caller on the other end of the phone, which Daruk understood to be some sort of business conversation. Just as Mr Lakhanpal turned towards his car, he stopped in his tracks and turned to his family.

"*Daruk, son, why in the hell are you wearing a dress?*" he asked.

5

THE PREMIERE

London, England, 2018

Lola danced around the penthouse with curlers in her hair. She applied a dark red lipstick in front of the bathroom mirror and then jumped up to the hallway mirror to perfect her eyeliner.

"I'm just so excited!" she cried. "Thanks so much for getting my mum a ticket, babe. She can't believe her luck!"

Ash smiled. "And your best friend, and your best friend's mum, and your colleagues, and…your sister?" he laughed.

"Yeah, yeah, thanks for their tickets too!" Lola rejoiced, darting back into the huge glassy bathroom.

Ash's top-floor apartment was immaculate. They overlooked Tower Bridge in London, on the edge of the River Thames. The balcony outside boasted a huge fire pit, hot tub and inviting outdoor sofas and chairs. Anybody crammed into the boathouses below, looked up and envied the huge suite, as they sat in the cramped confines of their boat gardens, bursting with hanging baskets and plants. This was the only greenery which could be seen for miles in the huge concrete city. The cleaners came twice a week, sweeping the spacious laminate floors, dusting the piano, and scouring every crevice of the modern open-plan kitchen.

Lola loved living there. She woke up every morning feeling *lucky*. Her East London background had not been quite so comfortable, but it had given her a closeness with her family that others envied, and coming from humble beginnings gave her an unshakeable pride and gratitude for her achievements as an interior decorator. She'd initially met Ash when he'd hired her team to create a studio set for one of his first films: "The Way Back Home". Her female colleagues had flirtatiously worshipped the ground Ash had walked on. Every morning he'd strut in bossily and give new instructions about the set. But Lola was unimpressed by his sweeping charm and arrogant attitude. She was stubborn, and didn't see him as any more important than anybody else, despite his fame and success. As her friends twirled around him in a desperate-for-approval fluster, making him cups of coffee and hanging on his every word, Lola had folded her arms and even politely disagreed with some of his suggestions.

"I'm just not sure that choice of lampshade connotes an impoverished vibe", she had said honestly, to her colleague's horror.

Ash had looked the young and beautiful Hispanic woman up and down, and folded his arms in interest.

"Oh no?" he asked, with intrigue.

"Lola, *what are you doing?*", her colleague Linzy urged under her breath, glaring at her. Linzy turned to Ash, who's eyes were still fixated on Lola's own. "What Lola means to say is that we love all the ideas, the colours, the era, the props, and we're working on completion for this Friday."

Ash nodded.

"Right…", he expressed, sensing Lola's dissatisfaction.

"It's just, it's from *Harrods*…", she argued.

"Yes, but from the cheap section!" Linzy pressed in a high-pitched fury.

But Lola continued to speak her mind, and that is what drew Ash in. He was so fed up of all the superficiality around him.

"Harrods doesn't *have* a cheap section. I mean, it just doesn't scream poverty to me. I just think you need something tackier. This shade actually has quite a nice finish", Lola continued, pointing at the delicate embroidery covering the lamp.

"Oh, for crying out loud, Lola, perhaps this family splashed out on a lampshade! It's not like it would have been extortionate!" Linzy snapped unprofessionally, blushing with embarrassment, and going to join the rest of the team who were clearly feeding off the drama and eavesdropping in the corner, whilst trying to fiddle with the shabby wallpaper of the set and hang cheap wall frames against it.

Lola shrugged.

"Excuse me, Mr La-Pal, I'll get back to work. We will fit the set with all the props your design team chooses. I'm sorry if my input was uninvited. I guess I just see things from my own perspective. My family would never have been able to afford a lampshade like that, see."

Ash watched her slip away, behind the fake walls of the studio set.

"Neither would mine, at one time", he whispered to himself.

He couldn't get the spirited woman out of his head, even after he arrived home that night.

The next day, Lola was the first to arrive to the film set and unlock the studio. She was the senior artist, after all. She marched across the room in her high heels, her mind focussed on work, and switched the lights on. Something in the living room set caught her eye. It was the lampshade. Sitting on the rundown wicker coffee table she had purchased from a charity shop in Notting Hill, was the lightbulb covered by the tackiest, shabbiest, white plastic shade she'd ever laid eyes upon. She lifted the post-it note which was stuck on the shade, and smiled, letting the butterflies which had so far been for everyone else, fly around deep within her. Ash's writing was surprisingly messy.

You were right, the note said.

*

Ash was a passionate, attentive, and caring boyfriend. This was why it troubled Lola that he'd been distant and incommunicative these past weeks. She knew he was stressed at work, but there was something else preoccupying him that he wasn't prepared to share. Ash, up until now, had always been so good at putting her first, at making time for friends and family above any of his film developments. Heck, he was heroic at doing that, sometimes it made Lola wonder whether he was even *fussed* by how successful he was. It wasn't that he appeared ungrateful, for he'd known hardship, and struggle, and poverty, just as she had. It was almost as if nothing was ever good enough to satisfy him, and this is what troubled Lola the most. That is where she'd hoped the counselling would help.

Finally dressed in a gorgeous black-velvet, low cut number which clung to her slim body, Lola bounced out of the bathroom and sensually walked over to Ash, who was engrossed in his laptop screen. Clean shaven and sporting a shiny tuxedo, he slammed his laptop shut and looked to Lola to fix the bow tie dangling loosely around his neck, but when he caught sight of her radiance, he stopped for breath, for the first time in days.

"Wow", he said, "you look *incredible.*"

Lola's plump lips lifted her cheekbones in a dazzling smile, revealing her pearly teeth. She reached for Ash's collar, but he grabbed at her hips and pulled her up against himself, running his hands gently across her bouncy black curls.

"You're perfect", he whispered, getting lost in her smile. She felt happily relieved by his engaging arms, as he'd seemed so vacant recently. He reached for the two champagne-filled glasses on the pristine coffee table.

"Actually, Ash… I'm not going to drink to-", she began, but she was interrupted by his blaring ringtone. Usually, Ash would silence his phone, throw it down onto the nearest soft landing and take his girlfriend in his arms and begin unwrapping her clothes at a time like this. Even if it would make them late. He always wanted to remind her that she was what mattered most to him. But today, he gently pushed Lola away and immediately tapped his phone to accept the call, dashing away towards the bedroom.

Knowing she'd be upset, he poked his head back out through the bedroom doorway and called, "Sorry I have to take this, babe", somewhat flustered. Then, he slammed the bedroom door shut.

Lola slumped down into the huge cream-coloured corner sofa and let out an exhausted sigh of disappointment. She knew Ash had a busy mind, a painful past, and hidden depths she hadn't managed to completely unravel yet, but she *hated* being shut out.

Ash rushed over to the huge oak dresser in the corner of his spacious bedroom. Lola had all sorts of eye shadows, mascaras and hair products scattered over the surface. He pulled at the top drawer, and dug out her decorated writing paper and hastily threw it on the table, reaching for a pen.

"I've found your guy", came the male voice on the other end of the phone.

Ash gulped. "And?" he urged, gripping the pen tightly and hovering his shaking hand over the paper.

"Well, his family moved from that address in Essex over ten years ago. His parents split up, and she took the three other siblings, but it seems, your man, Charles Wincott went to live with the father, although the father lives abroad now, in Spain. I then managed to get a forwarding address of his mum. I spoke to her on the phone posing as an insurance provider, she went through a whole quote with me-"

"Simon, cut to the chase, I haven't got long", Ash urged. "Where is he now? Where's Charles Wincott?

Did you find him?"

"Well, yeah I did, only he goes by Frances now. Well, Frankie. Frankie Wincott. That's his middle name, that's what made him so hard to find. He went to Oxford University, class of 2008. He achieved a First Class Honours in Business Management. He worked as a Senior Director for a huge investment bank in Canary Wharf for four years, and then he sort of, just slipped off the radar for a couple years. There are no records of him anywhere during this time. Now he has his own business as a landscape gardener, and lives in Surrey."

There was a silence as Ash tried to gather his thoughts. He and Lola had been looking at purchasing a property in Surrey after his next film release.

Of course he went to Oxford University, the pretentious bastard, Ash thought to himself, seething. *That sounds about right, he got a First Class Degree and wound up a Bank Director.*

"Ash?" came the voice, "this is what you wanted, right?"

Ash snapped back into the phone call.

"He's a *gardener*?" he questioned, confused. "Who leaves a senior role at a bank to be a *gardener*? It doesn't make any sense. He comes from big money."

"Who knows, Ash? Maybe the guy wanted a quiet life. He's certainly got one now. He charges reasonable rates to mow people's lawns and reconstruct their patios. Now are you satisfied? Is my work done?"

"Yeah. Yes of course. Thank you. Send me his current address and the link to his website. I'll transfer your money across now. Remember, it includes you forgetting this search and this whole conversation, got it?"

"Understood. Emailing you now. Goodbye."

And then the voice was gone. Simon worked as a private investigator in the USA, and Ash had first met the man when he was making a documentary about undercover work whilst touring the states with Lola, two years before.

Ash fixated on the scruffy scribbles on the paper in front of him.

Frankie Wincott. Oxford Graduate. Garden Landscaper. Surrey.

It was unsettling and cryptic. Charles, *Charlie* back then, had changed his name to *Frances*. *Frankie*. He grew up in a huge house in Essex. His family had owned four cars. And now he was a *gardener*. This is not what Ash had envisioned. How was he going to work this into all he had planned, these past years? There wasn't time to think now, as Lola burst through the door.

"Babe, we're going to be late. The limo is here", she said, although the excitement in her voice was gone.

Ash was too preoccupied in the leathery limousine to notice Lola wasn't drinking. They shared the luxurious space with some of the cast of the movie, including Ash's producer Sarah and her husband Mark. Sarah and Mark were good friends of Lola and Ash, and they'd enjoyed many a drunken taxi ride with them before. Ash made sure he joined in with the communal laughter of every joke, even if he didn't know what it was about. He chinked his glass at every toast, despite not listening to a single word that was said. He threw back every shot he was passed, even when he couldn't taste it. His mind was in a completely different place. A dark place.

The white lights flashed in a frenzy as they stepped

out of the moving lounge, and onto the red carpet. But the paparazzi's yells were hardly heard by Ash's ears; he was too busy running over the recent phone call in his mind. The crowds were huge, bundled up in their puffer jackets and woolly hats, waving banners and handmade posters in the air. Ash slipped his hand onto the small of Lola's back, leading her across the carpet. She was still star struck by it all, but she managed to mask her nerves behind her glittering smile.

Ash stepped across the carpet in a daze.

"Cast and director", a young, suited photographer ordered, leaping into Ash's personal space. "Can we have a photo with the full cast and director?"

Before Ash had time to blink, the enthusiastic photographer was marshalling up the cast in a tight gathering. Ash clumsily slipped into the far side of the picture, next to Samantha Walsh, the lead actress in "Dragon Train". But the gutsy photographer ushered Ash into the middle of the photo, before arranging all the actors and actresses around him. Then, the photographer crouched in front of the glamorous young group, clicking his camera and emitting blinding flashes of white light about thirty times, and shouting, "That's it!", and "Lovely!"

Ash searched the carpet for Lola, who was revelling in all the attention and posing for a photograph with Sarah. They held hands and lifted them in the air, laughing and grinning.

Suddenly, a voice emerged from the noise behind him.

"Director! Can we have a word with the director please?"

Ash spun around and was faced with a captive

audience of fans, leaning over the silver barriers, reaching for him and flapping various banners and autograph papers in his face. In front of the crowd was a stocky, middle-aged reporter with a black beard, holding his microphone out. There was a cameraman trailing behind him pointing the lens directly into Ash's stunned face, and a boom which was encroaching closely.

He just wanted to escape. It was overwhelming. All he wanted to do was be in a quiet room and carry out the private research he so desperately yearned for. But he found himself adopting a false smile and stepping into the interview.

"Absolutely", he agreed, obligingly.

"Ash La-Pal, firstly congratulations on "Dragon Train". Critics have said this could be your darkest movie yet, would you agree?" the reporter pressed.

Ash thought about the scenes of violence and psychedelic fantasy in the film.

"I suppose it is, yes. Though I think there's darker to come in the future, for sure", he answered.

"What does it feel like, Ash, seeing all these people gathered here today to watch *your* film; one that you wrote up on a piece of paper initially?"

Ash froze for a moment, entranced by the words: *a piece of paper.*

The story had been written up on a piece of paper. It had been drafted with genius. The enticing beginning, the thrilling climax, the heart-wrenching ending. But Ash hadn't written the story. And he was the only one in this whole charade who knew who had. He gulped, anxiously.

"It feels surreal. Very surreal", he said

uncomfortably.

Lola was glancing over at Ash regularly, haunted by the memory of Ash attacking the reporter at his trailer release earlier in the year. The interview continued for far longer than Ash would have liked, and made his head hurt. He grabbed a glass of bubbly on his way into the cinema entrance, and rudely pulled Lola away from yet another photographer.

"I need to get some air", he explained. "I feel a bit sick."

But Lola pulled back.

"Ash, what's going on? This is *your* premiere. This is *your* big moment! Look around! They're all here for *you*. Anyone else would kill to be in your position right now, and you're acting like-"

"Like what?" Ash asked crossly, forcing the untouched champagne glass into her hand.

"Like you don't even care! Like you have more important things to do", she whispered sourly, gripping his arm with rage. They were beginning to attract attention. Ash glared at the unwanted onlookers.

"Well, maybe I do", he retorted, storming past her and hurtling through the crowd.

He ignored the various calls and pats on his back as he charged through the packed-out cinema lobby.

"Ash! Tonight's the night!"
"Well done, son! What a turn out!"
"There's the man of the hour-"
"Asha, what's your poison?"

The corridor to the screen rooms were cordoned off with a red ribbon, guarded by two bulky security guards.

"I'm the director, I need to get through", Ash demanded.

The guards glanced at each other unnervingly.

"Sir, we've been asked not to-" one of them stuttered.

"... but for you, we will make an exception." The other interrupted in haste, unclipping one side of the ribbon, and beckoning him through.

Ash marched down the dark blue corridor, and past the two soundproof double doors which had been propped open, revealing the huge theatre inside. The red curtains were drawn. The front row had been reserved for him, and he would later be expected to accept an award and give a speech.

But for now, he carried himself to the end of the corridor, and threw the fire escape open. The chilling air filled his lungs, and he inhaled it deeply, as he slumped against the brick wall, falling into a crouch in the dirty, deserted alleyway. He listened to the faint noise of the crowds around the corner in the square, and the hum of the traffic.

He ran his hand over his gelled cowlick and tapped open his emails on his phone. He scrolled through various congratulatory messages, until he saw the email with the subject: "INFO".

He read it under his breath.

Frankie Wincott, 67 Hampton Street, Guildford, Surrey…

Bespoke Landscaper and Garden Designer. For quotes, please call…

Ash scrolled down to the bottom of the email where a link to Frankie's website had been attached.

The website was well designed and easy to navigate, it boasted several pictures of stunning flower filled gardens, water features, deckings with hot tubs, and patios. Reviews with five stars sped across the homepage:

"Better than I could have ever imagined"
"Wonderful friendly service"
"I won open-garden 2016, thanks to Frankie and his team"

Ash tapped the drop-down menu and selected 'gallery'. A few pictures in, and *there he was*. After all these years. He was a fully grown man. Ash's heartbeat began to hasten with rage. He grit his teeth, letting his fury bubble as he studied Frankie's face. He couldn't believe it. He'd finally found him.

Frankie's hair was just as fair as it had been all those years ago, when he was a teenager. His pretentious combover however, was now styled into a plain cut with a short fringe. He had a stubbly, slim face and ocean-blue eyes. His smile looked warm and approachable. But as Ash studied the thirty-something year old, all he could picture was the vile teenager he had encountered back then. He saw through this innocent photograph of an average looking man, and remembered the malice that had once filled his eyes.

"What's going on, Ash?"

Ash pressed his phone screen off and looked up to see a concerned Lola. She shivered in the cold, and wrapped her arms around herself, but as she walked closer, her face softened.

Ash remained silent, peering down the eerie alley way.

"Please, just talk to me", she said, crouching down next to him. Suddenly, he realised how unfair he had been.

He leant over and buried his face in her thick curls, kissing the top of her head.

"I'm sorry', he whispered.

"Was tonight not attention enough? You wanted a bit more airtime, so caused a scene?" she sighed, nestling into his neck.

"Something like that", Ash muttered.

"You're going to have to tell me what's going on sooner or later, Ash", Lola said softly, edging away from him. "I'm... *we're*... going to have a baby."

"*What?*"

Lola nodded nervously, "I've been trying to tell you all day, and then what with the premiere I didn't want to-"

He slipped his hand behind her head, gently held her hair, and pulled her lips against his, kissing her fiercely. He took his other hand and gently touched her stomach, and his eyes filled with joy.

"Really?" he whispered, ecstatically. And suddenly, all his spiralling thoughts became just one thought, which was how deeply he loved Lola and felt the luckiest man alive to be fathering her child.

"Really", she confirmed, "so I need to know you're with me, and that you're okay."

Ash paused for a moment.

"I'm with you", he said softly. "I'll love you and our baby, *for as long as I am standing.*"

6

THE AIRPORT

London, England, 2000

What was this feeling? Ash had never experienced anything quite like it. It engulfed his whole body and made the hairs on his little brown arms stand up on end. His teeth chattered together uncontrollably, and his whole frame shivered. He found his arms wrapping around himself, in an attempt for it to go away.

He was so cold. They alighted the aircraft nervously, clinging to the steel bannister, uneasy against the harsh silver blowing jets. His mother held Jayminee tightly in one arm, and used the bannister to steady herself as she cautiously made her way down the steps.

Daruk and Ash were in charge of the bags, clumsily hauling them down the temporary stairs.

Ash looked around at Heathrow airport. It was so

bleak. So grey. The aircrafts were deafening monsters, taking off and landing with piercing roars like the roaring of the thunder in monsoon season. Men in fluorescent jackets wearing little earmuffs seemed to be the only people to communicate with each other, and even that was through gestural signalling.

Ash hurried along after his brother, and they jumped onto the exceptionally clean bus. There was so much more space than on the buses in India, where it was stuffy, noisy and so overcrowded that you found yourself being pushed into somebody else's legs half the time. The people's faces were all so white and somber. They each clutched identical suitcases on rollers. Even the children seemed tame and quiet. Their hair was fair and red and black and brown, and their eyes were blue and green. The bus swerved over the concrete, heading towards the colossal white building of glass windows, billboards and signs.

Like robots, the people marched off the bus, and towards the terminal.

Ash looked to his brother nervously, but Daruk was eagerly taking in their new surroundings with a mind so open, just about anything could wander in.

Everything looked so immaculate and colourless. Shiny glass windows, great long passages of thin carpet, and metal steps on a magic conveyer belt which moved up and down, carrying people as if they were floating. Voices with strong English accents boomed out of the black speakers on the ceiling. Everybody seemed to be rushing, but there wasn't much chaos. It was all so regimented with people standing in front of small coffee shops, single file. Mothers clutching their toddler's hands and people walking in straight lines. The air smelt bland. No hotness. No richness. No aroma of chapattis frying, or sweet flowers, or wet lush grass. People didn't shout, or beep their horns, or whizz around like they did in India.

Soon enough, the young boys joined the queue for border control, and found themselves giggling once again and making faces at Jayminee, who was contently nestled into their mothers' neck, clutching at her sari. Roshni looked nervous, the paperwork in her hands was shaking a little. But she was following her husband's instructions like the hands which obey a clock.

"Pappa will be waiting for us, just the other side of those walls", Roshni exclaimed, matter-of-factly, although she wouldn't feel settled until they were finished with this whole ordeal. Roshni was a strong woman and wouldn't let it show that she was petrified about doing this alone. She resented her husband for not being with her, but she knew better than to argue with him at this time. Her priority was the children. She had to keep them safe.

Though all the signs were written in English and she could not read them, she knew Daruk was a clever boy. He would help. The plane journey had been tedious and confusing for her. Jayminee had cried a lot of the way, and she felt embarrassed and helpless. Everybody else's children were somehow so quiet on the aircraft. It was nothing like in India, where they would all be running free and quite often become another empathetic mothers' problem.

Ash had been terrified at take-off.

"It's going to be fine, brother. It's going to be fun! Now, are you with me?" Daruk had said, holding out his hand.

Their fingers interlinked as the plane hurtled across

the runway and lifted them into the air. Daruk gazed out the window with amazement, as the luscious, forest-filled, mountainous country grew smaller beneath them. Ash squeezed his brother's hand tightly, and kept one eye shut as he dared to take just a peak at the world below.

Soon after, they had both embraced the flight, figuring out how to work their little television screens within minutes and fighting over who got the window seat. Daruk was in the aircraft toilet when they'd first hit a patch of turbulence, and he hurried back to his seat, knowing Ash would be in pieces. He was.

But just as Daruk had assured him, they had landed safely. And now here they were.

At each border desk was a different member of border control, and they were all straight faced and intimidating, wearing their badges and uniforms as if they had something to prove.

They finally reached the front of the queue.

"Do you think they'll be a tree in our new garden?" Ash asked, hopefully.

Daruk stared at the customs desk, growing more and more aware of the unfriendly faces. But his ever-present positivity exuded from him.

"I'm sure there will be, brother" he replied, reassuringly.

"Do they have snakes in England?" Ash pondered, gazing at the billboards on the walls behind the customs desks. They displayed photographs of palace gardens, a brightly lit up city, with white Ferris wheels and towering golden clocks. But all the animals were behind bars, strangely, under the title, "London Zoo".

"I don't think so, Ash. No snakes", Daruk laughed.

Ash smiled. No snakes. Perhaps he'd like this country after all.

"*Daruk, come and translate for me*", their mother suddenly ordered, pulling her eldest son by the arm. He stood on his tiptoes until his chin surpassed the desk, and he could see the broad shouldered, square jawed, manly woman who sat behind the glass panel.

"Do you speak English?" she asked slowly, as her gaze flicked between Daruk's wide eyes and his passport photograph.

"Yes, I speak it", he replied proudly, smiling up at his mother.

The woman nodded.

"My colleague is going to help you. You need to wait here, okay?" she said, concerned, before standing up to reveal the belt around her uniform, which had a large golden medal attached to it. Ash thought it looked over the top and attention seeking. Daruk thought it looked exciting and important.

"*What's going on?*" Ash asked, wishing he could understand as well as his brother. Although they spoke English at school and with each other, there were still some words which Ash struggled to comprehend. What did the word *colleague* mean?

"*She's going to get somebody to help us*", Daruk explained to Roshni, who felt flustered by the queue of people backing up behind them, hearing their sighs of impatience.

"*Is there something wrong with our passports? I've brought all of the documents your father gave me*", she insisted.

"*I don't know, Mamma, she didn't say*", Daruk responded, as his mother held out Jayminee and forced the baby into his arms. Then, Roshni laid out various papers and files on the counter, trying hopelessly to remember which was which. Roshni was a strong woman, and she'd always found ways around her illiteracy, though it frustrated her and made her feel inadequate, often. When motor taxis came by the house to take the family on days out, to the swimming pool, or to the animal sanctuary, she often fought with the drivers when they handed her, her change. She had always understood rupee notes by their colours, and Mr Lakhanpal had taught her that a blue note was fifty rupees, therefore she would only accept this as change. When Daruk had tried to explain that a number of yellow rupee notes combined were equivalent to the same amount, and the driver wasn't trying to con her, she'd got cross and felt humiliated.

The large woman behind the counter returned, with a man by her side. He was wearing a different kind of uniform; a black padded vest, a chequered black and white cap, and a belt with a dangling baton. His aged face looked sincere, yet kind. The police officer smiled weakly.

The woman nodded at Roshni and pointed to the officer, who was waiting for them behind the counter.

"This man is going to help you", she said to Daruk, "follow him, son." Her expression had softened somewhat.

Daruk beckoned his mother, and the family followed the officer past the border, away from the crowds of immigrants and nationals, through some automatic glass doors and down a quieter, cool corridor.

What's happening to us? Ash worried to himself, reaching out his hand and grabbing at his mother's dress.

Father's probably got us a fast pass, skipping all the queues, Daruk thought to himself optimistically.

The officer then stopped halfway down the corridor and scanned a badge across the small silver screen on the heavy padded door, until it beeped. He opened the door and welcomed the family inside. The room was neat and basic, with a computer and desk, and several plastic seats splayed out on the thin corduroy carpet.

There were two other police officers sat down inside the room, chatting sternly, who immediately rose to their feet when the family entered. They gestured for Roshni to take a seat on one of the plastic chairs, and she did so obediently, dusting off her pink sari, and holding out her hands to Jayminee who was pining for her. She sat the baby down on her lap, tensely knocking her knees up and down to entertain the infant.

"Where's the interpreter?" the male police officer, who had brought them in, asked quietly.

But the two other police officers, one a young, blonde female, and the other, a greying man, shook their heads awkwardly.

"There isn't one available. Do they not speak any English?" the young woman asked the officer, as if the family weren't even present.

"The boy speaks English", the officer replied, "but this won't do. They were supposed to get us an interpreter of sorts", he said irritably. Then, the walky-talky clipped onto his chest started beeping, and an inaudible muffled voice came through, speaking, disruptively.

Daruk smiled cockily, translating to his mother.

"*They are going to ask me to translate*", he grinned.

"Look I need to leave. If there are no translators

available then you're going to have to use the child, but this won't go down well with Whitmarsh. It's completely unethical", he snapped. And with that, ignoring the family, he stepped outside, huffing.

Ash gawped at the two officers, swinging his legs on his seat, in impatience. The sleepless flight was starting to sink into his weary bones, and he yawned.

"What do these people's badges say?" Roshni whispered to Daruk, not taking her eyes off the officers.

"It says 'Po-Lees'… Police, they are police, Mother." Daruk whispered back.

The male officer sighed, he knew this was going to be challenging and was unsure whether he should go ahead. He paused for a moment, then sat forward. His grey hair was shaven neatly to the sides of his uncomfortable expression. The furrows in his forehead deepened, as he leant forward, flicking his gaze between Daruk and Roshni, and ignoring Ash completely.

"I need your mother to look at this picture, and tell us who the man is, do you understand? Is the man in the picture her husband… your father?" he asked, somewhat sympathetically.

Daruk nodded politely, impressed with himself for understanding their English accents. He turned to his mother and translated in their own dialect of Urdu, *"They will show you a photograph and you tell them if it is papa, eh?"*

Roshni nodded impatiently.

"Can you confirm for us, that this is your husband, Mr Anjani Eshin Lakhanpal?" the officer asked, handing Roshni a passport.

There was no need for Daruk to translate that. Roshni heard her husband's name and understood what she was being asked to do as the passport was handed to her. She opened it slowly, took one brief glance at it and shot her eye gaze back up to the officers.

"*It's him. Is there a problem?*" she asked. She hadn't realised how worried this situation was making her until she heard the shaking in her own voice. Daruk's tone changed too.

"Yes, that's him", he echoed to the officers.

Ash slipped off his seat and walked the few steps to his mother, opening the passport in her hands and staring at his father's younger face. Anjani had always kept his passport in the top drawer of his ivory desk. Ash missed their home already.

The male police officer looked to the ground, dismayed. The family looked at him in anticipation.

"My mother said that, the photograph is our father. Where is he?" Daruk repeated, with a touch more urgency. "He came to England three weeks ago, he said he would be waiting for us here."

The male officer shot a stressed glance at the female police officer, and she sat forwards immediately.

"I'm afraid we have some bad news", she said, speaking with a quiet and sensitive empathy. "Your father, Mr Lakhanpal, died last night in a road traffic accident. We tried to contact you as soon as it happened, but you were already on the flight. We are so, very sorry."

Her words sent shivers down Daruk's spine, penetrating his mind like a sharp stab with no warning. He was stunned, and so utterly confused.

It couldn't be *true*. Could it? His jaw dropped, but his eyes remained dry.

"*What is it? What is it, Daruk? What are these people*

saying?" Roshni urged irritably.

Ash had understood. He understood the words 'died', and 'father', and 'last night'. He too, could not articulate his very emotions in this moment, and could not possibly open his mouth to speak. He waited for his brother to translate, desperately hoping he had misunderstood the news in some way.

"Do you understand what I've said?" the policewoman asked, as Daruk remained silent, gawping at her. He slowly nodded his head, but his eyes were fixed on her in a vacant trance, trying to picture the scenario that lead to his father's death, trying to picture a life without him, in a split second.

Roshni reached over and gave Daruk a sharp pinch on the arm, awakening him.

"What have these people told you? Is your father in trouble with the police?" she demanded irritably, but then, about to continue her rant, she hesitated. She caught a glance of her other son, Asha. A tear from each of his striking eyes, tracked down his smooth cheeks, as if they were racing with each other. And she suddenly felt less impatient, less irritated, and more frightened. Not for herself, but for her children.

"They said, he has died", Daruk croaked.

7

THE THERAPIST PART II

London, England, 2018

"Welcome back Ash", Geoff said warmly, sitting down in the garden conservatory.

Ash sunk into the seat opposite, feeling far more comfortable this time round. He knew Geoff would put him at ease and not make him talk about anything which distressed him. He felt safe here. But he knew it was only a matter of time before he'd be forced to revisit his darkened past, which had robbed him of every happy memory he'd ever held dear, prior to that doom filled day.

"Thank you. How's your week been Geoff?" Ash asked, sipping at his takeaway coffee cup which he'd picked up on route to the counsellor's home.

Geoff beamed at him. "Oh, well thanks for asking, it's been rather tame really", he chuckled. "I'm much more interested in how your week has been."

Ash thought back over his week. He thought about the school break-in, which luckily hadn't made it to the papers; he thought about his film premiere, which had: "*Ash La-Pal's finest story yet*", and "*Film of the year; epic genius!*"; he thought about the news that he was going to become a father; and he thought about the search for Frankie Wincott finally being over. But although the hunt was complete, his uncertain plan was only just beginning, and how it was about to unfold, was going to change *everything*.

"My week's been okay", he replied, "dramatic as usual."

"Any particular feelings or emotions you've felt have been prominent this week?" Geoff asked, resting his wrinkled hands on the table and leaning forward in concentration.

Ash looked to the ground.

"Err…I suppose, um, anger. Rage. Fury", he said bitterly, gritting his teeth as he spat the sour words out. "But also, happiness, I felt happiness when I was with my girlfriend."

"Sure", Geoff said, intrigued by Ash's response. "What did you feel the night of your premiere? Was this where your happiness stemmed from?"

"No, no. I mean, don't get me wrong I was glad it went well. But it didn't really faze me. I'd already seen the movie in full", Ash explained, swirling the remains of his coffee around in the cup before gulping it down.

"But I mean the success of it all, seeing all those people congratulate you and turn up in crowds for *your* work, how does that make you feel?" Geoff pressed, reaching for his black leather notebook.

"It makes me feel like a fraud. It makes me feel guilty. It makes me feel... I don't know, numb? I just don't care to think about it really. I just see my job as a job", Ash said, earnestly. This was the first time he'd spoken about his true emotions out loud, in what seemed like forever. He was even surprising himself with how honest he was being, but Geoff made him feel so relaxed and safe, that it didn't torment him. It felt almost natural.

"Do you think you don't allow yourself to feel proud and happy about your work?" Geoff continued, writing softly in his notebook.

"It's not my work, Geoff", Ash said with self-loathing, "but the world will know about that, soon enough."

Geoff stopped jotting, dropped his pen and lifted his rounded designer glasses onto his balding head. He feared Ash was irritated and would soon start shutting down. He saw this happen a lot amongst clients, and it was his job to manage the breakthroughs, keep them noted, but never push the client too far.

He decided it would be best to change the subject, for now. He wanted to understand the route of denying self-happiness.

"You were telling me, in our last session, about your early childhood. You said that was a happy time. Can you pinpoint where it started to not feel quite so happy? Did you experience any sort of change, or grief, perhaps?"

Ash nodded. "Both", he said.

"Would you be able to tell me about where things started to go wrong?" Geoff asked, compassionately.

Ash's leg began to shake. "Yeah, yeah I can do that",

he breathed, gathering his thoughts, clutching at the armrest. "It all sort of turned to shit when we first moved to England", he began. The kind old counsellor listened, intently.

"My father had gone ahead of us, to secure his business and get us a place to live. And then, er, well we rocked up at the airport, my mum, my brother, my sister and I, and these police officers took us to one side and told us that my dad had died in a car accident."

"Oh, gosh. Please, go on", Geoff pursued, pushing his notebook away completely.

"I wasn't close with my father. He was a bit of a stranger to me, to be honest. I guess I was a bit scared of him, as well. We were always on edge when he was around, even my mother. He wasn't horrendous or anything, I just didn't really have much of a relationship with him. When he died, it was more that it messed everything up for our family. We'd had it so good up until then. Like literally, I'd grown up like royalty. We went to the best school in Northern India, and lived in this amazing house. But it turned out that that came at a price - my dad hadn't been an honest man." Ash said regretfully. "But I received a letter, from my uncle, my dads' brother that is, about twelve years ago, and it sort of explained to me why my father was the way he was. I suppose I made some sort of peace with him, in that moment."

"It's good to make peace", Geoff agreed. "So why didn't you return to India after your father had died?"

"We couldn't. We wanted to. My mother especially. But my dad was in so much trouble. He'd kept my mum in the dark about everything. He'd lied about so much. He sold our house in India and used a lot of the money to pay off the authorities over there. He was in trouble for running his factories like sweatshops."

"I see", Geoff said, quite unsurprised. "And so, there was no home to return to?"

"That's right. But aside from that, he'd lied about his new business venture in England too. Well, there was no venture basically. Nothing solid anyway. It was all a bit of a gamble and he'd already invested all our money into it, and it fell through. So, there was nothing left", Ash explained, hanging his head in shame.

He remembered how sick he'd felt when Daruk had explained to him about his father's corruption. It wasn't just the relentless working hours and inhumane conditions he'd placed his factory workers under, but it was the allegations of assault too. It made Ash seethe to think about how his mother had been burdened by such a man, and he felt ashamed to call him Father.

But he also remembered the conversation that Daruk had had with him that same night, when Ash vowed to be angry at their father forever. Daruk had sat beside him on the grass, outside of the asylum seekers refuge in London, back in the year, 2000.

"I can't believe Father left us nothing. I can't believe how stupid he was. How he treated all those people and those women", Ash had sobbed, dismayed.

But Daruk knew how to console his brother, always. Somehow, he knew the right thing to say.

"Ash, we are all just products of what has happened to us, until we decide to change. Do you know what that means?"

Ash shook his head.

"Not really", he replied.

Daruk used his hands to gesture. "If somebody

inflicts pain on somebody else, or treats them badly, it's because he was treated badly. And so, the cycle goes on, from generation to generation, until one person decides, enough."

"So, what are you saying? Somebody treated Father badly and that's why it's okay he hurt all those other workers?"

"No, it doesn't mean it's okay. It just means he didn't find a way to let go of the darkness inside of him, so he passed it on to others. You have to forgive him Ash, or the darkness will be passed on to you, and you'll pass that onto your children."

Ash dismissed the wise words, intent on holding onto his disappointment.

"Well, I don't forgive him, and neither should you. If you forgive him then it's like saying you agree with what he did to those women and all those workers."

Daruk picked at the grass.

"I don't agree, Ash. I will never agree. But, tell me how you feel right now?"

Ash thought for a moment.

"Angry and sad; I feel angry at him, and sad for us."

"Exactly, because you've let the pain be passed on to you. Forgive him, brother. And the pain will stop here, and we will promise each other never to pass it on, not to each other, not to anybody else."

If only that had been true, Ash now thought to himself, in the therapist's home. If only he had known in that moment, Daruk would go on to cause Ash more pain than he'd ever thought imaginable. After recalling the conversation, and the words he'd wanted to trust, he snapped back into reality, facing Geoff.

"We got assigned a social worker and had to seek

asylum for a few months before they found us a council house, in Essex."

"That must have been challenging", Geoff commented, listening attentively.

"It actually wasn't so bad. I mean, I don't remember being too unhappy at that stage. It was hard for my mum because she didn't speak much English, but she got involved with a women's asylum seekers support group, and there were women there from Madha Pradesh who she made friends with. Actually, I seem to remember my mum being a lot more relaxed after my father had passed away. My brother and I shared a room, well a bed actually, and we used to make dens and go out exploring London, and we made some friends with some of the others in the refuge, so it wasn't so bad."

"Did you maintain a good relationship with the rest of your family? Your brother and sister and mother?" Geoff asked.

"Yeah", Ash smiled deeply. "Daruk was my best friend growing up", he exclaimed, before quickly reaching into his pocket and pulling out his phone. He tapped it open and ran his fingers over the screen, scrolling through his camera roll.

"And this is a picture from the premiere last week, it's me and my sister, Jay", he explained, holding his phone screen out for Geoff to appreciate.

Jayminee, now in her early twenties, had inherited her mother's luscious brown complexion, delicate nose and alluring eyes. Her jet-black hair was sprayed up in a towering quiff and fixed with fancy silver hair pins in the photograph where her arms were thrown around her brother's trim suit jacket. They were both wearing huge grins, flashing their supremely white teeth, and their eyes seemed to mirror each others.

"That's a lovely photograph", Geoff exclaimed, gladly, "you look alike."

"Yeah, she's training to be a midwife now", Ash said proudly.

"So, you mentioned that you eventually got granted a house in the end, on a council estate?" Geoff pressed, "what was that time in your life like?"

Ash shuddered.

8

THE SOCIAL WORKER

Essex, England 2000

Ash pressed his face up against the car window, watching the traffic roll out on the streets, and the people bustle outside the moving vehicle. They were on their way to their new home, and had just crossed over into Essex.

The social worker, Marie Coles, drove slowly and carefully, gripping the gearstick with her black leather gloves, and making the changes smoothly.

Roshni sat in the passenger seat, and her two sons were sat in the back, either side of Jayminee in her travel cot. It was the first time Ash had been in a car since they'd arrived in England, and he clung to the door handle nervously. It wasn't until now he began to envision his father's car accident. He wondered if he had died instantly, or had had time to think for just a moment. He wondered if his father had thought about them at all, before he died.

The streets were pleasant and less busy and smoggy than London's. Daruk was happy to see a group of men dressed in white woollen vests playing a game of cricket on a large green, where others walked their dogs, played frisbee or laid in pairs on blankets, lovingly intertwined around their picnic hampers. Daruk loved cricket as much as he loved all sports, running, swimming, and football.

"I'm so excited to see the house!" Daruk exclaimed.

"No more shared toilets", Ash agreed.

"No more crazy Mrs Kitts next door", Daruk chuckled.

"Do you think Abdullah and Samra will write to us?" Ash asked, thinking of the friends they were leaving behind in the refuge.

"Of course, they will. We'll go visit them soon, too. Their new house sounds nice, they're moving to Lewisham and it's not too far away, brother", Daruk reassured him.

The brothers chatted among themselves, almost all the way to the new house. Ash quizzed Daruk on what their new school would be like, whether their family allowance would continue, whether they'd get a key worker to take them to watch *Dinosaurs* at the cinema, and how they'd decorate their bedroom walls, with dragons or pirates or tigers. They pulled faces and giggled behind the seat of their oblivious social worker every time she began singing along enthusiastically to the car radio. When they pulled into the estate however, the atmosphere changed, and the boys' sudden silence caused their mother to stir from her doze.

The front gardens were no bigger than a few strides wide. Strewn over the neglected grass were plastic children's scooters, tatty pieces of unwanted furniture, or bursting black bins which hadn't been collected in weeks. There was a considerable amount of litter all over the pavements, knocked over sign-posts, stray car tyres and defaced wheelie bins. Offensive graffiti covered every bus stop and lamppost, and broken glass glinted on every corner. There were youthful gangs, huddled on the street corners, some on BMX bikes, some on mopeds, all hooded and masked in balaclavas or scarves. Women, in less clothing than Ash had seen the tourists wear on Goa's beaches, were strutting around the estate with cigarettes in their hands, not paying attention to their young children who trailed along behind them. One held her middle finger up to a passing bus. Ash knew what that meant… Daruk had told him.

A heavily tattooed skinhead who looked as though he'd just escaped prison, jogged along past their car, glared at Roshni and then spat in the street, before aggressively tugging at the silver dog chain enslaving his pit-bull terrier. Two teenagers sat in a stolen supermarket trolley on the next bend, huddling over their lighters as if they'd nothing else to live for. But it was the teenage girl sitting on top of, whom Roshni could only assume, the girl's boyfriend, in a derelict park that made her grimace, hoping to God that her children couldn't see what they were up to. Her boys knew what sex was. She remembered the day that Daruk had told Ash about what he'd learnt from a friend at school, and Ash had come running into the house, in disgust, asking if it were true.

The houses were small and stacked up next to each other like dominoes, and they each displayed identical plastic window frames and monotonous brick work.

They turned a corner, and Marie slowed the car to a halt, pulling up outside a row of similarly constructed houses. Opposite the houses was a strip of poorly placed garages, and an empty, neglected green.

"Here we are", Marie enthused, though her tone was as disheartened as the boys faces. This was truly grim. The family clambered out of the car, and hurried into the house with their few belongings, trying to escape the barking and the shouting coming from the street behind.

The smell of damp greeted them as they stepped through the cramped hallway. An immediate left doorway revealed a small, square kitchen with simple cupboards, an aged green stove, which looked like it had been donated from the 1940's, and a rusting fridge. The floor was covered with a cheap plastic green lining, which lifted at the corners and revealed patches of black mould creeping up the chipped wallpaper. They swiftly moved through to a dark, confined lounge, with two black synthetic sofas, and a simple wooden table in the corner, on which sat a box television. The curtains, which shabbily covered the one back window in the lounge wall, were transparent, revealing the garden... if it could even be described as that. Low broken fences surrounded the small square patch of grass, uneven slabs of concrete patio and a washing line which looked as if it had been in one too many hurricanes.

Daruk peered through the final downstairs room of the squalid house, which was a dilapidated L-shaped bathroom, consisting of a dingy toilet, grimy bathtub and grotty sink. The shower curtain was a flimsy transparent piece of fabric, which looked like it had been hung up carelessly.

"Why don't I put the kettle on, and we'll sit down and talk about the boys' schools, and job prospects for yourself", Marie said optimistically, slipping off her shoulder bag, hesitant to put it on the carpet. Just as Daruk was translating to his mother, Ash interrupted the social worker-

"*Schools?*" he asked, "Daruk and I won't be going to the same school?"

Roshni told Ash to calm down in Urdu. Though she'd picked up some English over the last few months, she was very behind both of her sons. They'd been told the interpreter would arrive just after 2 o'clock. It was 1:55 pm, now.

"We'll discuss that when the interpreter arrives, my love. Don't worry", Marie reassured him, before she bolted to the kitchen, awkwardly.

Roshni sighed, looking fixedly at their new dismal reality. Although she wasn't fazed by the actual house, having grown up in an overcrowded shack far more basic, it was what lurked outside which frightened her.

"*You might as well go and pick your bedroom whilst we wait*", Roshni said apathetically, sharing her children's anguished looks.

"*But Mama, which one do you want?*" Daruk asked, as the boys turned towards the stairs.

"*I'll take the smaller one, you two are sharing and Jayminee will have the box room*", Roshni explained. She swept across the room and pulled both her sons' heads into her body, kissing each head in turn.

"*We're going to be okay, my darlings*", she whispered, and

they wrapped their arms around her waist.

At that moment, there was a sharp knock on the door, and they listened to Marie greet the interpreter. He was an Indian man, smartly dressed and small in figure. He had his identification badge clipped onto his navy-blue shirt, and he followed Marie, who was carrying a tea tray, into the lounge.

"Sorry boys, I couldn't find any juice but there were some teabags left over", Marie apologised, pouring the full teapot into three mugs. "This is Pradeep, the interpreter", she introduced.

Pradeep smiled at the children and shook Roshni's hand. It was reassuring to meet another adult who spoke her mother tongue, and on any ordinary day she'd have liked to ask him where he'd grown up, and why he had chosen to leave the beauty of India for this reserved and uninspiring country, but today wasn't a regular day. There was so much to discuss. Daruk and Ash sat down, close to each other.

The meeting seemed to go on for an eternity. Having the interpreter repeat everything caused an even longer delay, though it did feel comforting to have somebody there who understood their culture, their homeland and their way of being. Marie spoke about the jobs which Roshni could apply for, and how she'd already secured her an interview with a recruitment centre the following week. She spoke about government benefits and childcare options.

And then, she spoke about the children's schooling. This is the part that Daruk and Ash sat up straight for, listening attentively.

"Now, I know this estate is… is something to be desired", Marie said sarcastically, "but, as luck would have it, the schools here are totally oversubscribed. This means that both of the boys are eligible to go to schools outside of this catchment area… in far nicer areas. Far better schools."

Ash's heart thudded, distraughtly. Why did she keep saying *schools,* as if there would be two? He couldn't bear even the notion of having to go to different schools.

"Now, there is a school called Kingsgate, which is a lovely, high achieving school in the next town along. It's a comprehensive, and very multicultural I hear. I think it would be more than suitable for Asha", Marie enthused, as if she were working on commission. The reality was, she was as desperate as the family were to see any light in their new given circumstance.

Roshni nodded agreeably, although one could tell she sensed the discomfort in her sons' faces. She held her index finger up to them, as if to say *just wait a minute*. They remained silent, letting the social worker continue, although it took everything inside of them to bite their tongues. Ash ran his hand over his face, as he often did, when he felt anxious or stressed. Daruk edged closer to his brother, until the skin on their arms was touching.

"There is also a very exciting opportunity for Daruk. Given his impressive 98 percentile exam results and his school record from back in Kash… in India, I reached out to Beacon Cliffe High School; it's an incredibly prestigious, mixed private school, one of the best in-"

"Sorry, she says they can never afford a private school", Pradeep interjected, before returning to whisper the translation into Roshni's ear.

"That's just it - every year they release a scholarship. It's sort of like a charitable… sorry I'm not sure if that's the right word, well anyway, it's a scheme that the school runs so that exceptional or high-achieving individuals can enter the school, no matter what their background or financial status. That's the beauty of it, you wouldn't have to pay *anything*. They have an intake of one student per year group, per year, accepted through scholarship. I honestly think that with Daruk's grades, and his keen extracurricular record and sporting achievements, together with the fact that the school are seeking to be more...*diverse,* he'd be in with a good chance." Marie gloated, whipping out the school prospectus excitedly, and passing it over the interpreter's lap. Pradeep was whispering the translation so fast, that he barely stopped for breath. When he finished, Roshni held the impressive school prospectus in her hands and examined the photographs. The building looked epic, great grey stone walls and big stained-glass windows, courtyards and fountains and a huge lush school football pitch. The children in the photographs looked well presented, smart, and most importantly, happy. They were also, all very *white*.

"*It looks beautiful,*" she admitted, "*but I want Daruk to choose.*"

Ash hung his head in conflict. It was this conflict that kept him silent. He could not deny how great the school sounded. He had no doubts his exceptional brother would be accepted. He glanced sideways at his brother's face. The eyes which had always looked out for him. The smile that had always made everything better. The voice that made him laugh. For the first time, the ten-year-old challenged himself to be selfless.

Roshni looked to Daruk, as did Marie, as did Pradeep even, with expectant eyes.

Daruk loved sports. He loved football and he loved

school. He knew this school would provide him with the best opportunities possible, and inside, deep down, he believed he could get in. He'd never met anybody who was as good a footballer as him, or artist, or writer. But he didn't even bother to look at the prospectus.

"No. No, I want to go to the same school as my brother", he said firmly. "I've made my decision", he said. Ash looked up in disbelief, his heart warmed.

But Marie shook her head.

"Oh, Daruk you misunderstand. Even if you don't choose to apply to Beacon Cliffe, you and Ash can never go to the same school. Here in England, high school begins at eleven years old. You are fourteen, and Asha is ten. Asha has to go to a primary school, he'll be in year five, and you must go to a senior school, joining year ten, whether it is Beacon Cliffe, or another one."

*

That night, when Marie had left the house, and Roshni was busy double checking that all the doors were locked and secured, shuddering at the loud music and shouting she heard coming from outside, Ash and Daruk sat against the bottom bunk of their bunk beds, in their matching pyjamas, which they'd been gifted as a leaving present from the refuge.

"I'll see you every day after school, and you heard what Marie said, mine's just a little further than yours so I can drop you off and pick you up and we can still walk home together", Daruk said encouragingly, trying to cheer up Ash's deflated expression.

"What if I get bullied?" Ash grumbled, refusing to make eye contact with Daruk.

"Well, then those bullies better wish they weren't born, 'cause I'll be showing up at 3:30 pm won't I?", Daruk reassured him, with a nudge. "You've no reason to get bullied, Ash."

"I do. We're brown. People look at us differently here. I know you've noticed it, too."

Daruk shook his head, "Yes, but you're not looking to be friends with racists, are you? Who would want to be friends with them?"

Ash nodded bravely.

"Yes, you're right", he agreed, "and I suppose at our last school we were in separate classes anyway, so it won't be that much different will it, brother? Oh, except for *lunchtimes*", Ash exclaimed worriedly, but before he had time to fill his own mind with tormenting visions of sitting in a playground by himself and having rocks thrown at him, Daruk stood up.

"Ash, you haven't even got there yet! You've never been bullied in your whole life."

"That's because I've been with you! And nobody would pick on me when you're there", he cried, burying his head in his legs and folding his hands over the top.

"Ash, you've no reason not to make friends. You're going to make tons. They are all going to love you", Daruk said softly.

"I just don't feel safe here", Ash sobbed.

It took him a while to realise that Daruk had left the room.

"Daruk? Daruk?" Ash called, uncrossing his legs and wiping his face.

Great. He's had enough of me. He's finally had enough. Thought Ash, as he buried his head back in his legs.

The door soon opened again, and Daruk walked in,

carrying a pile of brightly coloured saris.

"Let's make a den. It can be our safe place", he smiled.

*

That night, the brothers slept side by side, under a canopy of orange and pink drapes. Daruk had moved the lamp from the living room into the den, and covered it over with the silk, dimming the light. It was their own little haven, shielding them from the world outside. They made shadow puppets with their hands, projecting them against their orange covering, like tigers and elephants and bears walking against the setting sun.

And that night, for those brief moments under the onlooking moon, Ash felt *safe*.

9

THE THREE

London, England, 2018

The Loft was an artsy, dimmed attic conversion above the studios where Ash's producers, writers, and team, held auditions and shot scenes in the huge indoor film sets down below. There was just one Velux window in The Loft, above the paint splattered wooden desk, which when cracked open, beckoned in the passing sounds of Ealing Broadway. The private studios had once been an old opera house and Ash had fallen in love with the vast building and scope for imaginative creations as soon as he'd viewed them. He would come up to The Loft to write and plan, and gave everybody strict instructions never to disturb him when the door was closed, although, he had allowed some of the designers to store their costumes up there, which they had neatly strewn over the one puffy armchair in the corner of the room. The glittery emerald dresses and striped gangster suit jackets, were just some of the outfits which were illuminated by the streaks of the morning sun, flooding in from the window.

Briefcase in one hand, and takeaway coffee in the other, Ash darted across the busy street outside, and passed the Romanian woman, selling *The Big Issue* magazine. In his hurry, he was only a few steps past the smiling woman, when his gut willed him to turn around.

"*Nobody chooses to search for food, Ash. It's the hand she was dealt*"

Ash patted down his empty pockets. He never carried change.

"It's okay", the woman said, in the most genuine of tones, "you can have this one for free if you need it."

The stranger gazed at him with kind eyes, and held out one of her many copies of *The Big Issue*. The creases in her skin were filled with dirt from the passing traffic. Ash paused for a moment, thinking deeply. This woman had nothing, and yet, she was offering him, he who had everything, something.

But it wasn't the words of his brother that convinced him. He no longer trusted that wisdom. It was the compassion in his heart which compelled him to give up his time, as it always was.

"How much do you earn in a day? If you don't mind me asking?" Ash asked the woman abruptly.

She was not offended. "It depends how many I sell, Sir", she replied, "eight to ten pounds, perhaps."

Ash tried to hide his mortification. *Ten pounds*. He'd spent more than that on his breakfast.

The woman looked at him with a patient gaze, as if it was refreshing to even be spoken to as a human being, and not some filth on the street. He guessed she must have only been in her early forties, but each crease in her dark skin added on another year of struggle and pain. Her smile reminded him of his own mother's, brave and hopeful, no matter what the circumstance.

Suddenly, two young girls linking arms, stopped in their tracks on the pavement.

"That's that guy from the premiere the other week!" one of them whispered loudly, whilst the other took out her mobile to try and steal a picture of the attractive young man. Ash blushed, turning away from the teenagers, and facing the woman.

"Look, I'm in a bit of a rush. But I'd love to help you out… not that you're in need of help, I mean, sorry, what I mean is, my mum used to sell *The Big Issue* too when we first moved to this country, and I know it's not the most enjoyable of work, but necessary. It means a lot to me that you'd offer me a magazine for free", he exclaimed. "I work just over there, in those studios. If you come with me, I'd love to get you some breakfast, we have a kitchen inside. I could have a chat with you about other work you might be interested in, if you like?"

The woman's eyes widened at the sight of the grand studios. She saw the type of well-dressed, important people who walked in and out of that place. They were also the same people who ignored her every single day, not even returning her smile. She couldn't believe this young man came from a mother who also sold *The Big Issue*. He looked like a movie star himself.

"That's kind of you, but I need to sell all of these today." She said, disheartened, gripping the pile of magazines which although burdened her, were her only lifeline in this cruel world.

Ash paused for a moment, and then, "I'll buy them all", he insisted impulsively. "My team could use a break, I'll give them all one of these to read today. Please."

The woman was so stunned she was almost untrusting. But something within the young man's eyes told her not to be afraid and assured her he knew exactly how she felt in this foreign land.

Ash lead her along the pavement, past the studio's shiny double automatic doors, where he waved good morning to the two security guards, and then showed her down a cobbled alley way.

"This is the side entrance", he explained, taking out his pass and bleeping it over the scan-lock. He pushed the door open, and the woman found herself in a busy, open plan, studio. There were no windows in the dim room, but white lights spotlighted the messy desks, strobe lights hung from the ceiling and huge black cameras on rollers were, seemingly, randomly placed in the middle of the room. Green screens were lit up, laptops were out, open and unattended, and an office scene had been set up in the middle of the room, surrounded by put-up cardboard walls. Within the office were two women organising the large desk and re-positioning the computer.

In the corner of the studio, was a cluttered kitchen, with a lit up spinning microwave and a boiling kettle which squeaked. When Ash walked in, followed by the strange woman, the small clusters of bubbly, young and artistic individuals suddenly seemed to rush to their feet and dart over to their abandoned laptops or break away from their gossiping huddles. But she was not unexpected, Ash regularly brought homeless people into their studio, and spent time chatting to them and getting to know their stories. They'd learnt this was just something Ash did.

"Good morning, Mr Lakhanpal!", came the chirpy calls from the various members of the team.

"Morning, guys", he replied. "Actually, everyone, can I have a word?"

They soon gathered around him, leaving their mugs of coffee and disorganised desks.

"I'm going to be working in The Loft today. So, if scriptwriters can send me the final draft of "The Valley of Flowers", scene three, by this afternoon that would be great. Mark, I liked that Irish kid best on Friday's audition. Offer him the part please, and remember to get his family to sign all the permissions. I'd like to shoot scenes two and three again this evening, because Jason was not in the right frame of mind at yesterday's shoot. And before you ask, I have had words. Call up your partners and tell them it might be a late one, I'm afraid. Designers, that office space is looking good, but the desk is way too cluttered, so clean it up a bit. I want it to look lived in, but organised. Over organised… if that makes sense."

Ash spoke with confidence and clarity, but it was evident he was highly preoccupied. He wasn't even remotely concentrating on any of the things he'd just said. He just wanted to get to The Loft.

"So, Ash…", Sarah wondered, eyeing up the shabby woman standing awkwardly with the pile of magazines.

"Oh, how rude of me, sorry, what was your name again?" Ash begged, turning to the woman and taking the pile of Big Issues from her. He placed them on one of the desks, pushing important drafts and pieces of paper to one side.

"My name is Cassia", she said meekly.

"This is Cassia, she's going to be joining us today. Don't be afraid to say 'hello'", he said, ushering his team away. Most gave the woman a warm smile before breaking away from the huddle and busying themselves in the studio.

"Sarah, Jade, can you do me a favour?" Ash asked the two women as he pulled them aside. They only ever wanted to please their director, no matter how absurd or random the request.

"I need one of you to sort this woman out some breakfast. Make it nice… you know, eggs, toast and that. Maybe some avocado, know what I'm saying?" he said flirtatiously to Jade, before placing his hands on each of her shoulders. She quivered excitedly.

"Then, can one of you go to the cash point and withdraw two hundred pounds. Just keep it on you, I'll give it to her at the end of the day, when I've got time to come down and have a chat with her."

Sarah rolled her eyes, bewildered.

"Umm… okay, but what do you want us to do with her until then?"

"Give her a tour of the place, make conversation. Let her use the laptop. I'm going to try and find a job for her here", Ash said.

Cassia's face lit up more brightly than the rays of a morning sun when she overheard Ash's words. But, as his two baffled colleagues eyed her up, she immediately looked to the ground, minding her own business.

"Ash, we do have quite a lot to do today", Sarah hissed, "as lovely as your charity cases are… she could be *anybody*!"

"Look Sarah, I know I've put you through a lot lately. I know everyone's under a great deal of stress. Please. Don't ask me why, I just need you to do this for me, okay? I'll come down just after lunchtime to check how she's doing. Perhaps we can offer her a cleaning job here."

"She might not be legally able to work here", Sarah argued.

"Then I'll pay her in cash", Ash said firmly.

"Fine." Sarah unwillingly agreed. She then took a deep breath and forced a fake smile.

"Hi, Cassia, I'm Sarah", she sighed, spinning her slim body round in a flurry so that her blonde loose curls waved around her head like the seats of a fairground ride.

Ash smiled satisfyingly, watching his producer lead the woman into the kitchen area.

"Oh, and before I forget everybody", Ash called, "help yourselves to one of these magazines throughout the day". He tapped the pile of unwanted Big Issues and raced toward The Loft.

*

Inside the secrecy of The Loft, Ash held the ageing letter in his hands. He'd only met his eldest uncle a handful of times, twice in Goa, and once in the UK. It was handwritten, and the writing looked desperate and rushed. It was dated August 2nd, 2006.

Dear Asha Anjani,

As I write this, it is uncertain how much time I have left. The doctors have advised me it could be weeks, but my tired body tells me, it is more likely to be days. Asha, I want to congratulate you on your short film, your mother sent me the newspaper clipping in the post. She also told me you have ambitions to go to London and pursue a career in the film industry.

I need to tell you a story about your father, because I have carried this shame for too long now. As you know, I was the eldest of nine children, and your father was the youngest. I'd left to go to college in Mumbai, in the summer of 1964, so I did not get to know Anjani well because he remained at home, just a child. One night, I returned to our home, from college. I overheard the abuse inflicted on Anjani by our stepfather. He was a relentless man.

I was big enough and strong enough to have fought him off, Asha. But I did nothing. I wish I could tell you it was a one-off occurrence, but it was evident that this abuse tormented your father every waking night of his childhood.

Asha, I have kept this guilt inside me for so long. I have kept this secret for most of my adult life, and it has consumed me in every possible way. I do not allow myself to experience joy. I do not revel in success. I only wish I could go back and do the right thing.

I did not do the right thing, Asha Lakhanpal, and it shames me to tell you this. I blocked out the screaming of my own little brother, I closed my ears to his cries for help. I left the house and I never returned.

When I met up with your father as an adult, I could see how his childhood trauma had broken him. He liked to drink, he liked to gamble, he liked fast women, and had a love of money. This is because he was trying to escape, Asha. I followed him to England to make things right, but it was too late, Anjani was already gone when I came. I needed to tell you this because I know you have never forgiven your father. I pray that you can forgive me. You must never run from the truth, Asha Anjani. The truth will always find you, or it will be the lie that kills you.

I tell you this to relieve my own conscience, on my dying day. I have made peace with God now. I have come clean about my sin. I also tell you this, Asha, because I have something to leave to you. Everything in my name, in my last will and testament, I leave for you. I pray you will bring pride back into our family name. You can do the right thing, Asha. You can make a way for your family. You can support them through honest work.

May God bless you, dear nephew,
Deeptendu Eshin Lakhanpal

Ash gently folded the letter shut, and placed it in the drawer of the desk in The Loft.

"You must never run from the truth, Asha Anjani"

His uncle's words streamed through every part of his mind, filling him with disgrace just as they had done when he'd first received the letter back when he was still a teenager. For *his* truth was even more shameful than his uncle's. He too had known a dark secret and kept it quiet. Perhaps cowardice had run in the family.

He thought about the money which had been left to him not long after receiving his uncle's letter. One hundred and fifty thousand pounds. It had been enough for a deposit to buy his mother a new house in a safe area and fund him through film school, even aiding his very first successful short film which had won a Film Festival Award and given other producers an interest in investing in his movies to come. But Ash knew, it was not only money that had fuelled his success, but the genius behind his work. The work which was not his own.

Ash ran his hand over his face, as he often did, when he felt anxious or stressed. He pulled out the Beacon

Cliffe High Yearbook. Then, he took the pair of scissors from the drawer and cut out the young photograph of Frankie Wincott, glueing it onto his double page spread of paper in his planning book. He ran his fingers over the haunting teenage face, which to the average onlooker would appear un-provoking and pleasant, but filled Ash with an offence so deep, it made his hands shake.

Usually, he filled his planning book with spider diagrams of film plots, character developments and initial scenes. But this was a fresh story. It was *his* story. And it was the darkest one he would ever write. He felt the urge to take a knife and stab the photograph unyieldingly, releasing his unthinkable fury. But instead, he calmly smoothed it against the white paper. He then took another cutting, this time, a pixelated printout of the adult Frankie Wincott, which he'd taken from the gardener's website.

He placed the images next to the other two men. And the puzzle was complete. Together, they were *The Three*.

Frankie Wincott, Billy Thatcher and Popeto Charpentier.

Ash looked at the newspaper cutting of the mugshot of Billy, who'd grown into an overweight, balding, ogre of a man.

"Drug smuggler who murdered his girlfriend with telephone wire sentenced to twenty-five years"

Ash satisfyingly cut out Billy's school photograph from the yearbook, which showed the chubby student posing cheekily and his white set of teeth shining through unattractive braces. He stuck the school picture of Billy next to the newspaper column, which had made national news a few years before.

"Billy Thatcher, 30, of Brentwood Essex, was arrested for the murder of his girlfriend, Charlene Baker, 36, when neighbours alerted the police after hearing raised voices of a violent nature and screams signifying Baker was in trouble. When officers arrived at the scene, they found Baker to have been strangled with a telephone wire, and Thatcher packing up over £100,000 worth of crack cocaine. Investigations since have suggested that Thatcher was a dealer responsible for the distribution of class A drugs to over eleven different counties within the UK."

Ash wondered what prison Billy was now captive in. He hoped he was rotting, even though that still would not be enough. Ash then took the printout of the Facebook profile picture of Popeto, who, in the photograph, was sitting on a yacht, his brown wavy hair blowing over his tanned face, surrounded by his sun-kissed wife and two privileged children, wearing matching nautical all-in-ones. Comparing this to his yearbook photograph, Ash observed that not much had changed in the face of Popeto, who'd been an attractive, budding athlete. Ash thought back to how they'd called him "Poppy", and he remembered how he'd thought at the time it was overly pretentious to call a boy by a girl's name.

He wrote out the three men's details underneath their photographs.

Then, he glared at The Three, plotting, scheming, seething, and *hurting*.

He took a red felt pen and circled Frankie's face. Staring at the stranger's pale blue eyes, he allowed his own eyes to well-up with hot tears. But he knew he must do it. He *had* to. The tears raced down his face as he typed the words into the internet search engine on his laptop:

'Most painful ways to die'

10

THE NEW KID

Essex, England, 2000

"And you promise you won't be late picking me up?", Ash urged, desperately wishing Daruk did not have to leave. They stood outside the black railings of Ash's new school, Kingsgate Primary, and stared at the playground. The grey stone building was modern and every window was bursting with colourful posters children had made. There were paintings all over the playground floor, where little girls in their chequered green and white dresses played hop-scotch and skipping. Boys dashed past in their green chimney sweeper caps, chasing each other and impersonating airplane noises with their arms spread out like wings.

A few young female teachers huddled together gossiping, and occasionally looked up to watch over the excitable mob of children. There was a swing set, a climbing frame and a football field peeking out from behind the school building. The autumn leaves had covered the pitch, boasting brilliant oranges and reds.

"I promise", Daruk reassured him. "Look, Ash, it looks like a great school. They've got a football pitch and everything!"

"Yours has a swimming pool", Ash grumbled, terrified of being the new kid.

"Ash, there's loads of Asian and Indian kids", Daruk whispered positively. "You won't be the only one."

Ash nodded, although he was overcome with nerves. He just wanted to run away. Every time he thought about setting foot inside the gates, his anxiety overwhelmed him. *What if nobody talks to me or says "hello"? What if I'm too scared to say "hello"? Who's my teacher?*

Daruk's voice had started to deepen now that he was fourteen. It made Ash feel even more protected in his presence. Daruk was dressed smartly in his burgundy blazer with golden broach, a crisp white shirt, black school trousers, scruffy black shoes which his mother had found in a charity shop, and a neat gelled haircut. His smile shone as brightly as ever, and his eyes were mischievous and full of life as he prepared for his first day at Beacon Cliffe.

"Are you not even a little bit nervous, brother?" Ash asked, staring admiringly at Daruk's calm expression and confident allure, wishing he could be the same as his older brother.

"Not at all. We're both going to be fine. It's an adventure. Well... I guess I'll miss you a little bit", Daruk said, poking his pink tongue out cheekily. "Come on", he said, opening the school gate.

He placed his hand on Ash's shoulder and they

strode through the busy playground together. Ash trailed close behind him.

Daruk caught the eyes of the playground staff, and danced straight up to the three young women.

"Hello", Daruk said happily, "this is my brother, Asha Lakhanpal. It's his first day today. We got told he would be in... what class was it, again, Ash?"

"Newton class", Ash confirmed, as the teachers gazed upon his cute face and recognised the nerves in his voice.

A plump, jolly woman in the middle of the huddle replied eagerly.

"Yes, that's right, all of our classes in upper primary are named after inventors or discoverers!" she said. "And, that also means I'm going to be your teacher sweetheart, I'm Miss Bourbon."

Miss Bourbon wore a pink cardigan and flowery dress which clung to her in all the wrong places. Her rounded glasses shielded her warm nut-brown eyes, and every time a smile spread across her soft face, Ash felt a little more reassured.

"So, have you done your homework? Do you know who Isaac Newton was?" she joked.

Ash shook his head nervously, but Daruk laughed.

"She's only joking, Ash. Isaac Newton was the one who discovered gravity, when an apple fell on his head."

"That's right", Miss Bourbon beamed, impressed by the teenager's knowledge.

Then, another one of the women turned to Ash.

"I'm Mrs Brown and I teach Carter class in year five, shall we see if your brother knows who Howard Carter was as well? Nobody ever gets it right first time", the thin, pale teacher beside Miss Bourbon suggested playfully. She had a whistle hanging round her neck and was dressed in sweatpants and trainers.

Ash nodded, beginning to relax. He looked up to Daruk, whose mind was wandering, determined to get the answer right. And Ash knew he would.

"Howard Carter, I am sure he was the archaeologist man, who discovered Tutankhamen's tomb in Egypt, in 19… 22. Yes, I think that's right", Daruk grinned cockily, and the three woman were stunned.

Ash grinned.

"He's a geek", he laughed.

"Well, you've arrived on a great day Asha, we're going on a forest walk this morning, and we've got the sports day try-outs this afternoon." Miss Bourbon explained, "And you must be off to Beacon Cliffe - my nephew goes there, it's absolutely fantastic!" she beamed, glancing at Daruk's broach.

Daruk nodded proudly, still elated that he'd been accepted into the prestigious establishment. His mother had been overjoyed.

"It sounds like you're going to have such a fun day, Ash", he encouraged.

"Right, let's introduce you to some of the class", Miss Bourbon said kindly, putting her hand on Asha's back. "Your big brother's welcome to come over, too."

She shimmied Ash towards a group of three boys playing with hula-hoops. One of them had strawberry blonde hair, big baby blue eyes and chubby cheeks.

"Good morning, Miss Bourbon", he said in a high-pitched voice. "Is this Ashley who you told us about?"

The small boy dropped the hula-hoop down to his feet, and stepped out of it.

"His name is Asha, and yes, I thought you could look

after him today, Joshua, is that okay?"

Ash smiled at Joshua, shyly.

"Yes, that's okay", Joshua sung. "Do you know how to hula?" he asked, spinning around, full of energy and handing out a hula-hoop to Ash, who took hold of it, feeling relieved by the friendliness. He was good at hula-hooping, too. Almost as good as Daruk.

"We're trying to do twenty spins each, or you have to do a forfeit!" one of the other boys explained, jumping up and down inside of his hoop. As he did so, his long blonde hair jumped up and down with him.

"Arthur's already had to do two laps around the playground, he's rubbish", giggled the third boy, who was Indian, just like Ash.

Ash laughed, took the hoop and stepped inside of it. He was concentrating so hard on rotating his hips and keeping the spinning ring balanced on his body, that he barely noticed his brother leaving the playground.

"Have a great day, Ash! I'll see you later", Daruk called, happily.

*

Ash's day was even better than Miss Bourbon had enthused it would be. Joshua, Arthur and Kulraj not only wanted to be his friends, but *fought* over who got to be his partner on the forest walk. Conversation flowed as they quizzed him about India and explained to him where they liked to sit at lunch, which girls in the class they liked and which he should avoid sitting next to. They told him he could be a part of their Christmas talent show act, though they hadn't decided what their talent was yet.

The four boys trotted through the forest among their class, stopping to draw flowers of interest which resembled the flowers on their work sheet. Miss Bourbon described it as a "science meets art" lesson. Ash wondered why there were so many teachers chaperoning their every move in the forest and imposing so many "out of bounds" areas. In India, Mrs Sharma would have just sent them down to the lake and told the class to be back by lunchtime, whilst she switched the fan on and put her feet up on her desk. Still, Ash was more than relieved to have made friends.

Crouching around a dandelion, the boys began to sketch. Although he still felt a little shy, Ash had relaxed considerably. He was glad to be outside under the canopy of fresh trees.

"I went to India once", Arthur boasted, "we went there on holiday, went to the beach, went to the kids club, had kebabs for dinner-"

"No, Arthur, you went to Ibiza", Joshua insisted, echoed by Ash and Kulraj's expels of laughter.

"Oh yeah", Arthur giggled, losing his balance and falling back into a bush of nettles.

"I'm surprised they take you anywhere", teased Kulraj.

*

When the school bell rang at 3:30 pm, Ash took his time coming out to the playground, where all the parents were waiting in little clusters, nattering and carrying children's bikes and scooters. He was chatting to Gracie, who he'd been assigned a seat next to when the register was taken, and Joshua of course, who couldn't leave him alone.

"So, remember to bring the flour for our brownies tomorrow in cookery, Ash. I'll bring the sugar and Lauren's mum will bring us the chocolate drops", Joshua recited, juggling his artwork, P.E. bag and lunchbox in his hands.

"I will, I'll ask my Mum", Ash beamed, already excited for what tomorrow would bring.

"Have a fun night, Ash", Gracie called, as Ash ran towards Daruk, who was leaning against the school fence, but for once, was staring down at his shoes, in a world of his own. This was not like him.

"Daruk!" Ash cried excitedly, racing up to him and flinging his arms around his strong body. The teenager had already loosened his tie, taken his blazer off and replaced it with a black hoody.

"Hello, trouble!" Daruk enthused, beaming at his brother's happy face. Ash was desperate to tell him all about his day. Daruk took hold of Ash's P.E. bag and slung it over his shoulder and they began the walk home, through the little town and back towards their estate.

"I made friends, just like you said I would", Ash said proudly. "Joshua is probably my best friend, but I like Arthur too, and Gracie and Lauren and Kulraj. Miss Bourbon's so nice, she let me say a speech about India in front of the class!"

"In front of the whole class eh, brother? Did that not scare you?" Daruk asked, impressed, as they turned a corner.

"Not really, because Miss Bourbon helped me with what to say and then the class all asked me questions, and then this boy called Connor farted and everyone laughed and it took the attention away", Ash exclaimed, continuing with the flowing commentary of his day. Daruk was as encouraging as always. He commented on Ash's stories with "that's great" and "good for you, Ash" and "I knew you could do it", although it took Ash a long time to realise, Daruk hadn't said a single word about his own day.

"What about you, Dar? Did you go in the swimming pool? Who's your best friend? Did you play football? What's your teacher's name? What did you have for lunch? Were they nice to you?" he spluttered inquisitively.

Daruk paused.

"Wait, did I hear your friend say you needed to bring something for cookery in the morning?"

"Flour" Ash exclaimed, "but I don't know if Mama has any or if she's got enough to buy some"

Daruk put his arm around Ash and pulled him toward the off license on the corner.

"That's okay, I've got some lunch money left over, let's see what we can find in here. You can't make brownies without flour" he said, grinning.

After the brother's picked up the flour, Daruk made sure Ash was too distracted to ask him about his day, again. He challenged him to find the biggest conker in the woods, and then to race him home. Ash was so relieved about his school experience that he didn't even notice Daruk limping during their race.

*

That night, as Ash was stripping off his clothes and leaping into his bottom bunk excitedly, Daruk locked himself in the bathroom and desperately tried to scrub the blood out of his school shirt.

11

THE SCAN

London, England, 2018

"I don't know what's so bad about Kings Cross Hospital", Lola remarked, ogling the quiet waiting room of the private medical group. It was immaculately clean, and there was no queuing, just a few well-dressed patients emitting Laura Ashley fragrances and reading magazines, whilst their husbands held their hands, in their pin striped suits.

It was the day of their ultrasound.

Ash was full of nerves. He paced up and down the waiting room, sat down next to Lola, shook his leg as if he was entertaining a small child on his knee, and then returned to the vending machine for the third time, without actually buying anything.

"Lola, they're completely understaffed at Kings Cross, and I'm not putting you and our baby through unnecessary stress", he insisted, rubbing his hand over her back.

Lola rolled her eyes, sat back in the padded green chair and returned to her women's magazine, as relaxed as if she were reading it on a beach on holiday.

"I'm just saying, it's all a bit over the top that's all", she whispered. "I would have been happy with the NHS, you didn't need to add me onto your care plan, I don't want you wasting your money."

"*Wasting*? How is it wasting? You mean the whole world to me, Lola-"

"I know, I know. And I care about our baby just as much as you do, Ash. I just get concerned sometimes…"

"Concerned? Concerned about what?" he pressed.

Lola sighed.

"Now don't get all uppity, but I just… well, I want our child to be well-rounded. I know you'll want them to have the best of everything and all that, and I know you'll always be able to provide that, I'm just not sure money is what's most important, and I don't want them to be pushed or sent off to some over indulgent private school or anything."

To her surprise, Ash wasn't angry, rather, relieved. He smiled widely, and took her by the hand.

"They won't be going to private school. I hate private schools", he said firmly. "Lola, I just want our child to be, *happy*."

Lola beamed, adoringly.

"And I'll be damned if I don't give you both the very best life", he whispered.

Lola giggled.

"Well, alright then", she said soothingly. "You can

go and get me a Coke from that vending machine you've been teasing, then!"

Ash leapt to his feet willingly. "Wait, I read something about fizz not being too good for the baby?" he worried.

"Oh, Ash! It's a Coke for goodness sake, stop your fretting and inject me with that sugar!" she laughed, pulling his hand towards her lips and planting a kiss on it.

He slipped away towards the vending machine. He *was* worried, and he just couldn't help it. *What if there was something wrong with the baby? What if Lola got pains in the night? What if he was at work when-*

"Miss Lola Orwell, the sonographer will see you now", called a kind, enthusiastic voice. Ash and Lola both looked up to see a young nurse, heavily made-up, with highlighted blonde hair pinned back in a bun.

Ash gulped, frantically pressing the vending machine buttons. The can fell out, and he grabbed it before grabbing Lola's hand. His palms were sweaty.

The nurse led them down a silent corridor, its white walls decorated with framed photographs of purple tulips and windmills.

"Here we are, your sonographer today will be Sunita", she said, showing them into the spacious room, which had a large hospital bed lined with white tissue, a computer with a rotating screen on a long silver arm, and a beaming brown lady, with a red bhindi stuck on her wrinkled forehead.

"Hello, hello, please come in", she beamed, in her strong Indian accent.

She was the first Indian they'd seen in this white hospital. Ash was glad of it.

Lola sat down on the bed, and Ash took the chair next to her.

"So, it's your twelve-week scan today. A big day, you must be very excited", Sunita exclaimed, reaching for the bottle of lubricating jelly.

Lola made herself comfortable on the bed. She appeared as relaxed as a woman going for a kip on her weekly sun bed. But as she rolled up her loose-fitting blouse, she revealed a stomach which churned with excitement.

"So, this is baby number one?" Sunita asked.

"Yes", Ash and Lola answered keenly, in unison. Ash examined the computer and equipment on the desk. It had been years since he'd been in a hospital. And for good reason.

"So, in a moment, I'll just ask you to confirm your full name and date of birth, and then I'm going to put some jelly on your stomach. This helps with the transparency and clarity of the scan", Sunita explained, and Ash listened as intently as if she were giving instructions for life support.

"Can we get the photos today? Ooh, I heard you can have it made into a keyring at the front desk, can we get one of those, babe?" Lola begged excitedly.

"Of course", Ash whispered, his heart racing. He leant in, over the bed, and Lola took hold of his hand, for his sake more than hers.

"And, most importantly, do you want to find out baby's gender today?" Sunita asked.

Lola's face lit up.

"I thought we could only find out at twenty-weeks?" She asked.

Sunita smiled widely,

"With your care plan, we can find out early, if you like"

The couple looked at each other, anticipatingly.

"We'd like to keep it a surprise, please", Ash stated, just as they'd agreed previously, despite Lola's constant indecision.

Lola bit her lip in conflict, again. "So, we'd literally be able to tell whether it's a little boy or a little girl, *today*?"

Ash shook his head. "Lola, no, we've discussed this. We agreed!"

"Oh, but the baby names, Ash, the clothes shopping… doesn't part of you just really want to know what we are going to name them?" she hesitated once more, but Ash stood firm.

"We'll buy neutral colours and we'll pick a name for a boy and a girl", he insisted.

Lola sighed dramatically.

"Okay, sorry. Right, I'm ready", she said, taking a deep breath.

"My full name is Lola Divinity Orwell, and my birth date is June the 2nd, 1985."

Sunita nodded.

"Okay, here comes the jelly. It might be a bit cold."

She smeared the clear goo on thickly, all over Lola's toned, tanned stomach, using the sonicaid probe. It rolled over her skin intensely. Sunita pulled the computer screen toward them so that it hovered over the top of Lola's muscular thighs.

Ash squeezed his girlfriend's hand, as they focused on the black, fuzzy screen in front of them, in nervous anticipation.

And then, there it was. The moving, beating,

pulsating, silvery outline of a tiny head, a curled-up spine, hunched up legs, little hands and little feet. In a shelter from the outside world, the little bundle of flesh was turning, growing, *living* inside of its own safe haven. Ash gazed at the picture in awe, seeing not just a computerised image, but a glimpse of his most treasured possession. His eyes filled with tears as he gazed mesmerisingly at every movement. Goosebumps covered his tense arms.

And suddenly, he could not hear Sunita's soft explanations, or Lola's elated responses, but, in a trance of quiet adoration, he listened to the beating heartbeat of the foetus, in rhythm with his own.

He was in love.

12

THE TWIN TOWERS

Essex, England, 2001

The footage looked like something out of an action movie, and not the Six O'Clock News.

The sooty, dusty eruption of cloud exploded from underneath the colossal high-rise, letting out a tormented rumble as the whole tower plummeted into the ground, filling the television screen with a thick dirty mist. Sirens wailed and screams chorused, as desperate people covered in white powder attempted to escape the chaotic despair of New York City.

The moving red strip across the bottom of the headlines, was filled with *"Breaking News: Terrorist Attack on World Trade Centre"* and *"Second plane hits South Tower"*.

Ash sat on the sofa, his jaw hanging open, completely stunned.

Roshni and her friend, Anita, who also worked at the

coach station as a cleaner, were sharing the small sofa and talking all the way through the programme, in Kashmiri.

"*Apparently most of the hijackers were Saudi Arabian*", Anita said in amazement, shaking her head disbelievingly.

"*All those poor families*", Roshni cried, putting her hand on her friend's sari.

Anita took hold of Roshni's hand and they grimaced at the television together.

"*265 dead on the planes*", Anita tutted. "*Conducted by a terrorist group*"

"*Al-Qaeda*" Daruk whispered, grimly.

They all looked over to Daruk, in surprise. He hardly spoke these days. What was al-Qaeda? Ash wondered, anxiously. There was so much he longed to ask his brother. But Ash remained silent.

Daruk was perched on the armrest of the only other armchair in the living room, quietly. He had hardly been out of their bedroom in weeks, not even during the summer holidays. But he simply could not turn away from this breaking news. His eyes were glued to the horror, and it sickened him.

The boys had attended their schools for almost a whole academic year, and after a six-week summer break, Daruk was now in his final year at Beacon Cliffe, and Ash, in his final year at Kingsgate. It was the year of Daruk's GCSE exams, and Roshni had high hopes for her son, especially after he'd been locking himself away so much, utterly engrossed by revision.

Although Ash *loved* his school, he was plighted by his brother's ever-growing distance. Daruk still picked him up from Kingsgate every day, always on time, and always with a smile. But the spring in his step had dwindled and the head he once held high, now hung below his slouching shoulders. His cheeky grin was no longer, and even the glimmer in his eyes was dimmed. His playfulness and conversation had become reserved and introverted. When the brothers arrived home from school each day, Ash would beg him to go and play football on the green outside, or to climb the trees in the wood, or to even build a fort in the garden like they would have done once upon a time. But Daruk always said that he was too tired or had too much schoolwork to do, and that he was sorry. He would ruffle Ash's hair, and tell him that once all his exams were all over, it would be just like old times again. But when Daruk rushed his way through supper every night, and then hid away in the den he had made in the corner of their bedroom, Ash lost hope of their closeness ever returning. Daruk had placed a little desk inside his den, and hung heavy, opaque bed sheets around the desk and chair, telling Ash it was his workspace and never to enter.

Roshni felt distressed by her eldest son's absent stares at the dinner table, one word answers, and sometimes snappy mood swings, but Anita had tried to assure her that all teenage boys went through this stage, and as long as he still maintained his manners and did his chores around the house, there was no real reason to panic. Of course, Roshni empathised with her other son, too. Watching Ash's deflated expression every time Daruk rejected him or pushed him away made her wonder what in the world could have caused the two inseparable brothers to fall out. But time and time again, Daruk told her that he was fine, to let him be or that she was smothering him. She would stop questioning him in fear of another argument or the worry that he would push her away even further.

The summer holidays had been strange. Roshni couldn't afford a mobile phone for Ash, and to her surprise, Daruk said he didn't want one. And so, through the summer break, frequently one of Ash's school friends would call the family's home phone, requesting for Ash to come to the zoo, or out to the park, or the beach. Ash *always* asked Daruk if he wanted to come, but Daruk just told him to have an amazing day, and to stop worrying about him.

"I don't have to go. I could tell Arthur that you and me are doing something instead. We could go down to the river with the dinghy?" Ash said enthusiastically, desperate for his brother to be persuaded. But Daruk had smiled at him kindly. "Thanks Ash, but I can't. You go and have a great time."

Although Roshni had managed to find a job as a cleaner at *The National Express* coach station, life was far from perfect. She felt trapped in the estate, and disheartened by its grim engulfment, especially when she thought back to their life in India. Her work was lifeless and unfulfilling, but she'd learnt to appreciate the simple pleasures within the struggle, such as the brief opportunities to gossip in her mother tongue with Anita, over a plastic cup of free tea in the coach station staffroom, or being invited to watch Ash perform in his school production of "Robin Hood", or listening to her daughter's first words.

Ash side glanced Daruk, as he slipped away from the living room and up to their bedroom. He sighed. Roshni and her friend remained engrossed in the headlines. Was there anything in all the world which would make Daruk happy again? If there was, Ash would do it. He was desperate. He thought back to the previous Christmas, in their grim estate.

Roshni had asked Ash what he thought his brother would like for a present. And Ash had suggested a Gameboy. When Roshni expressed that she couldn't afford one, Ash thought for a really long time. And then he asked his mother to take the money she would have spent on his own gift, and let it contribute to Daruk's gift.

"I'm sure Mama" he had said.

When the second-hand Gameboy arrived, Ash excitedly helped his mother wrap it up on Christmas Eve, as they sat around their foot-tall plastic tree. Ash hoped it would bring Daruk's bright smile back. He could barely sleep on Christmas Eve. He couldn't wait to give the gift to his brother. The Lakhanpal children all gathered in the living room on Christmas day, and Ash rose up on his knees eagerly, passing his brother the present.

"It's from Asha and I" Roshni had explained, gladly.

But when Daruk opened his gift and held the Gameboy, his smile was forced, and he looked pain stricken. Ash didn't understand.

"Thank you, so much" Daruk croaked. *"I really love it."*

Ash couldn't bare it any longer.

"What's wrong with you? We spent ages looking for that and you're still not happy! Why aren't you ever happy, Daruk? Why don't you like us anymore? It's Christmas and you've ruined it!" Ash had screamed, letting his tears fall.

Ash regretted his Christmas outburst every day. He just wanted his brother back.

*

Ash lay in bed that night, wishing he could ask Daruk about all the questions which were teaming through his mind, about the terrorist attack on the Twin Towers. He knew that Daruk was awake - he could see the low gleam of light coming from Daruk's torch on the top bunk.

"Daruk?" Ash gulped, pulling his covers up to his chin.

"Yes, brother?"

Ash was glad that Daruk answered him softly, although his tone was sad. He thought for a moment, as it wouldn't be long before Daruk told him to stop talking and so he wanted to ask his most urgent question first.

"Why did those people hi-jack the plane if they would die too?" Ash asked. "Surely that's stupid."

There was a silence.

"They are terrorists, brother. They believed they'd been sent on a mission by Allah."

"By Allah? So, you mean they're Muslims? But Sumraj and Sarfaraz are Muslims, and they would never do a thing like that", Ash urged.

"No, no don't worry Ash. Sum and Saf are good people. The terrorists were not like any Muslims we know. They weren't real Muslims, they were deluded. They thought they were doing something valiant by killing all those people, and by killing themselves, but they were doing something horrible. They'd been brainwashed."

Ash was glad for his brother's conversation, even if

it was about a topic which disturbed him greatly.

"I feel sorry for the families", Ash said sadly. "Anita said that some of the people jumped out of the building, and some of the ones on the plane rang their children for the last time to tell them that they loved them."

Daruk watched the ceiling, with tears in his eyes. He wanted to reassure his brother. He longed to play with him again, and make him laugh, and mend what he had broken. But in his depression, he couldn't bring himself to say anything at all.

"Daruk? Do you still love me, brother?" Ash asked, piercing through the silence.

Daruk could find the words now. He wiped his eyes, and hung his head over his bunk, looking down at Ash's innocent face.

"Ash, no matter what happens, or what you do and don't understand in this life, understand this, okay, brother? I will *always* love you."

Ash rolled over in his bed, scrunched up his eyes, and whispered "thank you" into the pillow, directed at the God he wasn't sure existed. Then he rolled back onto his back.

"*For as long as this tree is standing*", he whispered.

And Daruk smiled.

"You know what Ash, maybe next summer, when I've finished school and got a job, we can go back to our tree, back to India."

"*Really?*"

"Really. I promise we will be back there one day… back home."

Ash slept with a smile on his face that night.

*

The next morning, when Daruk and Ash opened their front door to leave for school, they were faced with a front lawn covered with litter. Toilet rolls had been strewn all over the grass, smashed up cans and broken bottles had been abandoned, their wheelie bin had been knocked over, tipping all of their waste over the ground, which spilled out like a cascading waterfall. Daruk stepped onto the uneven slated paves they called a path, and looked back at the house, where egg yolks dripped down their windows and red spray paint had graffitied their front door with; *"Terrorists"* and *"Go back to Afghan land"*.

Ash looked around the empty street, fearfully.

Daruk went to lift the black wheelie bin tiredly, and as he did, their next door neighbour used his muscular tattooed arms to wheel himself down the ramp outside his front door.

"Sorry, lads", he called, sucking on his cigarette. "I tried to call the police but they was already leavin'", he explained, squinting at the early morning sun.

"We're not even fucking Afghani!", Daruk spat, pushing the wheelie bin back over in a rage.

Stunned by his curse word, Ash timidly tiptoed around his brother, collecting up the cans and packaging, piece by piece.

"Aye, you don't need to tell me that. Thought those posh school bastards would've known it too", Jerry exclaimed.

Daruk's heart began to thud, but less in anger, and more in distress. *How did they know where he lived?*

"Posh school? Who were they?" Daruk asked anxiously, "what did they look like?"

"I didn't stop to chat with 'em, lad", Jerry scoffed, "but, they was three white lads on bikes. They 'ad the same red blazer on as you, and with the pansy little caps on, too."

Daruk ripped his burgundy cap off of his black hair, and pulled at it in his hands. *They knew where he lived.*

Ash listened intently, letting his mind be flooded with brutal scenarios.

But Daruk shut down his questions on their walk to school that morning, although Ash fired them at him like bullets, running to keep up with his brother's frantic pace.

"So, you know who trashed our house?"

"Leave it, Ash."

"Why don't we call the police?"

"No, Ash, we can't."

"Why won't you tell me who they are?"

"That's enough, I said!"

Ash stopped in his tracks, piecing everything together. He was almost relieved, when he realised, perhaps his brother hadn't really changed. Perhaps Daruk was still there, but his life was being made miserable. Ash could change it. He could make it better.

"This is why you've been so different lately, isn't it?" he insisted.

And that's what made Daruk stop. He turned around slowly, and looked at the little boy who he thought the world of, and exhaled, defeatedly.

"I'm sorry, Asha", he whispered, as a tear rolled down his cheek.

Ash couldn't remember seeing his brother cry before, not ever. His heart softened.

Ash moved close to him, rubbing his back and trying

to nestle his head beneath his arms.

"You can tell me", he exclaimed, "tell me what's going on, and we can make it go away."

Daruk gave him a squeeze, and wiped his tears away.

"I can handle it, honest", he sniffed.

They continued the rest of the walk in silence, with Ash trailing behind his brother, occasionally bursting into a jog to keep up. Ash's mind was teaming with questions about what went on at Daruk's school. He saw the look on Daruk's face when Jerry had mentioned three boys trashing their house. Daruk must have known who they were.

Daruk dropped his brother at the primary school gates, which were a lot busier than usual. Almost every teacher was outside on the playground, ushering the children straight inside.

"Straight into the assembly hall, everyone", the teachers called.

"I'll see you at 3:30", Daruk assured Ash, who nodded sadly.

Ash's day began with a long morning assembly, where his headteacher, Mr Blythe, educated the children on the terrible events that had occurred in America, the previous day. He explained that "we must not treat our Muslim friends any differently", and what had happened was "due to the severe brainwashing of groups of people in other countries." He told the children not to be frightened, and that "we will be having a minute silence to pray for all the families affected, right after lunchtime."

Miss Bourbon made all of the children paint pictures for their families, and reminded them that now was the time to tell them they loved them, and to be thankful for living in a peaceful country.

Ash recited his brothers words from the previous night.

"*I will always love you*"

He knew his words were true, and he comforted himself in them, as he stabbed his paintbrush into the paint pot which was supposed to be blue, but Joshua had turned green after dipping his yellow covered brush into it.

Ash worried about his brother all day and felt scared about what had been done to their house. Who were these three boys? He'd only need to wait until after school to find out.

*

Daruk picked up Ash at 3:30 pm, just as he'd said he would. His face was flushed, as if he'd been running, and his eyes were blood shot, as if he'd been crying. Ash felt more worried than ever. He felt scared about the attacks in New York, scared about the attacks on their house, but mostly, scared for his brother. What was happening? He was frightened to ask for fear of being snapped at, but he'd had enough of being shut out and kept in the dark. Getting a sense that even Daruk felt frightened was like his whole world was insecure.

"Daruk, what's going on? I'm going to tell Mamma", Ash demanded, as they began their walk home through the town.

Daruk was limping, biting his lip and trying to hold back the tears.

"I can't tell you", he said, trying not to break.

Ash tugged at his brother's arm, but Daruk winced

sharply, pulling it away.

"Why are you walking like that? What's happened to you? *Tell me!* Daruk I know those boys are bullying you, I don't have to tell Mum, I can tell Miss Bourbon, she can help." Ash urged desperately, as they turned away from the high street and headed across the green towards the woods.

"No", sniffed Daruk. "No, you can't tell anyone. I'm going to deal with it. It'll all be over soon."

"*It'll all be over soon*"

What did that mean?

"Daruk? Daruk, what does that mean?" Ash begged, running along the path into the woods. The tall trees blew fiercely in the wind, spraying their leaves over the boy's figures, as if warning them to get out. They continued.

"There he is", a chilling whisper came from within the trees.

Ash shuddered.

"What was that?" he asked, edging closer to Daruk, who put his arm across his little brother's chest, shielding him, and begging him backwards.

"They're a couple of faggots", another voice sniggered, from behind the trees.

Daruk spun around on the muddy clearing, in a desperate search for strangers. *Any* strangers. But there were no men walking their dogs, no children flying their kites, and no women pushing their prams today. They were all alone, with his perpetrators.

Popeto Charpentier was the first to emerge from behind a large oak tree, straddling his BMX bike and chewing sloppily on a piece of gum. Next, Billy Thatcher jumped down from the branch of a young sycamore, and as his chubby figure hit the ground, his cheeks wobbled.

Finally, Charles Frances Wincott, known to his friends as *Charlie,* appeared. He'd ditched his burgundy blazer since school was out, and had thrown on an expensive, white woollen cricketer's sweater, which made his fair hair look golden.

"I see you've got your faggot brother with you", Charlie taunted spitefully, edging closer to the two brothers. His friends echoed his remark with malicious sneers.

Ash scowled at him, but edged even closer to Daruk. He looked his brother up and down, knowing he was stronger, and braver, and *faster* than any of these boys could possibly be.

"Look Charlie, don't. Not while I'm with him", Daruk pleaded, stepping in front of Ash.

Charlie scoffed, and beckoned his friends to join him, who did so like obliging minions subjecting to their master. Popeto threw down his bike arrogantly and jogged to Charlie's side. Billy folded his arms in vindictive pleasure, feeding off Daruk's clear discomfort.

"I haven't done *anything* to you!" Daruk cried angrily, clenching his fists, trying to hold back his tears.

Charlie turned his head from side to side, winking at Billy and raising his eyebrows impishly at Popeto.

"Haven't done *anything*?" Charlie sneered. "Did you see the news last night, Poppy?"

Popeto nodded, spitting out his white gum in one harsh blow. It flew through the autumn air and landed on the fallen brown leaves in front of Daruk's feet.

"About two thousand people dead", Popeto

remarked.

Ash shook his head in disbelief, willing the confrontation to be over.

"You're a dirty, little, terrorist, Paki", Charlie seethed, relentlessly, "and we don't want you here."

"They're animals! Our school was clean before they came along!" Billy jeered, crouching down and reaching for a small rock. "They can't even afford to live here!"

"We're not terrorists, and we're from India, we lived in a palace!" Ash spluttered fiercely, regretting his words as soon as he'd spat them out. Daruk gulped.

A malicious grin spread across Charlie's face.

"So, the little monkey speaks?" he teased, glaring at Ash.

"A palace!" Charlie continued mockingly. "Unlikely, considering you're council house scum now. You shouldn't even be allowed on this side of town!"

Ash grit his teeth, seething and breathing heavily. The menacing boy gang began to close in.

Daruk turned to Ash, and spoke to him in Urdu. "*You must run, brother, I'll stop them*", he ordered.

All Ash wanted to do was run away, but his legs would not carry him. He simply could not bear to leave his brother. Even if it meant being battered to the ground, his innate loyalty kept him there, terrified but frozen. He felt safer beside his brother, even in the face of bullies, than he did being totally alone.

"*I can't leave you, I won't.*" Ash muttered, replying in Urdu.

"They're plotting!" Billy cried.

Charlie crept up to Daruk until he was standing directly in front of him, and Daruk could feel his breath on his face.

"I've heard how you Paki's in India treat each other. You throw stones", Charlie whispered, glaring into Daruk's undefeated eyes.

Today was not the day to mess with Daruk. He was tired. Tired of having the life sucked out of him. His inbuilt sense of worth and continual desire to protect his family willed his next actions.

Daruk lunged forward in a fit of adrenaline-fuelled fury, using his strong arms to push Charlie backwards, with all his might. Charlie fell with a thud onto the hard ground.

"Get the stones!" he cried vengefully, as Daruk grabbed his brother by the arm and they began running.

"Run, Ash. Run!" Daruk begged, and they sped together through the woodland.

But the stones soon caught up with them, sharply throttling their shoulders and backs with heavy hits that winded them. They kept running, but Daruk knew that Ash could never compete with his unmatchable pace. He slowed a little, hauling at his younger brother's arm. Ash's legs were much smaller than any of the boy's, and Daruk knew that his predators weren't far behind, especially when he began to hear the chain of Popeto's bike crunching, and the spin of the wheels on the leaves.

Charlie was riding it.

"Come back, you pussy!" he taunted, until he got so close to Ash that he lifted the front wheel of the BMX up, balancing on the back wheel, and then slammed the handlebars down, forcing the bike to drop down onto the backs of Ash's legs.

Ash screamed out in pain, as the bike scuffed the skin off his ankles and sent him hurtling onto the hard mud with a thud to the head. He scurried to his knees.

"Throw the stones!" Charlie ordered, holding Ash down by the scruff of his neck, and glaring at his bystander friends.

Popeto looked uncomfortable.

"I'm not sure, Charlie, he's just a little kid", he stammered, rolling a stone around in his shaking hand.

"Oh, give it here, you twat", Billy hissed.

But at that moment, Daruk, who had stopped and spun in his tracks, came careering through the air, sending his clenched fist into Charlie's cheek bone with the strength from every sinew in his body. His knuckles throbbed instantly with the contact. Charlie's head was knocked backwards, his body overcome with shock. And once again, Daruk swung his fist in a right hook which plummeted into the tender cheek of the dizzied boy. They all heard his cheekbone crunch, as it sunk into his face.

"Let him go!" Daruk screamed fiercely, holding his fist in the air ready to smack his peer again, but Charlie had already released Ash's collar, and held his shaking hands over his thumping, bloodied face, groaning in pain.

Daruk hauled Ash to his wobbling legs, and turned to Billy and Popeto, holding out his fists. Ash stood helplessly, breathing heavily, willing his brother's quick fists, and shedding tears of frightened fury.

Popeto held his hands up in surrender, shaking his head at Daruk and falling to his knees to tend to Charlie.

"What shall I do?" Billy asked Charlie, preparing to throw another stone.

"Leave them", Charlie spat, wiping a fierce tear away from his swollen eye. Seething, he stared Daruk directly in the eyes, and swallowed down a lump of sheer hatred.

"You may have gotten away today, you filthy inbred, but I am going to fucking *kill you*."

Ash and Daruk ran the entire distance of the woods, panting as they went. Daruk held Ash's sleeve, for his own comfort as well as his brother's. He felt mortified to have brought Ash into his living nightmare. It had gone too far now.

They passed the wide clearing where the trees were sparse, and an old gypsy van which frightened Ash sat, abandoned. Ivy grew over its walls and rotten steps. There was a steep drop hiding behind the lining of trees which surrounded the clearing, where the old railway ran underneath. The brother's ran over the top of the railway bridge and jumped a fence into a boggy farmer's field. The track through the farmer's field finally met with the alley way which led the boys up to their estate.

Ash was steaming on ahead, when he noticed Daruk had slowed down. He turned around, puffing and panting, to look back at Daruk, who placed his head in his hands, and began sobbing.

Ash shuffled over to him, not knowing what to say. Daruk was disgusted at himself for what he'd subjected his brother to. But Ash looked up at his hero, inspired by him in every aspect of the word.

"Thank you for saving me", Ash wheezed.

Daruk screwed his face up in anguish, forcing more tears to fall. He grabbed the scruff of Ash's collar, and pulled him into a close embrace.

And in that moment, just for that moment, ignoring all the hurt and the sadness and the shock, Ash felt safe once more.

13

THE HEADHUNT

London, England, 2019

Ash tapped his fingernails on the desk, in the dimmed studio. It was 9 o'clock in the evening, and he'd asked two of his scouting agents to meet him there.

Marcus was a mixed-race, hard-working and motivated young man, who'd confided in Ash about his financial problems, desperate to buy a house anywhere in London, for his wife and toddler. This is why Ash had invited Marcus to the meeting.

Gregory was a dreamer, who set ideas in motion. He was particularly trustworthy, and owed Ash a favour. Gregory was an old friend that Ash had met at a film festival back in their early twenties, and when Ash made it onto the big screen, he'd remembered the aspiring writer and had called him up, offering him a job.

Gregory owed Ash his whole career. That is why Ash had invited Gregory to the meeting.

Ash thought back on his day. He had gone to knock on the door of the reporter he had attacked on live TV, in the late part of last year. When the ginger-haired man opened up the door of his London town-house, he shielded his face with his hands, in fear.

"Please, I'm not here to hurt you" Ash had insisted.

"What do you want?" The man asked sharply, peering out into the street, in the hope there would be passersby.

"I'm sorry for showing up like this. I just wanted to explain myself. I wanted to apologise, in person. I am really sorry for grabbing you in the crowd at the Dragon Train Interview last year"

The man looked Ash up and down, suspiciously.

"They said it was the medication you were on, which caused you to do it. Obviously, I know that wasn't the case"

Ash looked to the ground.

"The truth is, I heard your voice in the crowd. I heard you say something."

The man looked puzzled.

"I was working that night. I just called after you, I said I worked for *Hello* magazine, and that my name was-"

"Charles Wincott" Ash finished, regrettably.

"Yes, that's right. Charles Wincott. I don't understand why it made you flip. You were being approached by all the other reporters as well."

Ash nodded.

"It was an unfortunate coincidence. I thought you were somebody else. I'm really sorry for what I did. I just needed to tell you that, and if there is anything you need-"

Suddenly, the studio door opened, bringing Ash out of his reminisce.

Anxious and confused about the reason for the evening meeting, the men came right on time, and walked into the studio one after the other, as if they had been conspiring outside. They immediately noticed Ash's unruly appearance. He hadn't shaved in a few days and thick black stubble covered his face, his hair was a mess, he had big rings under his eyes and he'd been wearing the same salmon shirt two days in a row - something he never did.

Marcus spied the half empty bottle of Jack Daniels sitting on the kitchen counter, directly behind Ash's head.

"Thanks for coming", Ash said wearily. "You didn't tell anyone, did you?"

Both men shook their heads.

Ash ran his hand over his face, as he often did, when he felt anxious or stressed.

"I've asked you here because I need you to do something for me", Ash began, reaching for a swig of his JD and Coke.

"Let me guess, no questions asked?" Gregory said, raising his eyebrows. He knew Ash only too well.

"No questions asked", Ash confirmed. "I'm serious."

Marcus and Gregory exchanged uneasy glances.

"Look, Marc I know you want to get on that property ladder, bad. And Greg, I know you want a promotion. I want to be able to make those things happen for you."

Elated, Marcus beamed,

"Mr Lakhanpal, Sir, that's *wonderful*!"

"I sense a big *but*…" Gregory interjected, ogling his old friend. Although Ash was his senior, he still thought of him as a friend first.

Ash took a deep breath. His head had been so tormented with anger and strife lately, that he was finding it difficult to see anything clearly. Including this plan.

"Okay, here it is. Marcus I can give you the deposit you need for a home in London, for your family. And Gregory, the same goes for you in the form of a salary bump, and you can take the writing lead on our next film. In return, I need you to… get a guy for me." Ash breathed, downing the contents of his glass.

Marcus' face looked stunned, his eyes widened with delight. "A house? A house in London?" he gasped, "I'll do it, Sir, I'll do *anything*-"

Gregory tutted at the foolish man. "Wait, what guy, Ash? Who is this guy?" he insisted, furrowing his dark eyebrows, which were a perfect colour match for his head of thick curls.

"He's just a guy I used to know. His name is Frances Charles Wincott, goes by Frankie these days. He once took something from me, you see. We've got history", he boiled, clenching his empty glass so hard that his knuckles turned white.

Marcus hesitated this time. "Wait, when you say you want us to *get* this guy… you don't mean…?"

"You want us to end him?" Gregory stressed, exhaling fiercely.

Ash slammed his fists down on the desk. "No, you maniacs! Who do you think I am? No offence but if I wanted a guy murdered, I wouldn't be asking daddy day care over here and bloody Spielberg in the making!"

Marcus sat back into his chair, letting out a sigh of relief, and slipping again into a brief daydream about a house in London.

"So, what do you want us to do with him?" Gregory pressed.

Ash leant over the desk and looked the men intensely in the eyes.

"I want you…", he whispered, "to *employ* him."

14

THE WOODS

Essex, England, 2001

It was Sunday night, 16th September, 2001. The Sunday after the Wednesday. The Wednesday they'd been caught in the woods. Daruk had skipped school on the Thursday and the Friday, telling Roshni he was too sick to attend. She only believed him when she felt his temperature, after Ash had held the hot water bottle on his forehead for ten minutes prior.

Daruk had made Ash *promise* not to tell their mother, or any of his teachers about what had happened to them. He told Ash that if he did, he'd get put into a juvenile prison for gross bodily harm to Charlie, and that Charlie's father was head of the police force. This was the only thing buying Ash's silence, but really, Daruk was buying time for a plan of his own. Bonded together by their hideous encounter in the woods, the brothers felt closer than ever, once again. Although Daruk was mortified for Ash's involuntary involvement in his troubles at school, he felt somewhat relieved that Ash could now perhaps understand. Understand why he had been forced to be so distant. To protect Ash.

Ash still feared the day his brother would have to return to school with those vile humans. But Daruk assured him, again and again, *"it will all be over soon"*.

Roshni brought the boys a cup of hot chai before bed. *"Do you think you will be well enough to go back to school tomorrow?"* she asked, handing Daruk his mug.

"Yes, I'm ready to go back", Daruk replied, sipping at his delicious drink.

Roshni nodded, and then bent down to Ash's bunk and kissed him on the cheek.

"I'll have one too, tonight", Daruk said shyly.

Taken by surprise, a deep smile filled his mother's face. She leant over the side of Daruk's top bunk, and kissed him on the cheek too, most lovingly.

"I love you both", she said, before she flicked their bedroom light off, and they heard her disappear down the landing and close herself in her bedroom.

The hot milk caused Ash to slip into an easy doze that night, but his eyes shot open when he heard the creaking of Daruk's upper bunk about fifteen minutes into his slumber. He watched Daruk's dark silhouette creep down the bunk bed ladder, and lightly pad across the bedroom. He quietly opened the door and snuck out. Ash wouldn't have followed him ordinarily, assuming he was off to the bathroom, had it not been for the fact that Daruk had slipped his trainers on before creeping out.

Curious, Ash crawled out of the comfort of his bed

and reached for his blue fluffy dressing gown, which was hanging on the bedroom door. He slipped it on, and slid his feet into his Indian slippers, one of his only original items of clothing to have made it to England, from Kashmir. They were Lakhan slippers, especially hand designed by his father.

Ash tiptoed across the landing and crept down the stairs, the front door had only just closed. When he reached it, he opened up the metal letter box and peered out into the night, where Daruk, dressed in a black hoody which he'd shoved over his head, was jogging across the road. Ash was crippled with fear; he *hated* the dark, hated being by himself and was terrified of the estate. It came alive at night with gangs and women that intimidated him with just one look. And yet, overcome with curiosity, the eleven-year-old found himself cracking open the door, and tiptoeing across the front lawn, his breath sending clouds of white mist into the cold air. Ash had only made it to the end of the front garden, when he saw Daruk stop by the row of garages opposite their home, and so he darted into Jerry's front lawn, crouching behind his shrubbery, peering out from his hiding spot.

They showed up quickly, the two hooded boys. They were a similar size to Daruk, both white, with black caps on, and tracksuit bottoms. Ash couldn't make out their faces. He squinted, desperately trying to see what was going on, but their murmurs were too quiet to comprehend, and although he watched their hands shaking, he couldn't see what was being *exchanged*. Whatever the object was, Daruk slid it into his hoody pocket.

Oh no, he was coming back. Already. Ash darted back

across Jerry's lawn and across his own front lawn, flung open the front door, and ran all the way up his stairs. He jumped into his bed and pulled the covers over himself, praying Daruk hadn't caught him. When Daruk came back into the bedroom, Ash peeked at his darkened figure, watching as he quietly unzipped his school bag, took the mystery object out of his pocket and dropped it into the bag. It made a gentle thud sound. Daruk then zipped the bag back up and gently placed it against the wall, before clambering back into his top bunk.

Ash hardly slept a wink that night.

*

The next morning, whilst Daruk was in the bathroom brushing his teeth, Ash, who had already put his uniform on and fixed his collar, crept over to Daruk's school bag nervously. He unzipped the bag, and picked up the strange object, which had been wrapped in a white cloth. It was a heavy piece of rectangular gold, with four perfect circles punched through it. Ash slipped his small hand into the knuckle duster, examining it. He could hear Daruk's approaching footsteps, and immediately wrapped the weapon back up and placed it back into the bag.

"You ready?" Daruk asked, poking his head into the bedroom.

"Ready", Ash sighed.

At breakfast, Roshni set the pancakes down on the kitchen counter, and put the kettle on. She was wearing her blue cleaning uniform fleece, and hastily spooning yoghurt into Jayminee's messy mouth.

She peered outside the front window, to see her lift waiting for her. Anita was later than usual.

"*Boys! Boys, I need you to drop your sister at nursery this morning*", Roshni called, as the two brothers, school bags on shoulders, appeared in the crowded kitchen.

"Okay, Mamma", Daruk agreed willingly, to Roshni's surprise.

Ash devoured his pancakes anxiously, as his mind spun with a thousand worries. What did Daruk mean by *it will all be over soon?* What was he planning on doing to Charlie with that strange golden object? Why did Daruk appear like a weight had been lifted from his shoulders this morning? The teenager ate his pancakes contently, making faces at Jayminee.

"*I hope you get on well at school today. I'm working late but I'll pick Jay up on my way home. I've left some dhal in the fridge for your supper*", Roshni said, in a fluster. As she turned to leave, Daruk stood up.

"*Mamma*", he said.

"*Yes, son?*"

Daruk paused. "*Thanks for everything, Mum*", he exhaled.

Roshni glanced at her son in suspicion, and then gave him a loving smile.

"*It's only pancakes*", she exclaimed. "*Have a great day, my darlings.*"

*

The three children walked through the estate together, hand in hand. Jayminee, who was walking now, or rather, tumbling along, held onto her brothers' firm grips.

Her nursery was a small, square, little building on the edge of the estate, next to the local library. It had a fenced off, flower filled garden with soft toys and plastic slides.

"Swing, swing", Jayminee spluttered, tugging on Daruk and Ash's arms. Ash looked to Daruk, and Daruk nodded warmly.

"One, two, three", he cried, as both brothers lifted her arms up, and swung her body backwards and forwards, through the air. She giggled happily. "Again! 'gen!", she begged.

As they carried the infant through the autumn air, on that crisp September morning, with the faint orange sun bouncing off their jet-black hair, it was almost as if the rest of the world did not exist. Not their enemies, nor their woes, nor their fears for the future. In fact, for just that simple walk together, everything that plagued their minds left, and they felt like *it was just them* in the whole world.

*

"I don't want you to go to school. Please don't go", Ash begged, finally all his angst coming to a head.

Daruk shook his head, "Ash, it's going to be okay. I'll be okay", Daruk reassured him.

"No, *he'll* be there. And after you beat him up, I'm scared of what he will do. Let me tell Miss Bourbon, she can help us, we can go and talk to her right now", Ash pleaded, as they arrived at his school gates.

"No, brother. I've told you, you can't tell anybody. You *can't*. Look, you saw what happened on Wednesday, I am *stronger* than Charlie. He can't hurt me.

If you tell anyone then I'll be taken away for what I did, I've told you about his dad", Daruk explained convincingly, and Ash felt trapped in an impossible predicament.

Daruk's tone had an underlying sense of nervousness and uncertainty.

"Today's the last day I'm going into that school, ever again", he said firmly.

"How is it? Why is it? What do you mean? Tell me. Tell me, right now!" Ash squeaked, frustratedly.

Parents and children passed the brothers on their way into the junior school, some stopped to greet Ash, but he ignored them completely.

"Ash, I need you to trust me, okay. Would I ever lie to you? I've got it under control. They won't be able to hurt us, anymore", Daruk insisted, placing both his hands on Ash's shoulders.

"Do you promise?" Ash stressed, dropping his bottom lip in an uncomfortable sulk.

"I promise", replied Daruk, "it will all be over soon."

Ash nodded. "And when all this is over, you'll play with me again, and be my brother again?" Ash urged.

Daruk let out a regretful sigh, and the rising sun set his eyes on fire.

"Asha, I'm sorry about before. I'm sorry for cutting you out, I was just so low. Forgive me. I will always be your brother. And yes, we will get our game plan back on. It's a promise."

Temporarily contented, Ash nodded. He felt strangely compelled to remind Daruk how much he loved him, but instead, he simply gave him a weak smile, and said "I'll see you at the end of the day, when you come to pick me up. You won't be late will you?"

Daruk rubbed his hand over Ash's messy mop of a haircut. "I'll be here, Ash. I will never leave you. I promise. And hey, maybe we can go and find that river you talked about all summer?" Daruk said, smiling.

Ash was enthused. "Okay", he beamed. "Love you."

"Love you, too", Daruk whispered, winking at him.

And with that, the teenager slipped away from the gates. Ash watched the sun gleam onto his athletic figure, which slowly disappeared down the street and into the horizon.

*

Bloodied knuckles, unforgiving strangulation, fierce rage, spitting, swearing, screaming, clawing, biting, wrestling, relentless beating, hot tears, racist remarks, slashing, cutting, *fighting-*

"*Asha!* Ash, it's your turn to roll", Lydia insisted, interrupting Ash's nightmarish daydream.

Ash snapped back into the moment, and picked up the dice.

"Sorry", he said, throwing them onto the game his small group had created in their design class the previous week. It was a game they'd named 'The Last One Standing', and consisted of silly forfeits and lots of jumping up and down.

"Asha, are you alright today?" Miss Bourbon asked, concerned, having observed her pupil's vacant and distant behaviour all day. It simply was not like him. He'd been thriving at school over the past year and had grown in confidence hugely. It was not uncommon that Miss Bourbon would have to split Ash up from his friends for talking too much at their tables and being silly.

Ash longed to be able to tell his kind and approachable teacher of everything that was playing on his mind. He wished he could tell her of the bullies, of how they'd trashed his house, of Daruk's mysterious exchange in the middle of the night, of the fight in the woods, of his fears for their walk home tonight, of his brother's confusing and vague words. It caused him much dismay when he turned to her and simply croaked.

"Yes, Miss, I'm fine."

3:30 pm took an eternity to roll around, but once it did, Ash bolted out of his classroom doors, knocking the sign over on the filing cabinet which read 'Newton Class'. He'd forgotten his lunchbox completely and was in too much of a rush to even say goodbye to Joshua. In anticipation, he raced onto the playground, where as usual, clusters of enthusiastic parents who waited to be bombarded with their children's paintings and schoolwork were standing eagerly.

Ash scoured the playground for Daruk, but his brother was nowhere to be seen. He hastily walked over to the usual spot where the young teenager would wait for him each day, but the school gates were bare, with nobody leaning against them. Although an immediate feeling of panic swept over him, the same kind that filled him when he'd lost his mother in the supermarket shortly after they'd arrived in the UK, he knew it was only *just* 3:30 pm. Daruk had been a few minutes late to collect him before, on two occasions. He circled the playground to double check.

Ash then returned to the school gates, and waited patiently, clinging onto the black steel railings and peering out onto the surrounding streets. With each minute that went by, and each chirpy parent holding their child's hand to pass him, he grew more and more distressed. He re-ran the words in his head to comfort himself:

"I'm stronger than Charlie"
"You have to trust me"
"I've got it all under control"
"I'll be here, Ash. I will never leave you, I promise"

But as much as Ash tried to focus on his brother's words, he couldn't escape his intrusive fears.

"Today's the last day I'm going into that school, ever again"
"It will all be over soon"

And,

"I'm going to fucking kill you"
"Kill you",

Charlie had said.

The playground began to clear, slowly and steadily. Ash listened to the dulled conversations of parents asking their children what they'd done that day, and telling them they had toffee apples waiting for them at home. Ash pulled on the zip of his winter coat, up and down, up and down, fidgeting anxiously. It wasn't just worry sweeping over him though, it was *anger*. Daruk promised. Promised! He said he would be there, and he wasn't. Now what was he supposed to do? Ash headed back across the almost empty playground.

"Are you okay, Asha? Mum running late?" Mr Richards called, clearing some coloured beanbags away and throwing them into the shed. As he did so, the whistle around his neck swung in the wind.

"Yeah, on the way", Ash lied, dashing into his classroom to find Miss Bourbon and Mrs Clay sat at a table on chairs much too small for them, doing some planning.

"Oh hello, Asha. Are you okay, darling? Daruk not here yet?" Miss Bourbon asked, but she did not appear too concerned.

"Can I wait in here, Miss? He's coming."

Miss Bourbon used the desk to push up her plump body, and wobbled over to Ash.

"There's After School Club going on in the library, why don't you go and join them? When Daruk turns up, I'll send him your way. It'll be more fun than you watching us do assessment planning", she suggested kindly.

Ash nodded, though he had no plans to go to After School Club. He dashed down the school corridor and passed the open library where a group of year threes and fours were dispersed on the small tables, drawing and reading. He continued to the back corridor, which lead out to the school field. There, he watched the after school football club, spotting his friends Luke and Darren. He walked the distance of the edge of the field, turned a corner, and found himself back on the now, totally empty, playground. Daruk had not appeared.

He sat down underneath the single oak tree next to the shed, rubbing his hands together and blowing into them to keep them warm. Here, he was out of sight from the football field and his classroom. He would wait here, stressing, fretting and incensed until his lying brother finally arrived.

His thoughts went round in circles - fuming that Daruk would do this to him, scared that he'd have to walk home alone. And then, slowly, his anger softened and he began to worry for Daruk, worrying where he could possibly be, whether he was alright, and he began to feel scared for his brother, and feel bad that he'd been angry. Perhaps he'd hit Charlie so hard that he'd been arrested? He hoped he had - hit him, that is, not been arrested. He plotted and calculated miserably, wishing that Charlie had got his comeuppance, and then some. He hoped Charlie screamed like a girl when Daruk beat him, and that the whole school would hear.

Ash had only visited Daruk's school once, when there was nobody to babysit him on Daruk's parents evening. Daruk and Ash had played with Jayminee out on the stripy cricket pitch, whilst Roshni was inside learning about Daruk's top grades, and his decision to turn down the offer of captain of the school cricket team. Ash had wondered at the time why Daruk hadn't talked about any of his friends, but Daruk had been so good at diverting away from the subject, Ash had been distracted.

The child blamed himself now though, fixating on the horrible thought that Daruk had been silently bullied this whole time. His thoughts ventured further, imagining the fear and anguish of facing bullies every day. It must have been so hideous for Daruk. Ash thought back to how nervous he'd been on his first day as the new kid at Kingsgate, and how Daruk had encouraged him and lead him enthusiastically to meet his teacher, saying that they were both going to love school in England. It broke his heart to think about how brightly his brother's face had beamed that first morning.

Ash didn't own a watch, but he knew that when the final whistle blew out on the football pitch, and the muddied and red-faced children came jogging back towards the school, it was 4:30 pm. They got picked up at 5:00 pm usually. An hour had passed, *a whole hour*. He could barely feel his fingertips, and the air had grown dim. He squinted to make out Darren's chubby body, jogging along and greeting his proud father who had been watching the last five minutes of the practice from the side lines.

Ash took to his feet and scurried out of the empty playground, and through the black gates.

He wasn't allowed a mobile phone yet, not that his mother could afford one. Daruk didn't have a mobile phone either. Ash wished that Daruk had accepted one now, so he could call it from the school reception. Although, Kingsgate reception was shut away and abandoned by this time. Ash remembered that his mum was working late, and she'd be home around 6:00 pm, so he'd have time to hash out Daruk's absence with him, before she got back. He toyed with the idea of going back to the classroom to see Miss Bourbon and telling her he was scared of walking home alone, but then she would know that he had lied about going to After School Club. *Oh, the anxiety*. There was only one thing for it, and one way home. Now, for the dreaded walk. Hopefully, there would be some people around in the woods, he thought to himself. And he'd better get moving, because it was growing darker.

Usually, it took Ash and Daruk about twenty minutes to reach the wooded area, but today, Ash got there in fifteen, he was jogging fast. *Just keep walking,* he willed himself. The first part of his journey had been okay. There were a few people dotted around on the first high street, as shops were only just closing.

Then, Ash approached the abandoned forest, and

stepped in. The trees towered above him, and the leaves whispered, haunting him. Perhaps he should go back to school? Would the teachers still be there, though? It was only *just* still light enough to make out the path. If he turned back to find the school locked up, then he would surely have to return to the woods in the pitch black, and there was no way of calling his mother or his brother.

He fought with the conflicting thoughts in his head for a moment, but then forced himself forward. Fuelled by fear and the bitter cold, he broke out into an affrighted jog. Each crunching leaf beneath his tired feet sent a cold sweat through his body and a quiver up his spine, unsure of whether it was his own footsteps he was hearing or somebody else's.

"Where are you, Daruk, why aren't you with me?", he trembled to himself. *Mum's going to be so mad at you for not picking me up and leaving me.* His eyes began to fill up with hot, wet tears, as he begged the journey to be over. He'd run about three-quarters of the way through the woodland and was only probably only another five minutes from the clearing and the old farmer's field.

Just keep going, just keep running, he told himself, repeatedly. And then his anger returned. He envisioned what he'd say to Daruk when he saw him. How he'd scream at him like he'd never screamed before, telling him how selfish he'd been not to let him tell Miss Bourbon about the house and the bullies and now deserting him to walk home-

Ash stopped in his tracks. Frozen.

He wanted to scream. But couldn't.

He wanted to run, but didn't.

He just stood still for a moment, crippled, by

disbelief.

Submerged in horror.

A sickly, prickly, hellish despair swept over him, from the darkest places of his mind to the depths of his soul, destructive in its wake, wiping out any glimmer of hope. He fought with every ember in his shaking body, and all of his mental might for it not to be true. He didn't understand it at first. Was this a nightmare, or a disturbed reality?

Suddenly, he felt the hot vomit creep up his throat and opened his mouth, spewing it out over the crinkled leaves, breaking through the silent woods with a loud retching.

Tears uncontrollably fell down his face, as he choked on them, gasping for breath, exhaling only silent screams.

He drew closer to the oak tree.

Daruk's body was motionless. Frost had already rested on his closed eyelashes and soft cheeks. He swayed in the breeze, his peaceful face folded over the noose around his neck, as he hung from one of the low branches. His feet swung above the ground, just as they'd swung their infant sister that morning.

"Help! Help! Help me! *Help*!" Ash screeched at the top of his lungs, sending a flurry of pigeons fluttering through the empty forest. He clawed at the bark of the tree, breaking his fingernails as he used them to haul his quivering body up onto the first branch. Panting heavily, he hoisted his shaking leg over the second branch, and straddled it, shimmying himself along until he reached the rope. He battled with the tight, thick strands of hemp, in a desperate attempt to pry them apart. His numb fingers stung with pain, until the knot finally loosened. The weight of his brother's body pulled down his arms suddenly, and Ash's head and neck followed, smashing against the branch. The weight was too much, and he listened to the dull thud of Daruk's body hit the leaves beneath.

When Ash leapt down carelessly, tingling pain shot up his legs, leaping from a height that he'd usually have climbed down cautiously from.

He knelt over Daruk's body, pulling the noose loose and gently sliding it off Daruk's head. He kept his hands holding onto Daruk's hair, and cradled his head. He kissed his face again and again.

"Wake up, wake up, wake up!" he cried, sobbing tears so forcefully that they started to soak Daruk's fringe. "Please wake up. I'm sorry. I'm sorry I didn't say anything. I'm sorry, please wake up. I love you. I love you. I love you!"

He gently rested Daruk's peaceful head on the leaves before pushing his own small hands down onto Daruk's heart. He pushed, up and down, up and down, up and down. He'd seen CPR only once before, watching the woman who'd performed it on the drowned boy at Dal Lake. She'd been too late.

And inside, Ash knew that it was too late for him, too. His heart was broken. But he needed more time. He continued. For a whole thirty minutes, the child continued to make compressions on his brother's chest. The same chest he had fought against whilst in a playful headlock, the chest which had homed a heart so warm, and the chest he'd clung to on a thousand piggy-back rides.

He pushed, and released, pushed and released, puffing and panting, weeping and spluttering, aching and despairing, until the darkness had fallen over the wood. And then he got up, and started running.

He ran in a straight line, until the black outlines of the trees had cleared, and he saw the light of the moon reflecting off the old gypsy van. He wasn't scared of what might happen to him anymore. He had lost everything. He squelched over the farmer's field, and towards the alleyway of his estate, where a group of four youths were huddled. Orange embers floated by their mouths, on the end of their roll ups.

"Oi, oi, sunshine, what's up?" one of them mocked, squaring up to the small boy. But when the teenagers saw the look on Ash's face, as if he'd been met by the devil himself, they stood to attention.

"Please, please call the ambulance and the police", Ash begged.

One of the boys immediately edged away, holding his hands out.

"Woah, what you on about? We ain't callin' no po po boy!", the ginger haired, freckly faced thug remarked defensively.

"Look at him, he's shakin'", said the other.

"What's the matter? What's happened to you?" the tallest boy asked, rubbing at his black cap.

"There's someone dead in the woods", Ash spat. "Can you call or not?"

"*Fuck*"

"*Shit!*"

"That's fucked"

"We can't call no police but-"

"It's my fucking brother!" Ash screamed, pushing through the huddle. He had never used the F word before, not once. Traumatised, he raced down the alleyway and onto the street, but the tallest member of the now dispersed gang had caught up with him.

"Wait! Wait, kid", he called, sprinting up to Ash. He pulled out his black phone and punched in the numbers.

"I'm calling 'em now. Ambulance first", he panted.

*

Yellow tape surrounded the scene, lit up by floodlights the police had placed around the oak tree. Forensic officers, covered in white overalls, masks and gloves, wandered in and out of the cordoned-off space. The ambulance engine was still murmuring, as paramedics and police officers stood respectfully, readying the stretcher which held the black body bag.

Ash stood silently, beside his mother, and the teenage stranger who had called the emergency services. His whole body was immersed in shock. He kept longing to be comforted by Daruk, and wanting to tell his brother all that had happened. Then he remembered he couldn't. He kept hoping that he might wake up soon, that Daruk would be hovering over his bed asking him what nightmare he was having, because he was screaming so loud. But the cold chilling air blowing against his skin reminded him that this was reality.

It'll all be over soon.

So, *this* is what Daruk had meant. How could it be? Ash felt so foolish. And in that moment, the child hated himself.

That was the last time Ash ever saw his brother again, aside from in his dreams. And, of course, his nightmares.

15

THE THERAPIST PART III

London, England, 2019

Geoff waited patiently as Ash held the journal entry in his hands. The wise counsellor had asked Ash to write a letter, addressed to his late brother. It was the most painful piece of writing Ash had ever had to complete.

He took his time, fixating on the words on the crumpled page. Knowing Geoff would be the first person to ever hear the truth. The truth of who he was, of his past and of his present. Of course, some sentences he couldn't read aloud. But over the past few months of attending Geoff's sessions, Ash had opened up emotionally, in ways he'd never imagined possible for him.

Daruk, my brother,

It's 2019. You vowed you'd be a famous footballer by this time, and you promised you would fly us back to India, so we could revel in the beauty of our homeland, in the wonder of our childhood.

When I think about life and love, and fate, I consider myself to have been the luckiest boy in the world to have been born into a brotherhood with you. When I was a child, I wasted so much time asking you questions. Now I am a man, I wish I had used my time more wisely. I wish I had used that time to tell you things instead. Tell you that you..."

Ash paused, running his tongue across his white teeth, wrestling with the lump in his throat.

"Take your time", Geoff said softly.

...tell you that you were my hero. That I admired your bravery. I recognised your strength. I cherished your smile. And, I loved your heart.

You made me feel safe. You made me feel important. You taught me about life, and love, selflessness, and sacrifice. I will never forget the reflection of the mountains, that shone in your eyes, as we walked to school each day. I will never forget the sound of your laugh, that echoed through the valley of flowers. I will never forget, the joy in your smile, when we swam in the waters of Dal Lake.

I will never forget believing your words, when you told me in our garden, that you will always love me, and always be there for me. You broke my heart the day you left me. You promised you would come back for me, and you didn't. You promised you'd never leave me, and yet you did.

I am sorry that all that is left of the little brother you once knew, is a bitter, enraged and darkened man. The day I lost you, I fear I lost a piece of my soul.

I am sorry that I have been a coward. I am sorry that I was such an anxious boy. That I could not bring myself to talk to the teachers, or the police, or even our own mother, about the secret you entrusted to me. About the events that lead you to take your own life.

Ash glazed over the next section of his letter, reading them in his own head, but refusing to say them out loud.

I am not a coward anymore though, brother. Your death has taught me to fear nothing, for the worst has already happened, and nothing can ever be done to hurt me as much as I was hurt that day, when you left me, for a world of peace. I promise you that I will bring about justice to your life, and justice to your death. And I intend to keep my promise.

Your brother,

Asha

He placed the letter down on the coffee table, and looked up to see Geoff wipe a tear from beneath his eye.

Ash waited.

"That is a beautiful letter, Ash", Geoff said finally. "It sounds like you have carried this anger around, and quite understandably, for a long time. That is a burden more than most will ever bear in a lifetime. But, there is a way to let go of the anger, Ash. There is a way, to be free."

"I'm not sure there is", Ash said solemnly. "What are you suggesting?"

Geoff gulped.

"Ash, to *forgive,* is to be free."

Ash had a great deal of respect for the aged, wise counsellor. But in that moment, he felt a bubbling rage rise within him, a bitterness so strong at even the notion.

"I will *never* forgive those boys for what they did to him. For what they took from me!" Ash seethed, shaking his head, disgustedly.

The counsellor said nothing.

"Sorry", Ash continued, "it's just, like, when I found him, that day, in the woods, I found a stranger. The Daruk I knew would never have done that to me. He knew I needed him. And he left me. I've tried so hard to understand, but I just can't. Out of everyone I've known my whole life, I would have said he was the boy who would have never given up."

"I wonder", Geoff posed gently, "if it isn't just those school bullies you need to forgive, Ash. I wonder if it's time you forgave your brother. Forgave *Daruk*."

16

THE SCRIPTS

Essex, England, 2001

It had been four weeks since Daruk's death. The house was all packed up, all besides the boys' bedroom. The family were ready to move in the morning. Marie had sourced the Lakhanpal's a small house in a quiet, safe, cul-de-sac in a suburb of Southampton.

Beacon Cliffe High School had given the family an extremely generous donation of money at Daruk's funeral. A month earlier, that kind of money would have been a miracle to Roshni, something from her wildest dreams, willing them a way out of the estate and into a new life. But now, she looked at the cheque, soullessly. She had slipped into a state of vacant depression. Her only reason for getting up each morning was to take care of her two remaining children. Confusion, guilt and grief kept her awake every night.

Roshni took the flyer advertising Daruk's memorial service off the kitchen counter and placed it on top of her suitcase, bursting into tears as she glimpsed at the photograph. It was an image of Daruk in India, wearing his best white cricket clothes and being lifted up by his team. His grin was as mischievous as ever, and his eyes were bursting with life. Of course, Ash was in the crowd of children surrounding him. Though he had not even been on the cricket team when Daruk's team had won the match, Ash had sped onto the pitch triumphantly. Daruk let Ash hold his golden cup that night, telling him one day he'd win it himself.

Roshni had asked for immediate family only to be at Daruk's cremation. She couldn't help but thinking, that if they'd have been home in India, the entire village would had filled every seat in the crematorium and be bursting into the aisles to pay their respects to Daruk's life. But as she fixated on the coffin, holding Ash's limp hand, and stroking her daughter's dismayed head in the empty crematorium, she felt as if they were all alone in this cruel world. All of their relatives were back in India, except for the late Mr Lakhanpal's eldest brother, who she had heard lived somewhere in Birmingham.

She had taken Ash to Daruk's school assembly memorial, too. He felt too weak to argue. The headmaster of the school, Mr Vondross, stood at the lectern in the huge sports hall, and gave a speech about Daruk's time there.

"We, as a school, are deeply saddened to have discovered the news of Daruk Anjani Lakhanpal's death, and we would like to offer up our deepest sympathies and sincerest respects to his family. We were only blessed with Daruk as a student for one year, but in that time, we all grew to know and love this quietly confident, hardworking, and polite young man. He excelled in sports, winning Player of the Year's Rugby Award, the Young Sportsman's Cricket Cup and scoring all three of the winning goals in the county final football match, against over seventy different schools in the area. His teachers had all predicted that his final GCSE grades would be A stars, though it is not his academic or sporting achievements we will miss, but his kindness, gentleness and smile."

Ash allowed the words to fill his ears with remorse. Listening to the perfect stranger speak about his beloved brother filled him with hate. *Quietly confident?* Daruk had been outstandingly cocky. *Polite?* He was ridiculously cheeky. No, these people didn't know his brother, *at all.* Daruk was like nobody else in this world. He was an *exceptional* human. He was special, too special for this stupid speech, too special for this pretentious crowd, too special for this earth.

Ash sought them out in the crowd as soon as he'd walked in.

Popeto had his hands in his pockets, and was staring at the ground, in a vacant, disturbed stare. Billy was sat on the back row, leaning back on his chair, gawping at the ceiling ignorantly, exhaling large sighs as if he were bored. Ash grit his teeth so hard in his scowl, that they slipped and he bit his lip, causing it to bleed.

He wiped the blood away from his lip, and looked at the bright red droplet on his finger tip. Then, he turned his eyes to Charlie Wincott. Charlie's parents had showed up to the memorial, and he sat in between them, a blank expression on his face. They were on the second row from the front. Charlie looked like an innocent little lamb, with his pristine teeth, well combed hair and expensive clothes, but Ash imagined smacking him in the face, again, and again, and again, until his nose caved in and his eyes were blinded. It gave Ash the only pleasure he'd experienced in a month to fixate upon this image. Charlie's well dressed, petite mother wiped a tear from her eye, and his father, a broad shouldered, fair haired and handsome man in uniform, bowed his head in respect, taking off his police cap. If only those parents knew how vile and wretched their boy was. Ash began to breathe heavily, until he could not take anymore.

The entire hall of teenagers were staring at him, with their mothers in their best dresses. They made Roshni stand out in her dark sari, which she had found in a charity shop. The pitying teachers gazes felt suffocating. And the noise of the silence was deafening, as the walls closed in. He couldn't take the discomfort any longer. He felt as though he couldn't breathe. It was all his fault after all. He could have done something, could have told somebody. He needed to get out of there. Suddenly, Ash stood up, causing the entire assembly room to turn their heads in his direction, and he ran. All the way out of the hall, down a corridor with a high ceiling, and through the first set of double doors that he could find.

The library was enormous and grand, and to his relief, completely deserted. Everybody was in the memorial assembly. Ash rushed into the room, panting. He felt bad for leaving his mother behind, amongst all those white faces, but he just couldn't bear the shame anymore. He walked to one of the huge library windows which was open, longing to feel the wind on his face, to feel something, *anything,* but this crippling reality. He would be safe for just a moment.

He felt so abandoned, so furious at Daruk, so shameful for keeping his secret, so enraged by the cruel boys that had ruined his life, but most of all, he still couldn't grapple with the shock. Everything he ever trusted was gone. His foundation in life had left him. Ash sat on the marble floor and peered into the glass cabinet, glancing at all the yearbooks which were on display. He then looked up at the towering bookcase, longing to step into one of the story books and become part of its tale, any tale, other than his own.

*

Roshni set her front door keys down on the table, miserably. Then, she placed Jayminee, who was fast asleep, down on the sofa where Ash's duvet cover lay. Ash kept his head down, knowing his mother was going to bring it up. And she did, though she was not cross.

"*Why did you run out of the assembly?*" she asked, folding her arms.

He perched on the arm rest, not making eye contact with her.

"*I don't know. I just didn't like being there.*"

"*They were praising your brother. It was disrespectful to run out.*"

"*They didn't even know Daruk. Not like we did*", Ash argued, scornfully.

"*Asha Anjani, what are you talking about?*"

Ash stayed silent.

"*Is this to do with the answer phone message I got from the school, the day your brother died? You told me you didn't know what it was about.*"

"I didn't, Mamma, I have no idea why the sports coach called."

"I'm sorry, Asha. I just don't understand! I just can't think! It was such a good school. I thought he was doing so well! Why would he do this? Why, Asha? Why?"

Roshni placed her head in her hands, and wept. Ash could feel her heart aching with regret and it made him uncomfortable. He just wanted to be angry.

"I don't know why he did it, Mama. I don't know why he left us", he croaked, stroking her back.

She placed her arms around his skinny waist, and looked up into his eyes.

"You honestly don't know? You don't know what made him do it? You know I will still love you, whatever it is."

Ash turned away. He scrunched up his face in guilt and all he could see was Charlie's evil eyes. He watched his brother collecting the weapon in the night. He envisioned their encounter in the woods. He saw Daruk breaking Charlie's cheekbone.

I'm going to fucking kill you.

And then, *"No, Mother. I don't know what made him to do it"*, he said shamefully. His bones shaking with guilt.

Roshni took the tissue out from her sleeve and rubbed her eyes. Gaining her composure, she quickly changed the subject.

"I can do it for you. Clear the room, if you like", she said.

"No", Ash refused. *"No, I'm going. I want to do it. I'll do it now."*

Ash went to his bedroom as agreed, to sort through Daruk's belongings, keeping those which were sentimental, and putting the rest in a charity box. He hadn't slept in the room since it had happened, entering only to fetch his clothes each day, and return to his new bed on the sofa downstairs. He didn't want to get used to a bedroom without Daruk, because it felt so empty. The sofa however, was like a strange vacation. It wasn't supposed to feel normal, so it was better this way. He couldn't miss Daruk in the living room when they'd never slept in there together. He wanted to preserve the memory of sharing the bedroom with his brother, and couldn't bear to be in there with his ghost.

The bedroom was cold, and dusty. He quickly fell to his knees, and began sorting as fast as he could. He threw various school books, and old shoes into the charity box. He picked out the hoody which Daruk wore the most, and snuggled into it, letting the smell of his brother comfort him, for just a moment, and then the sickening all-encasing sense of loss, loneliness and hopelessness returned. He threw Daruk's school uniforms straight in the bin, along with his school bag. Wait. *His school bag.* Ash unzipped the bag which had been returned to the family by the police, on the week it had happened. He found a four-week old lunchbox inside, but nothing else. He thought about the vanished knuckle duster which Daruk had snuck out to fetch in the night. It was all so confusing. So difficult to believe. And then, his brother's words haunted him again. And he felt sickened by his own stupidity.

"*It will all be over soon*"

He searched the room for Daruk's Gameboy. But Ash couldn't find it anywhere. It was the one item that Roshni had asked him to find, so that she could sell it, but it was nowhere to be seen.

Ash glanced at the tidy room, and the two piles of Daruk's belongings. There was barely anything to show for the boy who had guided him through life thus far, and been his everything. Perhaps Daruk had been an angel, Ash thought to himself, as he began to cry. Then, he took Daruk's old Swiss Army knife, flung it open in haste, and slashed at his forearm, letting out an angered cry. The blood dripped down into his hand profusely.

"I don't understand! I don't understand!" He wept.

Then, thinking of his mother, Ash pressed his fingers down on his wound, and sealed it with a scarf from Daruk's den. He wrapped the cloth around and around until the blood was hidden, and then he pulled the sleeve of Daruk's hoody down. Ash peered into Daruk's den. It was finally time to enter his brother's secret hideout. He'd been told never to go in there, and part of him wanted to respect Daruk's wishes, even now he was gone. He felt somehow like Daruk might still be watching him. But Ash's inquisitiveness and bitterness would not allow him to leave it alone.

He lifted the hanging bed sheet and looked at the desk inside. Surprised, he peered curiously at the unexpected items on Daruk's secret desk. There were six neat piles of paper, stacked up meticulously, and six more stacked up underneath the desk. Ash hovered over the hundreds of pages. On each pile seemed to be a title page:

A COWARD'S WAR
THE WAY BACK HOME
THE VALLEY OF FLOWERS
DRAGON TRAIN
THE LAKE OF THE LOST
WHERE SHADOWS GO TO REST

Ash stood amazed, at the mysterious collection of detailed, handwritten, stories. He looked over the careful plans, the plot lines, the characters which Daruk had carefully sketched and written profiles for.

Ash sat on the chair that night and began to read. He read into the night, until the sun crept up in the sky. He was enticed by the tales thought up by his brother's imaginative and beautiful mind. He cried, fixated, and even to his own surprise, laughed sometimes. So, this is what Daruk had been doing all those nights, *writing*. It had been his escape.

He found himself compelled to turn the next page of each story, desperate to relieve his own suspense. It was captivating. He felt like he was getting to know a whole other side of his brother, a mysterious and secret side. A new depth. He hoped the stories would never end, as somehow, he could hear Daruk's wisdom in all of them.

Wishing he could ask questions, wishing he could understand, he then lifted the stories into his own school bag, cautiously and gently as he heard his mother getting up for the day. He looked once again at the front page of the last pile that he stole away.

"The Way Back Home", by Daruk Anjani Lakhanpal, it read.

Perhaps Daruk had found his way back home. Ash only wished he could have gone with him.

17

THE GARDENER

Surrey, England, 2019

"You bought it? You really bought it? It's going to be ours! Our dream house!" Lola squealed excitedly down the phone. Ash assured her that he had purchased the property of her dreams, which they had gone to view the previous week. They would be all moved in by the time the baby arrived.

"But," Ash explained, "I want to do the garden up, as a surprise. So you're not allowed to come here until move in day, deal?"

"Oh, but Ash! I can hardly wait!"

"Lola", he said sternly.

"Oh, alright then, I promise! Can you get them to put the decking where we said, for the hot tub? And make sure the river is fenced off at the bottom, because I don't want our kids crawling in."

Ash giggled. "Of course. I'll have it done just like you said. It will mean I'm driving back and forth a lot to Surrey, but I promise you, it will be worth it."

The house was a stunning secluded Elizabethan estate, in the middle of the countryside. Best of all, there was a huge garden, with a secret door in the red brick wall, leading to another, completely hidden plot of land, albeit slightly overgrown and neglected. The main garden lead down to a wide still river, its banks teaming with willow trees. The couple had fallen in love with it on their first viewing, imagining their child taking their first steps in the secret garden.

Ash stood alone, looking at the neglected garden after putting down the phone to his girlfriend. He envisioned it transformed in his mind and thought about how much work was needed for the transformation. Not just in the garden, but in his life.

Back in his London penthouse, Ash didn't sleep at all that night. He lay there, with his hand fixed on Lola's seven-month bump, staring at the ceiling. He thought about the meeting he'd had with Marcus, earlier that day.

"Mr Wincott kept asking how we found his company, and why we wanted *him* for the landscaping project when there are so many others in Surrey which were closer", Marcus had explained.

"And? Did you tell him we'd been recommended him by word of mouth, and we're happy to pay all travel expenses?" Ash urged.

"Yes, exactly as you said and he said he was happy that Gregory had given him such a shining review. He even asked how his new water feature was!"

"And, was he still suspicious?"

"No, no, not after that. Greg did a good job earning his trust, plus, I think he genuinely loves his new garden." Marcus smirked. "He... he sounded like a nice man, y'know, Ash."

"Greg said he was", Ash said sharply.

"So anyway, he's going to come and meet us at the house tomorrow, to take some measurements, give you a quote, chat through the landscaping plan, that sort of thing", Marcus confirmed.

Marcus did a bad job at hiding the eagerness in his voice over the much-anticipated reward he would soon be receiving. He'd been doing nothing but searching houses in London recently, and had found his perfect family home in a quiet street in Paddington. He was keen to finish this whole façade so that he could get the ball rolling, but he remained patient, doing everything as Ash asked.

"Yes, good." Ash said bluntly. "Thank you for all you've done, Marcus. Remember, when I transfer you the deposit tomorrow, it includes forgetting all about this entire thing, okay?"

"Understood", replied Marcus, "though... look, boss, I don't need to know the ins and outs. I trust you have a valid reason for wanting to meet with this guy, or set him up to landscape your new place, but... no harm is going to come to him, right? I mean, Frankie genuinely sounded like a good guy."

Ash sighed, annoyed at Marcus' remark. He wanted to scream, *Look Marcus, do you want that house or not?* But instead, he bit his tongue, and simply said, "Look Marcus, I've got a baby on the way. I can promise you, I'm going to treat Frances in exactly the same way I'd expect to be treated by him."

"Alright, boss, over and out."

*

The next morning, Ash slipped into a pair of casual jeans and an unlikely T-shirt, with paint splashes on it. He'd taken it from the studio. He wanted to appear as differently to his usual self as humanly possible, and that meant no clean shave, no gelled hair, and definitely no freshly pressed shirt and suit. He'd never needed to wear glasses before, so he slipped on the trendy, black-rimmed pair of clear-lens spectacles. He looked unconvincingly at his new, odd reflection. He was still certainly recognisable to anyone who knew him from the magazines or TV, but to a stranger, appeared like any other ordinary workman. Better to add the baseball cap over his new fluffy hairstyle too. He was riding on the fact that Frankie, unlike Geoff, was not a film buff and would not recognise him as the acclaimed director he was. Even if he did, Frankie surely wouldn't be able to liken him to the small eleven-year old boy he had been back then. He had changed so much.

And yet, he stressed.

Surely Frances wouldn't forget the face of the little brother to the boy he'd terrorised back in high school? But Ash's accent had vanished completely, only returning when he spoke to his mother in Urdu. He was a grown man now, and not a quivering little boy. His once rounded face, was now square-jawed. His once puny arms, were now muscular and intimidating. His eyes were darker now, and his body was stronger. Even *if* Frances recognised him as the famous Ash La-Pal, there would be no way of knowing that the director was the same person as the little boy who'd vanished and slipped under the radar for all those years following Daruk's funeral. He'd kept a very low profile in Southampton, after all. He had also managed to keep Lola and his family away from the press quite well. He'd be meeting Frances under a different name, and he'd be posing with a different occupation; a family man who'd lived in England his entire life.

He couldn't worry any longer. He just had to proceed. His dubious new persona and outfit was complete.

Ash was used to being the director, but now he would take up his place as an actor, in a plot that only he knew the ending of.

He took a bus to his new estate.

Ash hadn't taken a bus in years. He sat in his casual clothes, blending in with the working class dotted around him. He pressed his head against the cold window, and gazed regrettably out at the concrete jungle which surrounded him. There were glimpses of green parks, all neatly trimmed and yet trapped by the streets which cut through their every wandering. They were governed by the tall, grey buildings which controlled them on every corner. Ash allowed himself to think back to the jungle which had encased his childhood. He visualised the untamed and wilding vines, how each tree was obscure and individual. He pictured the lush endless valleys, and the purple flowers that blossomed in the springtime and stretched over the rolling hills. He watched as the orange sun sunk into the horizon, setting the lake on fire. He saw the insects glinting in the waving heat, the snakes wrap around the ancient branches, and the deer prance through the forests bursting with a thousand colours. And then, he saw Daruk's face. The boy with the brightest smile, looking back at him, calling his name. He could still hear his distinct laugh. It was this laugh which reminded him why he was taking such a journey on the bus in the first place.

The garden plot which surrounded Ash's new house, was two acres in size, and was tucked away in the rolling hills surrounding Guildford. Through the small forest, which encased the grand house, lay the secret, walled, overgrown garden, with a creaking rotting door cut into the south wall, littered with ivy trails. Ash had bid for the house and land at auction, and when he'd gone to inspect its boundlessness, its thick weeds, its withering trees and unkempt shrubbery within the crumbling walls, he saw only its potential. Just like Lola did.

Ash strolled across the hills, and couldn't shake the anxious feeling in his stomach. He couldn't believe he'd made it all happen. He couldn't believe his own power. Frankie was going to be there when he arrived. After all this time. Vengeance would be his. But Ash knew that long, drawn-out revenge would taste sweeter than an impulsive attack, no matter how much he would have to suppress the urge to start a fight right away. He had to play the part. He had to do this, for Daruk.

Marcus finally came into view, standing in the main neat garden and outside the secret garden walls. Beside him, there he was. Frances Charles Wincott. *Charlie.*

Ash breathed in heavily, this was it. This was the beginning of putting everything that was wrong, right. He had to do this. For his family name. Or else he would never let go of the shame that came with being a coward.

"You must never run from the truth, Asha Anjani"

Ash gulped. *You can do this. You can do this.* He willed himself, just as he'd willed himself that fateful day, to keep running through the woods, although he'd been terrified to enter it.

Ash waved through the air at the two men, and slowly approached them.

His teeth grit together, relentlessly. It was a natural reaction. He pushed the intrusive anger out of his mind, focusing on the task in front of him as he looked Frankie's unassuming stance up and down.

"Hello, you must be Frances, or is it Frankie?" Ash forced, impressed by his own convincing greeting. Hopefully neither of the men noticed his teeth lock together inside of his jaw, biting down the hatred.

"Hi there, yes I go by either, but Frankie is fine", the thirty-something year old said warmly, in his perfectly enunciated accent.

Ash looked Frankie up and down. His body was thin, and his face was pale. His hair, though cut short and neatly, still maintained the same fair and youthful shimmer. But his eyes were surrounded by deep rings, and his forehead covered in creases. The same deep creases which guarded his eyes as he smiled.

"Nice to meet you Frankie, I'm Vince. I'm the landowner", Ash said confidently, he then stepped down to greet the men.

Marcus smiled nervously, "Hi again, Vince", he said.

Ash shook Marcus' hand first, and it felt as comfortable as any handshake should; slightly awkward, firm, but fine. One doesn't usually *feel* much at all, or very intensely at least, when they hold somebody else's hand, unless they are in love, of course.

But when Ash felt Frankie's warm fingers wrap

around his own hand, he felt a feeling as intense as that of being in love. It rushed through every nerve ending in his hand, and shot up his arm, through every sense in his bones. He was *in hate*. He held his breath until his hand was released from the devil's grip.

"Right, shall we go and take a look inside then?" he exclaimed, digging through the ivy and turning the old black steel handle of the door. It creaked open, and the three men stepped inside the secret garden.

"Wow, this is quite a project" Frankie stated, gawping at the wild mess. There were so many trees and branches, wildflower bushes and tall shrubs, that the men could barely see the other end of the garden where the ground met the far wall.

"It is indeed. But my girlfriend and I feel it could be a paradise", Ash exclaimed. He tried his best not to look Frankie in the eye, as it was difficult for him not to remember those eyes as they had been, tracking him down and running him over in the woods on that bike. Every time he glimpsed the man's face, his mind took him to those woods, watching the young Charlie's pleasured glare as he cornered his victims.

The three men trudged through the undergrowth.

"Wow, well, I would love to be able to make that happen", Frankie remarked enthusiastically, though there was a definite uncertainty in his voice, as if he were nervous, perhaps. Ash couldn't tell if it was his own paranoia or if Frankie's eyes really were all over him. He pressed on with the façade.

"I'm a property developer", Ash lied. "Although gardens and land are something I'm hoping to get into developing more, as well. So, you may well see me around quite a bit as you're carrying out your work. I love to learn", Ash stated, unsure of how his own words were even sounding.

Frankie paused.

"No problem at all. It's always nice for people to see each part of the transformation", he explained.

"That's right", Ash agreed. He was alarmed at even the ease of his own pleasantries, when the thoughts inside his mind showed him inflicting the utmost amount of pain on Frankie.

They stopped underneath the largest tree in the garden. It was a young oak.

"So, Frankie, we're dying to see what you've drawn up", Marcus said, placing his hand on the mighty oak.

Frankie smiled, and pulled out a large scroll from his back pocket. He unrolled the paper in front of the men. Marcus peered over Frankie's shoulder with genuine interest in the creatively sketched, beautiful design of a flourishing garden. Ash barely saw the drawing at first, his eyes were drawn to the large purple bruise which was half peeking out from underneath Frankie's shirt collar. It was only in this close up position that the bruise became visible. A fierce, familiar rage began to bubble up inside of Ash, as he suddenly wished Marcus would disappear, so that he could wrap his hands slowly around Frankie's neck, and begin to strangle him, slowly and painfully.

It took all of his might to suppress his anger, and bring himself to simply say, "Wow, this plan is better than I ever expected."

Frankie smiled gratefully. "So, I'd like to work around this oak, to preserve it," he began nervously. "We can fence it off, with a lovely little white picket. Then I was thinking, four paths throughout the garden, all wandering from the tree towards the four different sections of the garden. Originally, I thought shingle paths, but perhaps wooden slats, like decking, because you mentioned in the brief that your partner wants decking for a hot tub", he explained.

Ash and Marcus nodded in agreement.

"Yes, that's great", they murmured.

Marcus began to wonder how he'd even been pulled into this bizarre situation in the first place. It was so far removed from his usual daily work in the studio, although for him, it was actually a pleasant change to be outdoors, surrounded by nature. But there was an underlying discomfort in the pit of his stomach, as he dreaded what Ash was plotting. The fact that he'd suddenly found thousands for a deposit for a house had raised suspicions with his wife and she had been asking him all sorts of questions. It had made him think that this whole plot was far darker than he'd ever signed up for. But, after reassuring his wife that he'd received a huge bonus, there was nothing more he could do. He had to play his part.

"In this section, I was thinking a flower garden, with tulips and hedges cut into different shapes – I've designed horses, but they could be any statue or animal of your choice. In the far section, I was thinking a seating area, with a rock water-feature. And I hoped the other two sections would keep their wooded, forest-like feel. We can keep them slightly wilder."

Ash looked at the coloured sketch. Frankie had put so much effort into it, and it met his brief exactly. He could see why Frankie had received such glowing reviews for his work.

*

Later that day, the sun was setting over the hills, turning them to gold. Marcus was on the phone to his wife, just outside the walls of the garden, spinning her a lie. Frankie had cleared a whole section of undergrowth and weeds, collecting them in huge industrial green bags. He'd wanted to get started, straight away. Ash had spent the afternoon, hauling the bags into the back of Frankie's truck, and walking around his new estate.

"So, how long have you been running your own business, Frankie?", Ash asked, when they were alone together, inside the walls.

Frankie was tossing some of the last weeds into a sack, and finally crouched down on the cleared grass. He hadn't stopped all day.

"I guess it must be, nearly five years now", Frankie said, breathlessly.

Ash paused a moment, curiosity filling his mind. *Why had Frankie quit his career in London to be a labourer? Why had he graduated with a first from the best university in the country only to throw it all away on weeds?*

"Had you always wanted to be a gardener?", Ash pressed, carefully.

Frankie gazed into mid-air for just a split second, at the bumblebee who was on his way home, leisurely buzzing in the last streaks of the sun. He fixated long enough for Ash to realise that he was entranced by the question, uncomfortably entranced.

"No, not always", Frankie replied earnestly, smiling at the man kindly, the man who knew so much about him. In that moment, Ash realised that Frankie had no idea who he really was.

"I used to work for a big company in London. For a bank, actually. But I'd swap an office and a suit for a pair of old jeans and a t-shirt out in the sun, any day." Frankie sighed.

"Wow. That's a pretty big change." Ash remarked, intrigued, edging closer to the young man.

"Yeah, my father wasn't too pleased", Frankie scoffed.

Ash stared at him and observed the way his once high-and-mighty shoulders, were stooped and downtrodden. His harsh and unforgiving sneer had softened into an apathetic sigh. But Ash's heart was far from softening. All he had to do was picture Daruk's kind eyes, and his soul would burn with regret.

"So, it was just a passion of yours, and in the end, you traded it in for your career?" Marcus asked, who had finished his call, and had been eavesdropping on the conversation, now suddenly appearing in Ash's peripheral.

Frankie paused, once more.

"What I love about my work, is that you can change something really ugly, beyond all hope, into something beautiful", he said humbly.

18

THE BREAK IN

Surrey, England, 2019

It had been two weeks since Ash had introduced Frankie to the garden, and it was taking great shape. Frankie had singlehandedly stripped the ground of weeds and overgrown shrubbery, and on top of the forgotten wilderness, laid down a layer of young green turf. He'd dug a perimeter around the garden, and filled it with fresh soil, ready to home the wildflowers. Frankie had worked tirelessly, from the early mornings and into the evenings, long after his team had left. Ash had observed the hardworking man from afar, as he dug, and picked, and carried, and lifted, barely stopping for any break at all. When he did, Frankie sat down on the broken stones of the garden, his eyes wandering towards the sky, quietly lost in thought. He treated his workers with respect and spoke to them with gentleness, encouraging them to take breaks often, as it was an unusually hot spring.

Ash visited the garden usually once a day, as he'd been busy readying the nursery for the baby. Lola had chosen a pale yellow for the walls, with stencils of trees and animals that they'd chosen together. They'd bought a big white crib, and dozens of soft velvety toy animals, too. The more Lola buzzed with excitement, the more Ash became conflicted in his mind. He battled between his continuously tiring thoughts of rage, loss and hatred, and the sweet refreshing flutters of happiness every time they discussed names for the baby, or he helped Lola into bed, or they went shopping for a car seat, feeling closer to her than ever.

But he knew the time was fast approaching. The garden would be complete in a matter of weeks. His trauma would not allow him to live as a complete man until the deed was done. Until he followed through with his every plot, plan and sick fantasy. He reminded himself every day that he had to do this for himself, for his brother and for his family, past and future. Even when he felt convinced by Frankie's kindness. Sickeningly, sometimes Frankie's extreme willingness and patience reminded him of his own brother. He felt so confused. And it filled him with a deeper sadness, that he knew revenge was the only way to freedom. Despite everything Geoff had said.

Just the other day, when Ash was sitting on the edge of his bed, Lola had just finished brushing her teeth. She stepped out of the bathroom of the penthouse and completely out of the blue, she said, "Babe, I was thinking, if he's a boy, we could name the baby… Daruk?" she spoke tentatively, worrying about Ash's reaction. She had given it some serious thought, and although she'd never met Daruk, she felt so much closer to Ash when he opened up about his childhood. Every time Ash recalled a story about his brother, she saw his eyes light up, with glimpses of joy. But he soon shut down, forcing the memories away, changing the subject or clamming up sharply, as if he was immediately angered all over again. She had hoped that, perhaps, the more Ash was forced to use his brother's name, the more he would grow comfortable with talking about the past, and in time, truly heal.

Ash didn't know what to say. His immediate thought was, *oh, how I love you Lola*. He thought about a new Daruk in the world. Learning to walk, learning to talk, to play football, to get in to trouble, to laugh and to swim. He imagined his boy playing cricket, and riding a bike, and flying a kite. He toyed with the idea for a moment, almost allowing a smile, and then, like an unwanted guest at a party, he saw a vision of the tree fill his mind. He saw the noose, he saw the pain, he felt the fleeting peace in his heart rush away, and leave him with only sadness.

"No, no. I don't think so", he whispered painfully.

"It was just a thought… I understand. I researched what the name Daruk meant today", she exclaimed.

"And?" Ash asked, intrigued.

"It means *'tree'*."

*

The next morning Ash put off going to the studio, and drove out of the city, to the garden. He'd left Gregory in charge of his latest film. Gregory lapped up his newfound responsibility like a hungry animal. Ash parked up on the shingle, outside of the estate, and walked across the back garden to the walls which enclosed the project.

Frankie's black open-back truck was sitting outside the walled garden. The air was cool and fresh, and the sun was glazed over with gentle clouds. Ash opened the creaking door and was enveloped by the transforming beauty of the secret haven. Frankie had planted bluebells which danced around the feet of pink foxgloves around the outskirts of the fresh grass. He'd placed white picket fences to border the flower beds, and on the grassy lawns, the pretty clusters of daffodils and pansies circulated the hedges which Frankie had begun to trim into deer statues. It was impressive to say the least. Frankie hadn't noticed Ash's arrival, he was facing away from him, stood on a stepladder and sheering away at an antler.

Ash quietly crept back out of the door and tiptoed up to Frankie's truck. There, he found Frankie's blue backpack. It was dusty and uncared for. He glanced around the empty field and the entrance to the deserted forest. He cautiously pulled at the zip of the bag, being sure to listen intently to the sound of the sheers continuing over the wall. Inside of the backpack he found a plastic Tupperware box with a banana skin in, a sketchpad, and a set of glinting keys. He grabbed the keys, grasping them tightly so as not to let them jingle against each other. Ash ran his hand over his face, as he often did, when he felt anxious or stressed, and then gently slid the silver keys into the pocket of his jeans. Just as he went to re-zip the bag, his hand grazed against something hard in an inside pocket at the top of the bag which made a dull rattling noise. Ash hastily unzipped the inner covering and pulled out two plastic white pill pots. Curiously, he ran his hands over the medicine pots, reading about their contents. Sominex Sleeping Pills and Monoamine Oxidase. Ash snapped out his cell phone and took a picture of both of the pills pots, before throwing them back into the pocket, and zipping the bag shut.

He checked the time on his golden Rolex; it was 1:30 pm. He had a good few hours before he needed to return the keys - plenty of time to get them cut at the local jewellers in Guildford. As he trudged back across the empty field surrounding the gardens and toward his car, he typed in Monoamine Oxidase into the search engine on his phone. As the thread of results began to appear, spouting information about the anti-depressants, Ash got a discomforting feeling in the pit of his stomach. Was he just feeling nervous about what he was about to do? Was he, possibly, starting to disassociate the quiet and hardworking man he had observed the past couple of weeks, from the vile and evil teenager he once had been? *No,* he willed himself, he could not feel any sympathy. This could not be the faint embers of pity creeping up inside him. Could it? He couldn't allow it, he wouldn't. He was not the sympathetic, soft and weak child he had been then. He was fierce and mindful. He had calculated this for so long now, and only when it was finished, would he feel peace, and honour. He forced his uneasiness aside, and raced to his car, speeding towards the town, brushing all hindering thoughts aside.

*

At 7:30 pm, Ash waited, alert, behind the blacked-out windows of his Continental. His eyes were fixed on Frankie's small detached house down the quiet residential street. He tapped the steering wheel repetitively, breathing heavily, until Frankie appeared in his driveway. Ash watched Frankie climb slowly into his truck and pull away from the house. Ash then flicked his headlights on and off, flashing over to Marcus in his car, who was facing him across the street. As instructed, Marcus hastily revved his engine, and rolled away down the street, keeping a safe distance as he tailed after Frankie. Ash grabbed the keys he'd cut earlier that afternoon, slipped out of his car door, and tiptoed across the silent, floodlit street, with only the lampposts watching him. And suddenly, just for a fleeting moment, he was filled with a faint rush of hope. For the strange déjà vu which washed over him as he crept like a convict, caused him to feel like a child again, tiptoeing across the silent dark lawn where he had spied on his brother, buying a weapon in the dark. In that moment, Daruk was still alive, and there was still time to save him. There was still time to report the bullies to his teachers, to force him to leave his school, to run away with him. But as Ash approached the cold pale door of Frankie's house, he snapped back into reality. There was no hope left for Daruk now, and for this reason, there could be no hope left for Frankie either, his perpetrator.

Ash looked over both shoulders, listening to the gentle breeze. There was a distant murmur of rumbling engines on nearby streets, but other than that, he would have heard a mouse's stride. Considering Frankie was now a gardener, his small front lawn was neglected and uneven. It had one singular drooping plant as a centre piece, and some cracked slabs leading to the poorly painted door. Ash slipped the silver key into the door and twisted it open with ease. He then stepped inside the silent home. He ran his hand over his face, as he often did, when he felt anxious or stressed. Although the whiskey had helped calm his nerves a little, it had also made his judgment hazy.

Luckily, Frankie had left both the landing light and the hallway light on. Ash stepped across the spongy cream carpet and past the coat hook with various hanging outdoor jackets. He observed the photo frames on the hallway wall, none of which contained photos of people, but only simple pictures or paintings of flowers and plants. He swiftly took the first door on the right, which lead into a small, modest, and rather plain living room. Everything was very modern, from the pastel coral sofa and armchairs, to the widescreen TV set against the bay window, to the small electric piano which sat in the opposite corner of the room. Ash briefly glanced at the picture frames on the mantle piece below the mirror on the wall of the lounge, which again, held no photographs of actual people, but either paintings of seaside towns, or animals. There wasn't much to be found in the lounge, and it wasn't long before Ash found the same to be true of the small downstairs toilet and the kitchen also. It was all very standard, neat and tidy. There was nothing to give anything away about Frankie's character. The kitchen was fitted with modern counters and a breakfast table, and kept clean and tidy. There were no ornaments, no home sentiments, in fact, the more Ash delved around, he realised there was absolutely nothing to feed his curiosity. It looked like some sort of show home with no unique taste or originality.

Ash darted up the stairs, and as he did so, he slipped a glance at his phone. Marcus had text.

"Following him now, headed for town centre. Will update when he stops. Marcus."

Satisfied he had plenty of time, Ash began rooting through the sparkling upstairs bathroom. He opened the wall-mounted cabinet and sifted the bottles of shaving foam and hair gels to one side and picked up various pill pots. There were more sleeping pills and anti-depressants, but as well as this, there were some rolled up prescriptions from doctors. Ash stuffed them in his pocket, before going into the main bedroom. There was a wide cupboard on the wall, with huge sliding mirrors for its doors. Ash slid the cupboard open and tossed each shirt and tie to one side. There was nothing of any interest whatsoever. He sat gently upon the king bed, and rifled through the bed-side tables, but all he found was a book about wildflowers, some men's skin care cream and a phone charger. *Damn it.*

Getting frustrated, Ash left the bedroom, and entered the one remaining room in the little house. It was a small study. There was an open sleeping laptop on a desk in one corner, a bookshelf, and various old boxes and suitcases which were piled up on top of each other in the far corner. Ash tapped the laptop on but was immediately blocked by the password barrier which flashed up before him on the screen.

He moved to the bookshelf, running his hand along the bindings of each coloured book and occasional DVD.

"The Perfect Garden: Landscapers Edition"

"Birdsongs, 360 species"

"The Lord of the Rings: The Fellowship of The Ring"

"Business Today and how to make your business flourish"

And then, Ash pulled books from behind the first row, and fixated on their topics.

"PTSD: Working through Post-Traumatic Stress"

"Guilt; suppression or acceptance? One man's tale of restoration"

"Cognitive Behavioural Therapy"

"Re-train your brain: Back to being you"

Ash flicked through the various psychological self-help books with a deep intrigue, turning each page carefully, and stopping every time he found a highlighted section. Frankie had scribbled some notes down in each of the books, and Ash picked the ones of interest and lay them on the carpet, reading through the notes more urgently, desperate to find out anything he could about the man who ruined his life.

"You can face your trauma, or you can suppress it until it defaces you"

"Our deepest desires lead us into action"

"There is always a way out"

Ash began to seethe as he flurried through the pretentious self-help books, debating in his own mind why Frankie should even deserve the right to self-help. Was Frankie's evident trauma even the result of Daruk's death? Was it linked to his brother in any way? Or was it something else that had happened in his privileged life? Perhaps being thrown out of the cricket society at Oxford University for binge drinking, or losing his job as an investment banking director for embezzling funds? As Ash had got to know the timid and obliging Frankie, he had to admit, he had seen nothing of the merciless, unrelenting, monster who had gone before. But Ash knew, deep down, Frankie had to remember Daruk. He was the boy Frankie had chosen to inflict with pain. And for why? Daruk had endured brutal, relentless suffering at the hand of Frankie, so much so that it caused him to take his own life. And so, even if Daruk had meant absolutely nothing to the teenage bully at the time, surely Frankie would remember that he and his friends were responsible for his suicide. They had sat through the whole school memorial assembly all those years ago which must have forced the three boys into staring their decisions directly in the face. Surely guilt reaches even the heartless?

Ash tossed the self-help books to one side and began rifling through the boxes, which were stacked up against the wall, in a sudden fit of fury. All he had to do was picture Frankie's young scowl as he spat at Daruk in the woods that day, and it spurred him on. Now, rather carelessly, he opened the cardboard flaps of each box, and rummaged through their contents. There were more books, old files, and papers. Some were accounts, some were old pay-slips, and some were mugs and cups covered in bubble-wrap which Ash assumed meant Frankie had not been living here long. But then, Ash found a box full of old picture frames and small ornaments.

He pulled out the first picture frame, it was an old photograph of a blonde, teenage Frankie sitting in a pristine salmon shirt on the grass outside a large, superior home. He was laughing and cuddling a golden retriever, and his parents were sat on the grass, either side of him. In another picture, three young fair-haired girls surrounded Frankie. Although they appeared younger than he was, all four children shared the same eyes. This was his family. They looked happy. Ash ran his fingers over their innocent looking faces and then flipped the frame, *August, 1999*, the back of the photograph read. That was two years before Daruk had died. Ash dug further into the box, and pulled out the other photographs which had gathered thin layers of dust. There were other pictures of a young Frankie, surfing on a white beach, or holidaying with his family in tropical locations, pictured on yachts, or in ski gear in the Alps. And then, Ash found an early primary school photograph and it made him shudder. In a small class of twenty or so little children, sat in rows in a village hall, appeared a chubbier looking Frankie, about ten years old, and either side of him sat Popeto, with his distinct tan, and Billy, with even more puppy fat than he'd had as a teenager. *They must have been best friends for years,* thought Ash. He dumped the picture frames back in the box and pulled the old suitcase towards him, carefully pushing the boxes on top of it backwards so that they didn't topple over in his Jenga-like task.

Suddenly, Ash felt his phone buzz in his pocket, shocking him. He whipped it out and checked his messages, one from Marcus, and one from Lola.

"Where are you Ash? You said you were going round your Mum's, but she's just come round with some baby clothes. Good one. We need to talk. Lola"

Shit.

"He's gone inside a building just off the high street. I've researched it, it's a psychotherapy unit with counsellors and alternative therapies. I've tried to see through the windows, but

they're all shut up. I could see him in the waiting room before he went in though. I'll let you know when he comes out. Marcus"

Ash exhaled deeply, and then placed his phone on the computer desk. He pried open the old suitcase, and was even more surprised at what he found. There was a dusty photograph, with a black and white filter on it. It was a photo of Popeto Charpentier, in his late teens. He starred at the camera lens, as if posing for a lover. His dark eyes were fixed on the photographer with an intense intrigue. Attached to the photograph was a crumpled, dusty letter, with a paper clip. Ash read the handwritten letter.

Charlie,

Of course I haven't forgotten. I will never forget. In another life, it would have been you. You and me. You will always be the one that got away. But what has tied us together, is also the reason we must be apart. You know that. I will never feel again the way you made me feel.

Yours

P.

Ash stared at the letter, puzzled. Was Frankie gay? Popeto had been his lover? But Popeto had a wife now? It could explain why Frankie didn't have a wife, or children of his own. What kept Popeto and Frankie apart? Could it be anything to do with Daruk? Ash placed the unlikely letter back in the case before setting it back in its pile. He was so confused.

He then began sliding all the books back onto the shelf and tidied the boxes the best he could. What he had found, had certainly intrigued him, but his head spun with more questions. He rested against the wall for a moment. *Why did Frankie go to psychotherapy? Why did he have trouble sleeping? Why was he so depressed? Why did he keep his family locked away in a box? Why did he really become a landscaper? Why did he live in such a modest house? Was he gay? Did he remember Daruk? Did he even know he was the reason for Daruk's suicide?*

His phone buzzed once again. This time, it was Kenny.

"Got the medical records. Download the link to see them. Ken"

Ash immediately tapped the download link and anticipated the information of Frankie's doctor's notes. Perhaps this would give him some sort of insight.

He scrolled through the various appointments - prescriptions of the anti-depressants being issued way back, intermittently, since April, 2010. Referrals to hospitals for psychiatric tests and medical counselling, after numerous bouts of insomnia, self-harm and eating disorders.

Ash ran his hand over his face, as he often did, when he felt anxious or stressed. He placed his phone beside him on the carpet and leant against the walls once more.

Frankie needs to pay for what he has done. A life for a life. That's what's fair. That's what's fair. Daruk did nothing wrong. Frankie left Daruk with no other option than to kill himself.

Ash thought to himself, destructively.

He knew that he was running out of time, and the garden was going to be complete within a matter of days. The final centre piece and cement was about to be laid. Then Frankie's work would be over, and he would leave Ash's life just as quickly as he'd entered it. Ash needed to work quickly, and the more he stopped to think, the more he was riddled with a sickly feeling of guilt in the pit of his stomach, and of conflict. If his plan malfunctioned, he could jeopardise everything with

Lola, and ruin everything for their baby, who would be born next month. But he knew he could never fully embrace fatherhood until he had become the man he had always willed himself to be. He *had* to do this. Failure was not an option. It would all be over soon, and then they could finally live, as a family, with him a complete man. Ash suddenly remembered Lola's accusatory text, and it filled him with another rush of worry. He checked the study one last time, rose to his feet abruptly, causing quite the head rush. And then he slipped out of the room, down the stairs, and out the front door.

He stressed about what he was going to say to Lola as he cut through the quiet streets, revving his engine as he went. He'd been driving for about fifteen minutes when he felt his jean pocket for that comforting solid, portable device which connected him to the world, and realised it was missing. *My phone. It's on Frankie's carpet.*

Shit. SHIT.

Ash swerved the whole vehicle across the street in a frantic U-turn, without even checking for oncoming cars. The screeches of his brakes echoed down the quiet road, and luckily, he only received a few concerned glances from late evening dog-walkers.

"You idiot! You idiot!" he screamed, smacking his forehead down on the steering wheel as he sped up in a frenzy. If Frankie found his phone, then it would all be over. He approached the traffic lights as they were just changing from amber to red, and Ash slammed his foot down on the accelerator, zooming through the cross roads, and onward past the shut-up shops on the high street. He checked his golden Rolex; it was 8:45 pm.

"Marcus left at 7:30 pm… his appointment can't

have started until 8:00, or maybe 7:45?" Ash muttered to himself desperately, like a mad person going round in circles.

As he raced through the lit-up streets, carelessly flying over every roundabout and through each set of stop lights, he thought about what he had become, and wondered how differently life would have been for him, had Daruk never died. Daruk would surely be on the red carpet now, loving every minute of the fame and attention. Ash knew they would still be the best of friends, and every time Daruk would have received an award on stage, he'd have given his brother a huge shout out, because that's the type of person Daruk was. He was full of life, and excitement, and intrigue, but most of all, Daruk was full of love. Ash wondered what Daruk would make of him now, and his actions. Would he be proud of what Ash was doing? Would he be rooting for him, spurring on his vengeance? Honoured by how his little cowardly brother had become such a brave hero, avenging their family? There was just one problem with that deluded concept; Ash could never truly know what Daruk would feel toward him now. But he feared it wasn't pride. As the tears slipped down Ash's overstressed face in a race with his car tyres, he felt like anything but a hero. He had a girlfriend who thought she was being cheated on. He had a baby on the way who he was completely unprepared for. He had no idea how to be a father. He was a fraud in his work - praised and acclaimed for masterpieces which he'd stolen. He hadn't visited his mum in weeks. He couldn't sleep at night. He battled with continuous rage, and guilt, and sadness. And now, he was about to become a murderer. He toyed with the idea of just giving up now, of throwing himself off the road and in front of the next passing lorry. Ending it all, like Daruk had done. But he could never do that, not to Lola, or the baby, or his mum. He couldn't afflict the same pain on them that Daruk had afflicted on him, all by giving up. No, he had to finish the fight. It was the only way to find freedom. And once Frankie was dead, he'd go looking for the others. As he neared the house, he could hear the wise words of Geoff's voice fill his head. And it confused him even more.

"To forgive, is to be free"

Then he recalled another wise voice, and this time, it sent his tears streaming.

"Forgive him brother, and the pain will stop here"

There was no time to think. Ash pulled up to the house once again, and was relieved to find Frankie's car still missing from the driveway. He ran across the street, opened the front door once again, and bolted up the stairs. His phone was sitting on the carpet in the study, exactly where he had left it. He picked it up, to find the messages flashing up on the screen before him.

"Lola's very upset- what has happened, son? Love Mum"

"Don't bother coming home tonight, Ash. You're not the man I thought you were. Lola"

"He's on his way back now, get out. Marcus"

Ash spun himself around, and went to walk back through the study door, when he heard the key turn in the lock. It was too late, Frankie was home. Panic rushed through Ash's body, there was nowhere to hide in the study. He found himself darting across the landing and into the bedroom. He ran over to the front windows, but they were all locked shut, and there was a long drop down to the front garden. He glanced at

Frankie's abandoned truck in the driveway. There was nowhere else to go. Mortified, he dropped to his knees, and crawled underneath the double bed, breathing as silently as he could. His palms were sweaty, and he took a brief moment just to feel the spongy carpet beneath them, pressing his hands up and down, trying to feel anything but *this* hideous emotion of fear, not even the fear of Frankie, but the fear of himself and what he was doing.

He listened to the clutter and clanging of crockery in the kitchen beneath him, and the flicking of a light switch, before the footsteps came slowly up the staircase, sending shivers down his spine. Why hadn't he brought Kenny with him? The break-in at the high school had verged on exhilarating, but this was highly disconcerting and uncomfortable. He was suddenly overcome with a deep sadness, as he thought about Lola, and he longed to just be beside her right now, safe in the comfort of their own bed, listening to her soothing voice, and hearing her tell him that everything was going to be okay. Over the past year, he'd sometimes felt so close to her, closer than he'd ever been to any human, that he'd flirted with the idea of opening up to her about absolutely *everything*, but he was too afraid of bringing her into his darkness. Because once in the darkness, he knew better than anybody, it was almost impossible to see the light again. As the footsteps drew near to the bedroom, and the light was flicked on, illuminating his uncomfortable surroundings, Ash began to silently weep.

He watched the pair of feet pad across the carpet and felt something light be thrown onto the top of the bed. Ash peered out at the spread of mirrors and could see that Frankie was unbuttoning his shirt. Frankie exhaled nervously, and was breathing deeply. Ash watched the man unzip his trousers and throw them down to his ankles, before swinging his shirt off. He spied the thin young man, standing there in his boxer shorts. Just as Ash was about to shut his weeping eyes, he saw the scratches. Deep, bruising, red lashes all over Frankie's stomach and back, journeying all the way down to his thighs. Ash's tears slowed, as he looked curiously at the man's frail, slashed up body. Frankie only stood in front of the mirror for a moment, but it was enough time for Ash to see even the purple protruding scars all over his wrists and forearms. It was baffling. Ash grimaced at the gruesome sight, wondering what had caused such pain.

Ash knew, deep down, that these scars were self-inflicted. But why? He watched Frankie stare at himself in the mirror, loathing his reflection. And then for a split moment, he could have sworn that Frankie's eye gaze flicked beneath the bed, finding his own frozen gaze. Ash's heart skipped a beat in panic, but Frankie swiftly walked to his bedroom door and grabbed a white towel from the door hook, and left the room.

Ash exhaled in utter relief, as he listened to Frankie shut himself in the bathroom, and heard the all comforting sound of the shower power on. Ash crawled out from beneath the bed, and rushed out of the bedroom door. He padded hastily down the stairs, clicked the front door open, and stepped out into the safety of the night-time air. When he reached his car, he leapt inside it and drove all the way home without looking back. Still, all he could see in his mind were those curious, brutal scars.

19

THE TRUTH

Surrey, England, 2019

It had been almost eighteen years since Daruk had died. Ash glanced at his golden Rolex. It was 3:30 pm - the time Daruk had promised he would be waiting at the school gates for him, all those years ago.

Ash sat in his car, which he'd driven across the sludgy field and to the beginning of the woodland, and was now peering out from his nestle. He hadn't been to the garden in three days, not since he'd broken into Frankie's house. He'd paid Marcus and Gregory their dues, and Marcus was now well on his way to making an offer on his dream house in London. Ash had patched things up with Lola, spinning her every excuse under the sun. And now he was on his own. Only he could finish what he'd started.

He held the old, crumpled photograph of Daruk in

his hands, fixating on the memorial service flyer. He read the pages once more.

Daruk Anjani Lakhanpal
1986-2001
Loving son, brother and friend. As long as the orange sun rises and sets in the sky, we will remember you. We will love you. With all that we are, for all that you were.

Ash had no time to feel sadness now. He folded the flyer in half, careful not to crease Daruk's bright face, and placed it in his pocket. The words washed over him with the same penetrating sadness as they had the day they were printed. He had only predatory eyes though now, as he waited for his prey. He needed to stay focused. It was finally time. He felt the events of his entire adult-life piling up on his shoulders. Every nightmare, every sick and twisted fantasy, every messed-up desire of his heart was about to be concluded.

Frankie soon emerged from the walled garden and got into his truck, rolling away across the field just as Ash had anticipated. He was off to pick up the remainder of the wet cement, to fill the centre piece of the garden. This was the very last task to complete. Ash gulped. There was no turning back now. He willed his legs forward.

Ash picked up the rope from the passenger seat of his car and slid the black revolver into the back of his pants, letting his chequered shirt fall over the top of it. Then he slid the black cap over his thick hair, slammed the car door shut, and walked over to the walled garden. He breathed in the warm air, knowing it would be the last time he'd breathe without a man's blood on his conscience.

When he opened the door to the garden, and stepped

inside, he could not believe his eyes. He was truly astonished. It really was a *paradise*. More than he could have ever wished for, envisioned, or imagined. He had only ever seen a garden this beautiful once before in his lifetime. And it was *his* garden, as a child.

The wildflowers were so abundant, that they competed for space, reaching up from the flower beds in enchanted tangles that stretched up the old crumbling walls, spilling out their pastel beauty in pale pinks, whites, and yellows. Some of their petals were like cups, and caverns for the bumblebees, and some of them stretched their petals out wide, to be a landing spot for the butterflies. The soft grass was stripy, laid with strips of pale and dark green. The hedges were magnificent carvings of stags, trimmed to perfection. There were wooden secret pathways, which wound through the flowery shrubbery and baby willow trees, which Frankie had placed sporadically. White picket fences bordered each pathway, matching the fence which guarded the young solid oak in the centre. There was a little pond with floating white water lilies that spiralled around, flowing from the small rock-based water feature which pumped a trickling stream down one side of the whole garden. Shimmery white tables and chairs dotted the lawn. Frankie had even laid out a croquet set on one area of the lawn and set blossoming flowers in watering cans along an indented shelf in the wall. He'd hung a ceiling of old candle holders and lanterns, which beamed from side to side, attached to each wall, like a canopy of lights, which Ash knew would look spectacular once dusk began to fall. Ash stared at the empty, dug out hollow in the ground, directly in front of the oak tree. This is where the fountain would be cemented in. There was already a layer of wet cement in the base of the pit, which stood about three feet deep.

Ash stood, overwhelmed by the craftsmanship and design of the place. In any other circumstance, he would regard this as a sanctuary of bliss and beauty. But he had his own work to do now, and nothing about it was going to be beautiful. Ash took a deep breath and hauled his tired and aching body up the first branch of the oak tree. Its branches were strong and mighty, as always. With his legs either side of the high branch, he swung them backwards and forwards, walking his hands along, shimmying himself until he was directly over the top of the empty cement hollow. Then, he took the rope, and as his tears fell numbly, he coiled the thick hemp around the branch, and held it there with a tight fastened knot. Then he scrambled back down to the base of the tree and stared up at the noose.

Ash held out his shaking hand, and grasped the noose, swinging it backwards and forwards through the air. It was such a basic piece of material, but it sent rushing waves of torment through every part of his body. He gulped down the tears, and ran his hand over his face. Every bone in his body was shaking, and his teeth began to chatter together uncontrollably. He'd had only two shots of whiskey in the car, but with nothing in his stomach, he felt a wave of tipsiness. Ash slumped himself against the oak tree, waiting for the sound of Frankie's engine to return. It felt like an anxious eternity waiting against the tree, just as it had been an eternity that day he'd waited for his brother, who had never arrived at the school gates.

To his surprise, only a few minutes had passed when Ash heard the rumble of Frankie's truck just outside the door of the garden. He leapt to his shaking feet and clumsily clambered towards the door, reaching for the gun in the back of his jeans. He had only ever fired a gun once before, on a stag party, at a shooting range in Croatia. But he had hated the sound it had made and the impact it had had on his body every time he'd pulled the trigger. Now, with the feel of the cold steel in his sweating hand, he grappled it for comfort. Heart racing, he slowed down as he approached the door. It swung open slowly, and Frankie appeared, in a pair of old scruffy jeans and a thick plaid workman's shirt. To his surprise, Frankie didn't look startled to see him. He stared into Ash's bloodshot eyes for a moment, looking at the overtired, bristly, mess of a young man, and a look of dismay spread across his weakened face.

Ash fought with the shaking in his hand, trying to tame his nerves as he flung the gun backwards and forwards through the air.

"Hello", Frankie whispered, gazing at the barrel.

Ash was frozen, terrified Frankie was going to run. Petrified he had messed it up, already. But to his utter disbelief, Frankie stepped forward into the garden, and gently closed the creaking door behind him.

The two men stood about a yard apart from each other, staring into each other's eyes. Ash looked in bewilderment. Frankie in dismay.

Ash grasped the loaded gun with both hands, and held it out in front of him, pointing the barrel at Frankie's chest. His arms were still shaking, and his legs wobbled like jelly.

"Move to the tree", he whispered, keeping his eyes transfixed on Frankie's unfazed and expectant gaze.

Confusingly, Frankie then did something which

bewitched Ash to his core. The young man lifted both his hands slowly up in the air, in surrender, and smiled pensively.

"Okay", he said calmly, as he gently walked towards the young oak tree in the centre of the garden. Ash followed him, keeping the gun pointed closely at the back of his head. Frankie held his arms up all the way through the roaming flowers, until he reached the foot of the oak tree.

Frankie then looked up at the noose, and as Ash crept around beside him, he saw a glassy layer of tears rise and shield the gardener's sky-blue irises.

"What's the matter with you?" Ash asked.

Frankie's submission and calmness was making it difficult to play out the violent rage he had planned in his head all this time, whereby he threw himself over the monster and sent his fists flying into his skull.

Frankie stood at the empty hollow dug out in the ground beneath the oak tree for a moment, allowing one tear to drip through the air and fall into the wet cement base layer which filled the bottom. His tear sunk into the glimmer of wet grey soil.

"Answer me", Ash demanded, "are you not going to ask me why I'm doing this?"

Frankie turned to stare Ash square in the face. But he was not scowling, nor did he appear evil. He simply smiled again, tiredly.

"This is it, Ash La-Pal. This is how it's supposed to be", he croaked, his voice wobbling as he held back his fear. Ash glanced at the darkened wet patch, which had formed around Frankie's crotch, seeping through his jeans. He was trembling.

Completely stunned, Ash's eyes widened in disbelief.

"*What?* You know who I am?" he asked, edging closer to Frankie, with the gun still pointed directly at him, shaking his hands aggressively.

Frankie nodded.

"I've always known", he said softly, "ever since the day you first hired me."

Ash shook his head in confusion.

"But how? But, why would you accept? What's wrong with you?" he demanded, lowering the gun down only once, to run his hand over his tearstained cheeks. Then, he held the weapon tightly, still pointed in Frankie's direction, but down by his side, soothing his aching arms.

"I always knew that you'd come and find me one day, I guess. I've always known it", Frankie exhaled, nodding at his captor.

"But *why?* Why would you come and work for me?" Ash asked bitterly. "Are you used to having film directors with vendettas after you or something? I don't think you *do* know why I'm here… or why you're here… or who I *really* am."

Frankie sniffed at his tears as he looked to the ground in a deep shame. And as if by an inner willful instinct which took all his might, forced his head up to look Ash directly in the face.

"I know who you are, Asha La-Pal. I know every film you've ever directed. I know where you live. I know where you went to uni and I know where you work now", Frankie said.

"Well, everyone knows that. Anyone can know that. I'm in the papers pretty often", Ash spat. "Why do you think I'm doing this to you?"

Frankie shook his head agonisingly.

"I've followed you your whole career, Asha. That is not how I know who you are though. I know you from when we met in the woods that time, when you were just a kid. I know you because you are-"

Frankie paused for breath, and then the grown man began to sob.

"I know you, because Daruk Lakhanpal was your brother."

Ash's mouth dropped in astonishment. It was surreal. It was as if all his thoughts, anguish, and anxieties, his worst fears, and deep rooted nightmares, which nobody had ever been able to possibly understand, were now being understood by the one person who had caused them all in the first place.

"So, you *do* remember Daruk? You remember who he was", Ash said quietly, begging to understand.

"Of course I do!" Frankie urged. "Of *course* I remember him, I… I think about him every day. He's never left my mind… he's never left my life."

"Then you must know it's all your fault!" Ash screamed, ripping his cap off and letting his fringe fall over his forehead in a fury. "*Why* would you come and work for me if you've known me all this time? Are you setting me up? Have you got people behind these walls with you? Or are you just insane?"

Frankie shook his head shamefully.

"I thought you were going to do it the other night. When you were in my house. I thought you were going to kill me then", he explained, whimpering.

"You knew I was in your house? Of course… I knew you'd seen me! You looked right at me! What is wrong with you? Why wouldn't you call the police? Are you some sort of maniac? Answer me! Answer my questions! Stop crying! You don't deserve the right to cry." Ash seethed, hocking the saliva back in his throat and spitting aggressively at Frankie's feet. He thought back to the day Frankie had spat at his brother's feet, and all of his rage consumed him as, in his head, he went back over the scenes of what Frankie had put them through.

Frankie nodded and wiped his tears away submissively with the ends of his tatty sleeves.

"You're right", he sobbed, trembling in fear.

"Well? Explain yourself. Why would you let me employ you, when you know I know what you did to him?"

Frankie grit his teeth in pain. "Because, I want to die! Don't you understand? My life has not been a life. I want to die for what I did to your brother. I can't live with it any longer."

"Oh no!" Ash roared. "No, no you're not doing this to me. I will *not* pity you. Becoming the victim? It's too late for that. I'm not the same little wimpy kid anymore. You can't fool me. You don't get to play a hero now - you lost that right. I don't seem to remember you giving us any mercy when you found us in the woods! You were evil. What you did was evil. My brother did *nothing* wrong. And he hung himself all because of you! All because you were a massive racist!" his words bellowed through the air, sending a pigeon fluttering out of a distant tree.

Frankie ran his shaking hands through his hair, and then bit down onto his right hand harshly.

They stood together in the silence, intensely. Sweat dripped from both of their brows in the tension. And then, Ash ripped out the memorial from his jean pocket, waving it in the breeze with his one free hand so that it unfolded. With his other hand, he relaxed the gun for a moment.

"Look at it. Look at it and read it", he ordered, holding out the flyer before Frankie's disturbed face.

Frankie's lip quivered, shying away from the leaflet as if it were a ghost.

"I said, read it!" Ash spat, throwing the paper within an inch of Frankie's nose and lifting the gun up into the air threateningly.

Frankie came face to face with the photograph painstakingly, in a desperate attempt to find the words which were trapped beneath the lump in his throat,

"Daruk Anjani Lakhanpal... 1986 to 2001. Loving son", Frankie gulped, "brother and friend."

"And the rest", Ash ordered, as tears trickled over his trembling lips.

"As long as the orange sun rises and sets in the sky, we will, we will... remember you. We will... *love you*. With all that we are, for all that you were." Frankie gasped for breath as he hysterically bawled his eyes out.

Ash paused a moment, absorbing the sight of the genuinely distressed and tormented man. He had seen the scars on his body. He'd read the medical records. He knew of the sleepless nights. But he could not forget what had been before. He could not feel any mercy.

"Why did you hate him so much?" he asked, picturing Daruk's face in his mind.

Ash thrust the gun against Frankie's temple, then pointed it at the ground.

Frankie fell to his knees obediently, and Ash slowly crouched down as well, resting on the grass, swinging his legs over the edge of the dug-out hollow in the ground.

"I... I was different back then. I was a coward. Daruk joined our school and he was the best at everything. He was the best rugby player, the best football player and the best cricket player. He got all the best results in class - he always knew all the answers. Even on his first day."

"So, that was a reason to make his life a living hell?" Ash demanded. "Because he was *good*?"

"No, no of course not. I... I remember when he arrived on his first day. It was the cricket try-outs, before break time", Frankie explained. "I was the cricket captain the previous year, and Daruk showed up and the coach said he wanted him as the new captain because he'd never seen a boy get that many wickets before."

"So, basically, you were jealous of what he could do?" Ash concluded sourly.

"Well, yeah, I suppose I was at first. But it wasn't for myself, I mean, my dad used to push me pretty hard. He used to demand things of me. And, back then, I was too scared of him to stand up to him. I tried to be the best at everything. I tried to be the son he wanted. But when Daruk came along, I just couldn't compete with him. But the one thing that I had that he didn't, was friends. He didn't really, because he'd just moved to our school." Frankie said shamefully.

"So, it was because you envied him, not because we were brown?"

Frankie sighed.

"Yes. It only started because I was threatened by him. And then later, something else happened... and I was just so scared of my father finding out-"

"What happened?"

"It was… it was on the afternoon of Daruk's first day. He didn't know his way around the school, and he stumbled into the old theatre thinking it was the science lab. I was in there…with someone."

"Popeto Charpentier?"

"How did you know?"

"I guessed. Carry on", Ash ordered.

"I was just so angry he'd walked in on us. I thought he was going to tell somebody. If my father found out about us he'd have *killed* me. I tried to tell him I was gay when I was thirteen, and he grabbed me by the neck and held me up against the wall. So, I panicked, I thought it would be easier to scare Daruk rather than reason with him. I was ignorant back then. I thought that maybe he had a religion or something which would have disagreed with it, I don't know what I was thinking."

"But, what did my brother say? I don't think he would have had a problem with you and Popeto, my brother wasn't like that, he never judged anybody-"

"I know, I know! He didn't! He said that he didn't care, he said that we're all just human." Frankie sobbed. "But then I just found myself squaring up to him, and I hit him. And he made some wise crack, outsmarting me and I just felt humiliated in front of Popeto and… and I decided to have it in for him, for anything and everything: being Indian, you guys living on a council estate… it didn't matter what, I used it against him."

"*How* did you bully him?" Ash asked, placing the gun on his knee.

"What?" Frankie asked, perplexed as to why his captor could possibly want to unravel such truths.

"How did you bully him? What did you do to him?

It must have been pretty brutal, considering he took his own life."

"Um, I used to taunt him, and call him names."

"What names?"

"I can't remember... all sorts."

"Remember. *Tell me.*"

"Um... I called him a Paki a lot, I guess. And Monkey Boy. Raghead too. I said he didn't deserve to be in our country and on our benefits. I said he was povvo all the time."

"What else did you do to him?"

"I used to wait for him with my friends and we'd steal his lunch or if he had any money, we'd take that. When we'd corner him, I beat him up pretty hard. The others would... hold him down. I knew I wasn't as strong as him."

"Popeto and Billy? Your two friends from the woods?"

Frankie nodded grimly.

"Did you feel no shame? Had your mother not taught you right from wrong?"

"My mother?" Frankie whispered, shuddering a little. "She did. I guess I knew what I was doing was wrong, because I hid it from her. And my dad, like I said, he was only interested in good results and us achieving."

"So, you had a pushy father? Am I supposed to feel sorry for you? Being pushed doesn't excuse what you did," Ash exploded, "it's not like you were uneducated. You literally had no heart."

"I know, I know, of course it doesn't excuse anything. I'm not trying to excuse myself. Ash, I would do *anything* to go back and change what I did. There hasn't been a day gone by when I don't think about what

I did, about what happened. I hate myself for it. I hate myself, truly. I want to punish myself. I want to pay for what I did. That's why I came to work for you. Do you think I didn't know what you'd do to me?"

Ash let out an agitated groan, as he tried his hardest not to let the man's honesty compel his empathy, or soften his heart. He ripped at the grass, tearing blades up and tossing them into the dug-out hollow whilst he thought. They watched the green shoots sink into the cement. Then, trying to understand, Ash finally opened his mouth to speak.

"So, all your self-harm scars, all your trips to the counsellor, that's all been because you feel bad about what happened to my brother? It's always been about him?"

Frankie nodded. "Of course."

"You must have beaten him up so bad, for him to think there was no other way out. I just can't believe he ended his life. I thought Daruk was the most resilient and strong person in the whole world. You reduced him to nothing. He gave up because of you, he must have been so scared." Ash said, picturing Daruk hiding away in the toilets, eating his packed lunch by himself. It broke his heart.

Frankie spoke slowly, "He… he was resilient, he was strong. I don't think beating him up was the worst thing I did to him."

"Well, what was?"

Frankie's eyes widened in disgust.

"I… I took away Daruk's only friend."

"Which friend? Daruk had a friend in that place?"

Frankie nodded. "Of course. When he first came, he had quite a few friends. In class and out on the field.

But I took them away from him, one by one. I couldn't stand him having a little army against me. I was selfish. I was cruel."

"What, you just told them to stop being friends with my brother?"

"I paid them."

"You *paid* them?"

"Yes", Frankie said morbidly, digging his nails into his wrist.

"Stop doing that, it's disgusting", Ash snapped, glaring at the man's scarred wrists.

Frankie stopped immediately. "Sorry", he croaked.

It was strange - speaking of his brutality towards Daruk after being silent for so long, made Frankie feel somewhat lifted, to finally not be running from all the guilt he'd held on to for so long.

For Ash, hearing of the trauma, made him feel oddly close to Daruk again, and he wanted to know *everything*, even though each home truth hit harder and more painfully than the first.

"There was one friend Daruk had, called Thomas, Thomas Matthews. They sat next to each other in science. I told Thomas to stop hanging out with Daruk, and he refused. He said Daruk was his best friend. I offered him cash, I said I'd give him goalie on the football team, but he still refused. He said he would rather be Daruk's friend, any day."

Ash smiled faintly, feeling fondness to the brave stranger he'd never even heard of. Thankful there was at least one kind human in that place.

"And?"

Frankie looked to the ground in disgrace.

"We cornered Thomas in the toilets. I thought he

was going to tell the teachers about what we were doing to Daruk. Billy held him down and I shaved the side of his head with a razor, and we set his collar on fire with a lighter. I told him that I'd make it worse every day until he stopped being friends with Daruk, and, eventually, he did. I remember laughing at their fallout."

Ash was devastated. "What did Thomas say to him?" he pressed.

"He said he didn't want to be his friend anymore. That they had nothing in common and that he'd only ever been nice to him because he pitied him. I think he was too ashamed to tell him the real reason was because I'd threatened him."

"What did Daruk say? Was he upset?"

"Of course he was upset, but I think deep down he must have known what was going on. He told Thomas that everything was going to be okay, and that he would never hold it against him."

Ash's tears stung. He sat silently for a moment, grieving. And then his rage returned.

"But, I saw you went to University. You were in all the societies. You worked in London for years. You can't have felt bad your whole life. Don't lie to me."

Frankie nodded.

"I never wanted to go to uni after high school. It was my dad's dream, not mine. But he'd offered to pay and I felt obliged. Yes, I went to Oxford, I was off my face most of the time, in between my studies, just trying to escape. It's all a bit of a blur. Later I got a job in the investment bank. But I had a complete breakdown there, I couldn't take it anymore. I needed a job where I didn't have to think. So, I left, and became a landscape gardener. That was the last time I spoke to my dad. And

I haven't seen or heard from my mum since I was at school."

"Why not?"

"She walked out on us, a long time ago."

"Why?"

"It was… it was because of what happened."

"What? To my brother? That doesn't make any sense. You mean you told her you caused him to kill himself?"

"She found out that I'd been bullying him. She said she was ashamed to call me her son, and she left us, and took my sisters with her."

"Wow", Ash remarked. "Yet, you never actually tried to say sorry, for what you did. You just tried to run from it, your whole life. To protect yourself. Did you ever once think of us, of what you did to my family? You ruined us."

Frankie gulped, hesitantly.

"I… I did. I followed your lives. I wanted to reach out to you, so many times. But I… I wasn't sure if it was disrespectful, or would have hurt you more. So, I tried… I tried from afar."

"What does that even *mean*?" Ash snapped.

"It doesn't matter. Forget it. It's not important."

"Tell me now. Tell me what you meant by that", Ash spat, pointing the gun.

Frankie held his hands together tightly. "I just, I wanted to do something for your family. I knew it could never make up for what I'd cost you… but I just had this urge to make sure you were all okay, somehow. So, I… well I went on a little venture of my own. I don't know what I was thinking, but you'd disappeared off the radar, you, your mother and sister. It's when you were living in Southampton. I just wanted to find out where you'd gone and that you were okay. I managed to trace an uncle of yours, and found he was living in a care home in the UK. I went and volunteered to read to the residents of the care home, and I read to your Uncle Deeptendu on his death bed. We talked, a lot. I didn't tell him who I was or that I knew you, but I asked him about his family. He told me that all his relatives lived in India, all except you, your mother and sister. He was losing his mind a little bit, with the illness, but he started telling me about how he regretted the way he had left things with you, how he regretted the way he had walked out on your father. And then it came to me, when your uncle told me he was leaving everything in his will, to you. I looked over his will one night when he'd fallen asleep, he didn't own an estate in England, and just had a failing business and a few sentimental belongings. But, I had access to my trust fund by this point and so-"

"The money!" Ash interrupted, in complete shock. "The money my uncle gave me, it was never his, was it? It was never his money. It was yours."

Frankie nodded solemnly, "But the letter was all him. He meant every word he wrote. He wanted to apologise to you, he wanted to explain about your dad. I just, I transferred the money into his account just before he died, so that it would be passed to you through the courts. I wanted you to be okay."

"You gave me one hundred and fifty thousand pounds! I built my whole career on that money, and it was from *you*." Ash spat out the words as if they were sour, in a state of disbelief.

Frankie, in remorse, bowed his head once more.

Ash ran his hand over his face, as he often did, when he felt anxious or stressed. He was absorbing everything he had heard. He stared at Frankie, who had stopped shaking and trembling, and was gazing calmly up at the noose hanging from the tree, somewhat peacefully. The tears on his cheeks had dried, and he was faintly smiling as he looked towards the rope.

Ash tried to piece together the facts, though his mind was spinning with a mixture of vivid, violent images of Durak being brutally beaten up, and graphic play-outs of Frankie slashing at his body in self hatred, as a grown man. He envisioned Frankie hunting down his uncle and concocting a plan with him. He thought about the money he'd received, all those years ago, and how it had helped them out of poverty. How it had afforded his mother a new house.

In that moment, Ash truly believed that Frankie was a changed, sorry, and broken man over what he had done. Ash knew he regretted even being born. His adult life had proved that. Suddenly, some wise words, from a very long time ago, spilled into his mind, fitting the moment poetically.

"We are all just products of what has happened to us, Ash"

He hadn't understood back then what his older brother had been talking about. But now, he did. He thought about the darkness which Frankie's father had passed onto him. Which Frankie had passed onto Daruk. He thought about the darkness which was passed onto Billy Thatcher, and in turn, ended Billy Thatcher's girlfriend's life. He thought about the darkness which had been passed down to his own father, Anjani Lakhanpal, by his stepfather. And then, he thought about Daruk. The brother so determined not to pass the darkness on to anybody else. Who decided *enough*. And so, the boy had indeed been selfless- taking the darkness with him, in his death. But Ash was most hurt by this. Had Ash not made it clear to him how much he'd needed him?

No, it was not enough.

It was too late.

The past could not be undone.

Ash took a deep breath.

"Frankie, I believe you, you know. I actually *believe* you are sorry for what you did. Your life has been ruined almost as much as my mum's was, as mine was. My mum's never lived down the guilt, she thought it was all her fault, you know. Do you know how painful that is? Waking up every day, only because she had me and my sister to take care of, but really, just wanting the same ending that took my brother?" he said sadly. "Do you know, I trusted Daruk more than anybody else in the whole world, and he let me down as hard as any person can let another person down, and it was all because you pushed him to it. The old Daruk would have *never* given up, not ever. He would *never* have left me. But you dehumanised him and diminished him, until he was a shell of a boy! That's what *you* did, because you had no heart. You know Frankie… it's not enough that you're sorry. My brother was my best friend. He was the closest thing to me. He was the most popular boy in the whole school back in India. And it makes me sick that he didn't have a single friend in his life, the day he died. And it's because you took them all away. You didn't just take anyone, you took someone really damn special. You took him from all from us. I'm not that same kid you met in the woods anymore, I'm not a coward. I'm not a wimp and I'm *not* scared of you."

"I know Ash, I know."

"I'm going to do what I should have done a really long time ago. I'm going to *fucking kill you*. I'm going to hit you for every hit you gave my brother, and then I'm going to watch you hang."

The words flew out of Ash's mouth in fury, but he was trembling as he spoke. Part of him still wanted to just run away, find a safe place, hide, and cry forever. But he would not back down, not this time. He propelled his body through the air, and landed with a thud on top of Frankie. Wrenching his legs together in a tight vice, he straddled Frankie's torso, and sent his shaking fist straight into the gardener's cheekbone. Frankie didn't resist, but clenched his fists around the grass, and screwed up his face, shutting his eyes in anguish.

Ash punched him again, this time sending his left hand into the whimpering man's eye socket. Frankie's brow cracked beneath Ash's knuckles, sending a sharp pain up Ash's wrist.

"I hate you! I *hate* you!" Ash cried.

The harder he hit Frankie's face, the more droplets of blood spurted through the air and covered his grazed knuckles. He was consumed by hate, sadness and rage. Nothing was helping. Nothing was easing the pain.

He stopped, purely from exhaustion, and lifted his fists from the quivering man, who's face was swelling and covered in puddles of blood and tears. He looked like something from a horror film, with a swollen eyebrow which drooped over his eye, and a cheekbone which had turned itself into his skull.

Was Ash sickened by the sight of him, or, was he

sickened by the actions of his own hands? He wasn't sure. He leapt off the man, and as he did so, the gun he had placed in his back pocket slipped out and plummeted into the wet cement in the hollow pit. He gasped, listening to the sound of the gun sinking. Scurrying across the grass on his hands and knees, Ash swung his legs over the hollow and dropped into the cement.

"Don't! Stop!" Frankie groaned in agony, but it was too late. Both of Ash's ankles were submerged and swallowed by the thick, gloopy, cement. Though it was still wet, it was so heavy, pressing down on top of his feet, that he could not lift them. It was an intoxicating, trapping, claustrophobic feeling, sending quivers of panic down his spine. The gun had sunk.

And Ash's immediate reaction was to search for it, but, just as he went to thrust both hands into the toxic sea, Frankie crawled to the edge of the pit, leaning over it,

"Ash, don't! It's quick-dry!" he panted, "you'll never get your hands free!"

Ash let out a roar of frustration and rage, desperately trying to wriggle his feet free, but they were stuck. He wobbled, and threw his hands against the side of the pit, holding onto the grass for grip.

Frankie lay on the grass, panting and running his hands over his bloodied face.

"Get away from me, I'll kill you. I'll kill you!" Ash screamed, his eyes darting around for an escape.

But he was in a hopeless, tormented nightmare, and now, Frankie was in complete control. Had this whole thing been one huge act? Was there still an evil heart in Frankie's body, that had just been waiting to sabotage

Ash this whole time?

Frankie weakly scrambled to his feet and wiped his bloody hands over his shirt. He was shaking hard.

"Let me help you", he breathed.

"No", Ash spat. "You get away from me. I don't need your help. I don't need your money. I want to kill you. I am going to murder you."

"Does anyone else know you're here?" Frankie asked, trying to think straight.

Ash looked the man up and down curiously, threatened by his hidden agenda.

"Yes. Yes, Marcus is coming soon, he was going to help me seal everything up. He will be here any minute so you won't get away with hurting me. Marcus has a gun too", he lied.

Frankie nodded. "That's not why I asked", he said, "I just want to make sure somebody is coming who can get you out when I'm gone."

"I will find you again. You can't run anymore, Frankie. I will kill you. It's a promise", Ash scorned.

And then, something which took both of the men by surprise, happened. Frankie let out a small, pathetic, chuckle. And then he sighed, with an all-believing, all-encompassing, release of genuine breath, which relieved his pain, his anguish, his disgust and all of his shame.

"I don't doubt that, Asha Lakhanpal", he said. "You have the same determination your brother did."

And then, the troubled, broken man, staggered towards the noose.

Ash's eyes widened in disbelief, gawping as Frankie dragged the nearby white metal chair beneath it. Then, quivering, Frankie used the noose to haul himself up onto the chair, so that he was standing on it, with legs of jelly.

Ash's heart began to race. He wanted to scream, but no sound would rise from his voice box. He stood there, frozen, compelled by a spell of fascination. Everything inside him had willed for this moment, for as long as he could remember. Every embittered part of his pained heart had wanted this, to bring him freedom.

And yet, as he watched Frankie pull the noose over his bloodstained face, and tighten it sadly around his own neck, there was a part of his heart, which he had long forgotten even existed, which ached, with an even deeper sadness. It was the sadness of the fleeting realisation, that no amount of anger or hatred, and not even this sick conclusion, could bring his brother back. It was the part of his heart, that was wise.

"Ash," Frankie said, as he pulled the noose tight around his neck, "there's something I need to tell you, before I go."

Ash waited, still frozen. Unable to speak.

He then nodded slowly, feeling the sudden, all-consuming churn of uninvited *empathy*.

Frankie gulped, and then hesitated. And then, he closed his eyes for a moment, as Ash waited for what felt like an eternity. When Frankie said the words, the words changed everything. They swarmed through Ash's conflicted mind and penetrated his heart with an unrelenting, all convicting, unbelievable, truth. Because finally, it made sense.

"Ash" Frankie whimpered, *"Daruk didn't kill himself."*

Ash stood completely still, letting the words wash over him, too shocked to breathe.

Frankie's eyes met with his. "You deserve to know the truth. You shouldn't be angry at Daruk, and your mum shouldn't blame herself. Daruk didn't give up. He never gave up", he breathed, shamefully, as though it was killing him to say the words.

Frankie held the noose around his neck as it began to choke him, causing his voice to croak and grow faint.

"That day, the day Daruk died, there was a terrible accident."

Ash shook his head in anguish, disbelieving.

"What kind of accident?" he whispered.

20

THE BOY WITH THE BRIGHTEST SMILE

Essex, England, 2001

Daruk gazed around at the sea of white faces waiting to enter the sports hall. Their whispers made his ears burn with discomfort.

"It was Daruk who gave Charlie that bruise, apparently."

"I think Charlie's gonna do him at break time."

"Daruk could beat Charlie to a pulp, everyone knows that."

"I hope Daruk batters all three of them to be honest, everybody thinks they're pricks."

Thomas Matthews hung his head in shame, listening to the comments, glancing over at Daruk regretfully.

Then, robotically, they streamed into the exam hall. Daruk's peers were like clones, heads down and lips silent, obeying an invisible dictator of control. The desks were all lined up in rows, each separated a few metres from the next. His year group marched to their seats nervously. Daruk wasn't afraid of the mock English exam, though. He was quietly relieved that a test so regimented and closely supervised, meant that he was safe from the ambushing of Charlie Wincott and his friends. Charlie was thankfully sat nowhere near him in the exam hall, although Daruk could feel his pale eyes burning on his back, probably conjuring up his revenge from the fight they'd had the previous week in the woods.

There was nothing left for Daruk here. He had endured this school for a year too long. He looked around calmly, in the knowledge that it would all be over soon. He felt surprisingly peaceful. There was just one last battle, before he conquered the world.

The headteacher blew the whistle dramatically, and there was a loud gust of pages turning on each desk, as the students revealed the test question. For the next hour and a half, Daruk poured his heart out, onto the page, earnestly. It was a freeing feeling, writing deeply and truly, knowing nobody was ever going to read his work.

For a moment, Daruk got lost in his words, slipping into the paradise inside his imagination. There were tears in his eyes as he thought about all the things he'd wished had turned out differently, and the life he had lost in Kashmir. Then, he decided to face his captor, and turned around, resting his gaze upon Charlie. The boy was face down, writing his own test paper with intense concentration, the purple bruise on his cheekbone still swollen.

Daruk was intelligent. He knew there must be a missing piece in Charlie's life that meant he was so consumed by bitter hate and anger. After all, Daruk knew anger was just an outlet of deep sadness. He gazed at the boy a while longer, compelled by a sense of sheer determination. He was ready to face his demon and win back the life he'd lost.

He was the boy who never gave up.

After he was expelled, Daruk knew he would never have to see Charlie ever again. And the family social worker had been speaking of finding them a better house for weeks now, in a new area, in Southampton. Daruk would be free.

The teenager finished the last sentence in his paper, and quietly, began tearing the page out of the test booklet. He didn't want any of these people judging his work. And he wouldn't be around to see how they'd graded him anyway. Drawing as little attention to himself as possible, Daruk folded his page of writing up and slipped it into his trouser pocket, leaving his blank booklet on his desk.

Then, Daruk watched the clock.

He thought back to the day he had first concocted his plan. It had liberated him. Mr Timmins, his school drama teacher, had explained that "*any fighting within the school, results in permanent exclusion*". And that was when Daruk realised, he didn't have to put up with his perpetrators, or the misery with which they filled his life, anymore. He would get himself *expelled.*

When the Head blew the sharp whistle, there was another flurry of test booklets being closed as everybody in the sports hall exhaled a breath of relief. But, for Daruk, he inhaled a breath of anticipation.

When he collected his school bag from the pile of bags left on the edge of the sports hall, he hastily slipped his test paper inside, and grabbed the knuckle duster which he dropped into his pocket. Then, he rushed through the corridor of teenagers who were chatting about the test and headed for the boy's toilets. It was the start of break time. Daruk knew that Charlie, Popeto and Billy all played football on the school field at break time, and that's where he would find them. And that's where he would start the fight. The fight which would get him expelled, and set him free.

Shaking, Daruk sped into the empty toilets, and stared at his reflection in the mirror. His eyes had grown so dark, and his face was pale and lost. Who was he, now? He envisioned Ash's bright face, and it willed him to continue. He couldn't bear the trauma that he'd subjected his brother to in the woods that day. They had hurt Asha, and that was one step too far. He was ready to fight.

He gulped.

Daruk slipped the knuckle duster over his fingers, and clenched his right fist, feeling it's steel, tight-fitting protection. Then, he ran his hand over his face, and headed out of the door, but somebody was waiting for him in the corridor.

To his surprise, it was Mr Hogan, the head of sports.

"Daruk, I need to see you in my office, right now", he said sternly.

Mr Hogan had always been fond of Daruk, and he favoured the boy quite significantly, due to his impressive abilities as an athlete. Daruk had never seen him cross before. The sports teacher had realised that Daruk appeared unhappy at school and was puzzled by his apathy when he'd been offered positions as sports captain multiple times, and turned each offer down. He'd assumed there might be some racism among Daruk's peers, but had never caught the perpetrators.

The teenager followed the man into his office, which was decorated with glass cabinets boasting cups, medals and photographs of students' achievements over the years. There were also the leader boards in each sport the school took part in; football, sprinting, cricket, rugby, athletics and the like. Daruk Lakhanpal's name was at the top of every single board, in a league of his own. He'd broken every sporting record in the history of the school.

That meant nothing to him now. He sat down in front of his teacher's desk, and as he did, he slipped the knuckle duster back into his bag.

"Do you know why I've called you in here, Daruk?" the young, bearded teacher asked.

"No, Sir."

"Daruk, I was invigilating your exam this morning. I saw you putting something in your bag at the end of the test, and then you rushed off to the toilets. I need to know whether it's a cheat sheet, Daruk. We take cheating very seriously in this school, and there's no reason for you to cheat-"

"It wasn't a cheat sheet, Sir. I'm not a cheater." Daruk argued, agitatedly. The thought that his plan was slipping through his fingers was distressing.

"Then what was it, Daruk? You clearly had it with you during the exam. I'm going to give you one last chance to tell me the truth, and then I am going to examine your school bag."

Daruk looked at the ground and thought for a

moment. He was desperate to get out of the school. If Mr Hogan rifled through his bag he would surely find the knuckle duster. Would that be enough? He could only hope.

"Sir, it was an English paper. How could I have cheated? There were no right or wrong answers", Daruk said, firmly.

Mr Hogan frowned. "Pass me your bag then, son."

Daruk handed the bag over, gladly. He watched as Mr Hogan examined the contents, sifting past his lunchbox and his fluorescent green Gameboy, barely noticing his torn out test paper. Then, he saw the shiny object. Stunned, he glanced up at Daruk, disbelievingly. He placed the knuckle duster on the desk.

"Daruk, this is a weapon", he gasped. "Why are you carrying this around?"

"I've never used it before, Sir."

"That's not the point. I'm not sure you realise how serious it is to bring a weapon to school. It's criminal."

"So, I guess you're going to expel me then, Sir?" Daruk asked with anticipation, bouncing his leg up and down.

The teacher furrowed his eyebrows in concern.

"Daruk, if you're in some sort of trouble, you can tell me. And we will go to the head teacher together, and explain the situation. I just don't understand, a boy of your skill and ability could be a world record holder, you're Olympic standard. Why are you throwing away all your talent? Are you in a gang? I know the estate you live on is a challenging place to be, but-"

"I'm not part of a gang, Sir. It's nothing like that."

"Daruk, I don't want to see you go. You have unmatchable capabilities. But you need to start talking, is there a problem at home?"

"No, Sir. Honest. I just want to go home."

The teacher fiddled with the knuckle duster, fixating at its new finish with not a scratch to be seen.

"You've really never used this before?" he asked, in a predicament.

"Never", the boy answered.

"I'll tell you what I'm going to do, Daruk. You know I have to disclose that you've been found with a weapon. I'm going to call your mother now-"

"She's at work, Sir. She won't answer."

"Well, perhaps if we keep you here after school, when she's finished, she can come in and see us."

"I have to pick up my younger brother after school, Sir, I can't be late for him."

The teacher reached for the telephone on his desk, and called through to the head teacher's office. His receptionist answered.

"Oh, that's right, I forgot about the meeting." Mr Hogan sighed, as he put down the phone.

He turned to Daruk.

"Okay Daruk, this is what's going to happen. The Head is in a meeting all day, he's gone off site. I'm going to confiscate this weapon and suspend you for the rest of the day. I suggest you go straight home after picking your brother up. Tomorrow morning, with the head teacher, I will call your mother, and we will need you both to come in so we can discuss an appropriate course of action."

Daruk nodded, *elated*. He could go home and he hadn't even had to punch Charlie again.

*

It was 11:30 am when Daruk set off down the country lane leading from his school's estate. He knew in his heart, no matter what came of the phone call home the following day, he was never going back. He wouldn't do it. He was free. He didn't care what lie he had to make up to his mother, or to his head teacher, but he would think of something. He would think of something so bad that it would mean he'd never have to set foot on those grounds, ever again.

Daruk felt the autumn sun on his face as he breathed in the chilling air. He then burst into a sprint, as fast as he could, down the path towards the town. It was exhilarating. He felt like a bullet, finally released from a barrel, or a bird from a cage. He didn't need to live in misery anymore.

As he passed freely through the town, he thought about how he was going to take Ash out to the river that evening, and how he would be able to give him his full attention, laughing and playing with him. He thought about the prospects of the new house that Marie Coles would find them in Southampton, and moving to a new school, with a fresh start.

Daruk felt a new lease of life, as he set foot into the woods that day, allowing the golden leaves to crunch beneath his scruffy shoes. He smiled and looked to the branches of the trees, which were reaching to the sky. It was all going to be okay now. The past was gone, and the future was his. Daruk was excited to see Ash. He knew he could make up for pushing him away. After all, his brother was forgiving.

Suddenly, Daruk felt the harsh throttle of a sharp stone hit the back of his head. He spun around,

devastated at the sight of Charlie and Billy.
Would they stop at nothing?
Why couldn't they just leave him be?

Daruk rubbed the back of his messy hair, soothing where the stone had hit. Then, he clenched his fists in preparation, fuelled by the adrenaline running through every inch of his quivering body. He was ready. He knew it would be *bad* this time, after what he'd done to Charlie. They were skipping school to get him.

Daruk glanced around the abandoned woods. Not a soul in sight. He was completely alone.

There was a steep drop behind the trees which outlined the border of the woods, where an abandoned railway track lay beneath. Or, he could run deeper into the woods, but Billy was on his BMX, and Daruk wasn't sure he could outrun a bike, even if it was ridden by an unfit pig of a teenager.

"Look, I'm leaving the school. Isn't that what you wanted? Why can't you just leave me alone?" Daruk exclaimed, glaring into Charlie's piercing eyes.

"Just leave me alone!" jeered Billy mockingly, looking at Charlie for approval.

But Charlie's eyes were fixed on his prey. He felt intimidated by Daruk's muscular arms and pulsating neck. He knew the Kashmiri boy could pummel him, but he couldn't let go of his determination to destroy him. After all, Daruk had humiliated him in front of the one boy he wanted to impress the most; Popeto Charpentier.

"You think if you leave our school then that'll be it? I know where you live, Raghead." Charlie repulsed, spitting at Daruk's feet.

"Charlie, I could really hurt you. Just like I did last

week, but it'll be worse this time. I'm telling you, to leave me alone. I'm giving you one last chance", Daruk reasoned, edging closer to the two boys. "I'm not afraid of you."

Billy gulped, remembering the crunch of Charlie's cheekbone when Daruk had smacked him before.

But Charlie stepped forwards and peered into Daruk's eyes with a disgust so strong, even he felt controlled by it.

"Who do you think you're talking to, brown boy? I'll finish you", he promised.

And then suddenly, Daruk felt his ankles be pulled from underneath him, as he fell to his knees with a thud. A strong set of hands then pushed down on his back, sending his face flying into the mud.

"What now?" Popeto gasped unsurely, quivering as he held down Daruk's hands.

"Take his bag", Charlie ordered.

Daruk spat out the dirt that had entered his mouth when his face hit the ground.

"Get off me!" Daruk cried. "Get off! Popeto, I know it's you. You don't have to be controlled by Charlie!"

Billy ripped the school bag off Daruk's back and got a sick thrill out of pinning Daruk down with his heavy body. Popeto then backed off, disgraced by what he was a part of. Charlie crept up to the boy who was being held down in the mud, and towered over his struggling body, feeling the surge of power come back to him. But it was not enough. He slowly placed his foot on the side of Daruk's face, and pushed down on his skull, sending it deeper into the mud.

"He's got a Gameboy in here", Popeto remarked, rifling through Daruk's schoolbag, trying to create a distraction from the torture that was going on. Although he was afraid of the consequence. Popeto watched uncomfortably as Daruk inhaled the mud, growing ever enraged at the foot trampling down on his head, and the ogre on top of him which impeded his power.

Although his hands were being held behind him, and he was weighed down by Billy's ugly frame, Daruk used *all his might* and the determination in his chest to launch himself off of the ground and fling his perpetrators away. Billy flew through the air at the force of Daruk's strength, and Charlie lost his balance, falling backwards. This gave Daruk a split second to rise to his feet, and he kicked his foot forcefully into Billy's groin. Billy groaned in agony, falling to his knees and clutching himself.

Popeto threw the green Gameboy over Daruk's head and it was caught by Charlie, who sprinted over to the edge of the trees, towering above the drop. The bully held the green Gameboy over the railway track, dangling it teasingly.

"The monkey's been let out of his cage!" Charlie seethed, gritting his teeth in hate. "Come and get your Gameboy then!"

"Give it back!" demanded Daruk angrily.

Popeto raced over to the drop nervously, leaving Billy on the ground, still sore.

"Give it to me", repeated Daruk fiercely, thinking about the Gameboy his mother and Ash had so thoughtfully got him for Christmas.

"It's so old", Popeto laughed weakly, although his voice was verging on desperate. "I bet his mum bought him that Gameboy. They don't even make them like that anymore!"

"Come and get it! How many men did your mum have to sleep with in the ghetto to buy you this?" Charlie whispered, holding the green toy ever higher in the air above the drop.

Daruk swung his arms out to reach for it, but the Gameboy barely brushed his fingertips. He looked at the drop below, where the rocks jaggedly poked out of the muddy verge and over the concrete patch where the old railway track had finished. Charlie propelled himself even higher, standing on what was left of a crumbling old red brick bridge.

And then, Daruk watched as Charlie's menacing eyes changed. In a second, he saw the boy's pale blue iris's fill with regret, and a silent scream open Charlie's mouth. Billy had limped over to Daruk, creeping up on him from behind. And with his chubby, greasy hands, the monster pushed the boy, the boy who never gave up, the boy with the brightest smile, and he fell through the air. Flying through the cold autumn breeze, Daruk saw the flashes of the golden and brown leaves, flurrying around him. He heard the faint cries of instant regret fall out of Popeto and Charlie's mouths, and the cackle of Billy Thatcher. Charlie held his arms out over the drop, willing the boy back in immediate panic. But as Daruk soared, he didn't think about what had been done to him. He thought about all that had been done *for* him. He thought about the country, which exceeded all subliminal beauty, and raised him up. He thought about the jungle, the mountains and the lakes. He thought about the garden, the palace, and the school encased by a forest of banyan trees. And, he thought about the brother, the brother who'd be waiting for him. The brother he wished he could embrace, one last time. Yes, in his last moments, Daruk felt only love.

And then, Daruk died.

*

"What have you *done*? What have you done, Billy?" Popeto wept, crouching over Daruk's still body. He frantically tried to feel for a pulse, placing his two fingers beneath Daruk's strong jawline. There was nothing. He hovered his shaking hands over the boy's chest, but as all three boys leant over their classmate, they could see his neck was broken.

Popeto scratched at the leaves on the train track, retching and spewing up on his knees.

"Oh, please. Please!" he cried despairingly, letting the guilt engulf his body.

"I didn't mean for him to die, you twat! It wasn't my fault!" Billy fumed. "Charlie was leaning over the drop, I didn't know it was that steep! I didn't think he'd break his neck, did I?"

"How could you *not* know?" Popeto exclaimed. "We used to mountain bike by the drop all the time, you know how steep it is, you liar! I saw you push him! We need to call the ambulance, the police-"

"No, you can't! You won't, you won't or I'll kill you, too!" Billy stressed, squaring up to Popeto. "If you call the police then we'll all go down. We'll go to fucking juvie! We were all in this together, you were the one who cornered him from behind Poppy, you held him down, he'd have gotten away if it weren't for you, you little rat."

"Oh, what have we *done?* What have we *done,*

Charlie?" Popeto begged, holding his wet face in his hands.

Charlie was knelt next to Daruk, haunted by his motionless frame. Completely silent, totally shocked. His face was white and clammy, and there was a wet patch seeping through his groin.

"He's gone", Charlie whispered, in a morbid trance. "I deserve to go to prison. I deserve to die."

"Oh, shut up, Charlie. Shut up! None of us are going down for what we did. You *hated* him. We all did", Billy accused.

"I didn't", Popeto cried. "I fucking didn't. I should never have gone along with it."

Charlie looked at Popeto, apologetically. With the utmost regret in his eyes. If only Daruk had never seen them together that day. If only everything had been different. If only, he hadn't been so afraid.

"Look, let's just get out of here." Billy demanded, looking up to see if anybody was around.

The woods were quiet.

Charlie looked fixedly at the mud on Daruk's face and the faint footprint on his cheek. He wiped it off with his sleeve, and tears filled his eyes.

"I'm so sorry", he whispered. "I'm so sorry, it wasn't you, it was me. I'm so sorry, Daruk"

"They'll know it was us. Think about all we've done to him", Popeto said, sickened by the thought. "The whole school knew we were out to get him, all the shit we did to him in the corridors and the toilets and the changing rooms! They know we're missing from school too! We'll go down either way."

"No, all we need is an alibi. We could cycle to town now and rob a shop and then the police will come and, *wait,* Charlie - your dad!"

Popeto's eyes widened. "Oh wait, yes! He's the chief of police. He could cover for us. Call him Charlie, maybe he'll help us."

"I can't call him. He won't help us. He already hates me."

"But he's your dad!" Billy argued. "He's the one in charge. He can create an alibi for us. Call him Charlie, *call him.*"

Then Popeto turned to Charlie, and held his hand.

"Please Charlie, I don't want to go to prison. I never wanted to be part of this. I just did it all for you. Do this for me. Please call him."

21

THE TRUTH PART II

Surrey, England, 2019

Ash's lips quivered, as his tears tracked uncontrollably down his cheeks. He couldn't bring himself to speak. He couldn't quite believe his ears.

Frankie tightened the noose around his neck even more, although it caused him to squirm in discomfort. His voice croaked out the words as if they were on fire.

"Your brother never left you, Ash. He was coming back for you that day. He was on his way to pick you up."

Frankie then watched, as the man before him, stuck in the cement, released agonising, deep and disturbed high-pitched cries, one after the other. They were the cries he had been holding onto, for his brother.

"I'll be here, Ash"

"I will never leave you, I promise"
It had been true.
It was true.
That made it hurt, a million times more.

Ash squealed in agony, like a small child who cries out in the night and cannot be consoled. He placed his head in his hands for a long time, before gasping for breath.

"But he was hanging there. I saw the noose. I was the one that broke him free!" he spluttered, defiantly.

Frankie shook his head weakly. Ash could hear the air fighting to escape his crushed windpipe.

"After we climbed down the drop, Popeto and I tried to bring Daruk back, but it was too late. I didn't know what to do, so I called my dad. He was in the police back then, he was the chief superintendent of the whole county. He drove to the woods and came to meet us. He'd brought a rope in his van, and he helped us cover it up. It all happened so fast, he directed everything. He told Popeto to go and keep watch because he was crying so much and kept throwing up. And then my dad, Billy, and I lifted the body, and we hung him on an oak tree." Frankie sniffed, "We took everything out of his bag that might have had our fingerprints on. And my dad drove us all back to my house. He rung up the school and told them that he'd caught us all truanting in my bedroom, smoking weed, a couple of hours before. So, there was an alibi for our absence. And then, we just had to wait. Dad made sure he was the first on the scene as an officer when the police were alerted about a death in the woods, and he closed the whole case down, as a suicide. We were all sworn to secrecy. All of us."

There was a grim silence, as the story seeped through

Ash's veins. He knew in his heart, it was the truth.

He never left you. He was coming to pick you up that day.
He never left you.

How could he ever have doubted Daruk?

This was Daruk, the brother, the *only* brother he'd ever known to be true. The brother who would never have left him. The boy who never gave up.

And suddenly, Ash didn't feel angry anymore. He was heartbroken.

He looked up at the man responsible. Frankie was readying his squirming legs to kick the chair away from beneath his feet.

"Asha, I'm truly sorry", he breathed.

Ash looked into the man's eyes, and for the first time, saw a human. He could hear Daruk's voice in his head, again.

"Your reality doesn't have to be your destiny"
"Forgive him, brother, and the pain will stop here"

"Stop", Ash whispered. "Don't do it. I don't want to watch you, anymore. I can't watch."

Frankie hesitated, "I'm ready to do it, Ash. I want to do it."

"No. That's not what my brother would have wanted. And you owe him. If you're really sorry, you'll come down from there. Nobody should have to see somebody hang."

At that moment, both men were startled by the sudden rumble of a car engine trolling across the field outside and growing ever louder.

22

THE DELIVERY

Surrey, England, 2019

Frankie was torn, but obligingly pulled off the noose around his neck and freed himself of its grip. As he did so, he realised he felt more relief inside of it, than outside of it, as he faced his grim reality. Ash twisted his body awkwardly, panicking at the sight of the door in the distance.

Frankie stepped towards Ash and fell to his knees above the cement pit, shattered and gasping for breath.

"Marcus? You said Marcus was coming, right?" he asked.

Ash ignored him and they waited in anticipation before the door slowly creaked open.

"Ash, Ash?" the woman's soft voice called out.

"Oh no, please no", Ash whispered, mortified.

Lola held her large bump with one hand, and with

the other, ran her fingers along the wall, as she gazed around at the garden, taking in its beauty with wonder.

"Ash? Ash are you here?" she called again, timidly peering around at the first path.

"Who's she?" Frankie whispered, "your sister?"

"Worse than that, she's my girlfriend. And she's carrying my baby." Ash gulped.

Frankie staggered to his feet, mustered up the strength to clamber onto the white chair and tried to untie the thick rope from the tree as he reached up, but his face was throbbing.

"It's okay, I'll help you explain", he whispered.

"I don't want your help", Ash said harshly.

"Ash, Ash where are you? I can see your car outside", came Lola's voice.

"She sounds frightened", Ash muttered under his breath, hearing the rope finally fall to the ground and land with a thud. Frankie leapt down from the chair, and threw the rope to one side.

"Lola? Lola I'm down here." Ash called out into the trees.

She stumbled along as fast as she could, following his voice down the little wooden pathway, until she was confronted with the small clearing where the two men were. She glared at the cement encasing Ash disturbingly, and then her eyes darted up towards Frankie, who was standing weakly on the grass.

"Ash!" she gasped, throwing both of her hands over her mouth in shock.

"Lola, Lola I can explain", he begged, coaxing her to move around the pit so he could see her properly, from his twisted position. She moved towards the bloodied man who had collapsed on the grass.

"He needs help, we need to help him!" she screeched, wincing at the sight of the cuts and bruises all over Frankie's face. He looked into her eyes, silently, giving her a faint smile. Then, she dropped gently to her knees, and crawled over to the pit where she reached for Ash's hands.

"Ash, what has happened to you?" she asked. "I know who *he* is. I know everything."

"What? No, Lola, it's not what you think-"

"No, no it is exactly what I think. I thought you were having an affair, but this is ten times worse! You came here to kill a man, look at the sight of him. I don't know who you are", she said, letting go of his hands.

"Lola, I'm sorry. I'm sorry, please just give me a chance to explain."

"There's nothing to explain. I know he's the one from Daruk's school. I spoke to Nina, Kenny's wife. She found the three grand from you appear in his bank account, he told us all about your little break-in. And I've seen all your plots up at The Loft and how you came here to hang him. I know he's Charles Wincott. Or Frances or whatever you wanna call him! I know everything. I can't believe how much you've lied to me."

She caught a glimpse of the noose which was beneath the tree.

"Oh, it's true", she gasped. "I don't even know who to call for help now! Do I call the fire brigade to get you out of there? Do I call the ambulance for him? Or the police for *that*?"

"No, no don't call anyone", came the moaning voice, and Ash and Lola both turned to look at the mess of a man. "I've got some tools that can get him out", Frankie confirmed, "and I'm fine, really."

Lola sighed deeply, saddened to her core.

"I wanted it so much, not to be true."

"Lola, I'm sorry. I just, I needed to… he took my brother away. It was all his fault." Ash wept. "I wanted to tell you. I wanted to tell you so many times. I went to counselling like you asked. Please Lola, I'll do anything to make it better. He's not dead. I didn't kill him."

Lola shook her head, "No, but look at him, you've beaten him senseless, he's halfway there. And I'm guessing he would be dead if you hadn't got yourself stuck in that cement pit. Ash, I know you did what you did because you're traumatised, and yeah, it's so messed up. But it's more than that, I've got no place for lies in my life, not with my baby."

"*Our* baby! It's our baby, Lola. And you're *my* girlfriend! Please, I'll do anything Lola, I'll do anything. I'll make it better. I wanted all this to be over before our baby comes. I did it for you, for *us*. So that we can be a family, we can start again."

"That's not the point, Ash. You think I can't be with you because you've beaten up a man and you tried to kill him? The same man you hold accountable for your brother's death? I get it Ash, you wanted revenge. Don't get me wrong, if anyone touched my family I'd be driven to do the same as you. That's not even it, if you'd just have let me in on your thoughts, we could have gone through this together. I would have come to counselling with you, we could have worked through it, *together*. I'd never have given up on you, if you'd just given me the chance. But you shut me out so many times. I tried to help you and you hid this whole part of your life from me. And now, I just can't trust you. I feel like there's so much of you I don't know. And it scares me that you don't have any mercy. Where's your empathy?"

Ash was disgusted at himself, and mortified that the person he loved most knew the ugliest parts of him, now. But as he listened to his girlfriend breaking up with him, all he could do was blame Frankie. After all, this was all his fault. *They* murdered Daruk.

Frankie staggered to his feet once more, but the throbbing in his head caused a dramatic dizziness, "I'll go and find my tools", he mumbled, but then he collapsed gently onto the grass, falling to his knees again. "I just need a moment."

"Oh, shit. I need to call an ambulance for him. My phone's in the car", Lola breathed.

"I'm fine, honestly. It just hurts that's all. I just need a minute", Frankie explained, spitting his back tooth into his hand.

"See, he's fine", Ash urged. "Lola, look please don't leave. I'll call a friend to come and get me out, and then we can talk about this. I'm ready to be a good father. I can give you everything."

"Ash, it's too late for that. I'm going to the car and I'm going to call an ambulance."

"No!" both men shouted, in unison.

"His face looks like it's about to fall off!" she said crossly, rubbing her bump protectively and looking at her boyfriend with the deepest disappointment.

"It could have been so different, if you'd only told me, Ash."

Ash groaned, "I couldn't. How could I? What would you have thought of me?"

"More than this", she whispered.

And then, Frankie sat up, and cradled his legs in his

arms, resting his chin on his knees, and rocked back and forth gently to ease his pain. "Lola, that's your name, right?"

Lola looked at him worriedly and nodded.

"Stop talking to her!" Ash said territorially, but he was soon silenced by Lola's darting glare.

"Yes, that's my name… Charlie?" she said softly.

"I go by Frankie now. Lola, can I tell you something about me? Because your boyfriend didn't."

Ash dropped his jaw in fury, but Lola willed Frankie to continue.

"I didn't come from a family that really showed love for each other. My mum never held me, and my dad told me he was ashamed to call me his son. On Daruk's first day at our school, he got lost and so he stumbled into one of the old classrooms. He walked in on my boyfriend and me, we were only kissing. But I was so afraid he'd tell someone."

Lola listened to the man intently, whilst Ash grit his teeth bitterly.

"I wanted to drive Daruk out. I thought that if I was the best at everything, I might be able to make my father proud of me again. But when Daruk started to play sports, he was twice the boy I was, and more. He knocked me off every leader board. I used to bully others to feel important, to feel in control, to feel on top. But I think when I met Daruk, I wasn't just jealous of his talents. I was jealous of his life. I was jealous of the love. Because even though they lived in that shitty council estate and they didn't have any money, love stared me in the face every time I heard Daruk speak about Ash, or when I watched him stand up for his brother in the woods, or talk about picking him up every day from school. I envied that, I didn't have anybody who loved me like Daruk loved Ash. I wanted to know love like that."

Lola's stare softened, and she glanced at Ash down in the pit, who was still unwillingly silenced. For the first time, she was beginning to understand how close the two brothers had been. How special their bond was. She reached out her hand to him, and Ash slid his palm painfully inside of hers, feeling her grip encase him. They both willed themselves to look towards Frankie, and this time, Ash was inclined to listen.

"Carry on", Lola whispered.

"My point is, it was a lack of love that drove me to do what I did back in school. And it was the presence of love I guess, that drove Ash to do what he did today. I think he was hiding himself from you, to protect you. *Because* he loves you. I think it was love that drove him to avenge Daruk. I don't know anybody who would love me enough to kill for me, or who would die for me. So, if you're going to leave him, you should know more about the love he came from, because I'd say that's a love worth having in your life, for your child. I think Ash has been angry this whole time, because he thought his brother abandoned him. That would make it hard to trust anyone I think. But, Daruk never killed himself. I killed him. I murdered him in the woods with my friends, and my father made the whole thing look like a suicide. We got away with it. Ash found that out today, that's why he attacked me. But he stopped."

Lola's jaw fell open in amazement, and she turned to Ash.

"Is it true? Is what he's saying true?"

Ash stared into her deep dark eyes passionately,

craving her comfort.

"It's true", he finished.

Lola shook her head, astonished.

"So, your brother was murdered", she whispered in heartbreak.

The three adults were silent for a moment, as the solar powered lanterns which hung above the garden began to shine through the dim air, emitting a magical glow and illuminating each and every rock, statue and flower.

"I really loved him", Ash breathed sadly, and Lola nodded, trying hard not to cry.

"I know you did", she said, as her heart broke for him. "I just don't think you can ever move past this, I don't think *we* can ever move past this, unless…"

She stopped, breathing sharply, touching her stomach.

"Are you okay?" Ash begged.

"It's fine, just a slight pain", she replied, eyeing up the white chair, a little way away from her on the grass.

Frankie reached for the chair, and, still sitting down, dragged it towards Lola, but Ash reached his arms and waist over the top of the pit, past the woman, and snatched at one of the chair legs, "I'll do it, I'll get it", he said, glaring at Frankie, who immediately backed away.

Ash strained to position the chair above the pit, and Lola clambered up on it, and leaned forwards, peering down at him.

"We can move past this. Tell me what to do and I'll do it. Counselling, I'll turn myself in to the police, we can move away, I'll quit my job-", Ash listed, but Lola shook her head.

"None of that's going to work, Ash. There's only one way you can be free", she whispered, smiling sadly, at the impossible truth.

"I'll do it. Tell me. Just don't leave me. Please don't leave me."

"Ash", Lola gulped, "you have to *forgive* him."

Another silence. Frankie looked up in bewilderment.

"I'm not saying forget about what happened. I'm not saying that. I'm not saying you have to see him ever again. But you have to do this, for you. It's the *only* way you will ever be free in your mind. It's the only way you will honour Daruk, because he wasn't a boy of hate. He was a boy of love-"

"I can't."

"I thought as much."

"I *won't*", Ash said abruptly.

He shook his head and pulled his hand away from Lola's soft touch. It killed him.

Lola reached into the pit, and stroked Ash's cheek, wiping away his salty tears.

"Well then, I can't stay. I can't stay with you. I'm sorry Ash. I can't live with a prisoner. With someone who's not free. I want our baby to know love, and only love. I'll miss you… so much."

Lola stood up, and turned to face Frankie.

"I… I don't know what to say. Thank you for telling me the truth. I guess you'll work him out of that mess, won't you?"

Frankie nodded, in turmoil.

"Goodbye", he said.

Ash and Frankie looked at each other, and for the first time shared a common thought.

They both wished in that moment, that things were

different.

"Ouch! Ow! Ah!" Lola winced, as she stepped a few feet away from the men. She pushed her hand against the oak tree, leaning on it, and with her other hand she clung to her stomach, panting.

"What is it? What's the matter?" Ash cried, throwing his torso over the edge of the grass and clawing his nails into the soil, begging his feet to become unfixed.

Frankie crawled to his knees, but remained respectfully distant from the young woman, submitting to Ash's judgemental stare.

"Ouch, it hurts, Ash. My stomach, it's tightening. It's the baby", Lola said desperately, falling to her knees.

No. no. *no.*

"It's okay, honey. I'm here. It's going to be okay." Ash spoke the words so confidently, but his eyes were darting around the scene in a desperate attempt for *any* idea. He was truly trapped.

"Ouch!" Lola screamed, falling to both hands and knees. She breathed quickly, puffing and panting, "Ash… I think it's a contraction!"

Ash's eyes widened.

"What do you want me to do?" Frankie asked.

"Nothing! Stay out of this", Ash snapped, pulling at his phone in his pocket. The screen was black, the battery totally dead. He tossed the useless block of plastic onto the lawn.

"Lola, darling, pass me your phone. I'll call an ambulance", Ash ordered, as he agonisingly watched her suffer on all fours, clutching the grass beneath her hands, breathing in and out, in and out, just as they'd practiced in their anti-natal classes.

"I told you, it's in the car. My phone's in the bloody

car!" she breathed, turning her head towards the creaky door in the wall, which now appeared to be so far away.

Ash looked to Frankie regretfully. "Well, get your phone out then!" he ordered.

Frankie pulled his phone out from his back pocket, and shakily fought with it as if it were a slippery block of soap. He rushed it over to Ash. "I've got no signal. I never have it in the garden", he said, holding out the screen to Ash, worried he wouldn't believe him.

There were no bars of signal. Ash groaned angrily. "Okay, go outside, and find signal… Please", he begged.

Frankie nodded, "I'll find it!" he promised, and then he began staggering as fast as he could, across the lawn.

"Ahh! Ahh! My waters have broken. I think the baby is coming, Ash. I'm scared." Lola panted, turning to face Ash, and in that moment of desperation, wanting only a safe delivery, she looked to her boyfriend lovingly, forgetting all that had gone before.

"Frankie will get the ambulance, baby. It's going to be okay. It's *all* going to be okay", Ash reassured her. "I'm here, I'm with you. Can you crawl towards me?"

Lola began to walk her hands towards the pit, but the tightening drag in her stomach overpowered every inch of her body, and she screeched out in pain.

Frankie had disappeared through the door in the wall, out into the evening, tripping and stumbling as he went.

They were totally alone.

Ash had no control. Just as he'd had no control the day he'd found his brother in the woods. He'd tried everything to bring him back.

Ash clawed at the grass helplessly, reaching inches away from Lola's fingertips. In the smallest steps, she edged closer to him, until their fingers were intertwined, and she squeezed his hand with all her might.

"I think this baby is coming, like, right now! It's not going to wait", she said, terrified.

Ash's heart was beating so hard it felt like it was going to explode through his chest. He'd planned out the birth so many times, in his head. They'd be in the biggest, cleanest, private hospital room, and he'd have decorated it with photos and flowers. He would be sitting by her bedside, holding her hand every step of the way, and there would be only the best nurses and doctors on hand.

With each torturous scream, his perfect vision slipped further away, and he wriggled in the pit helplessly, looking at the woman he loved, suffering on her knees, as the white lights hanging over her illuminated the pain on her face.

"Okay, keep breathing, baby. Keep breathing, we'll do it together. Breathe in, breathe out. Just like they taught us", he said soothingly, rubbing her hands, and reaching for her hair. He grazed her soft curls with his fingertips, brushing them out of her eyes.

She squealed in agony, scrunching her face up so that creases swam around her eyes and cheeks.

"I'm with you, I've got you", he soothed.

"I've forgotten what to do. I've forgotten", she panicked, begging at his eyes. "Please Ash, please, I'm scared for our baby…"

"Don't be scared. Don't be. Frankie's going to come back. I know he will. I remember what to do. I remember. Should I check that dilation… dilation thing?"

"Absolutely not!" Lola puffed. Though when she

was filled with the next excruciating shudder of pain, she felt like something was wrong.

"Oh, I don't know. I don't know. Just do something, anything!" she begged.

He ran his hand along her back, begging for a saviour to the situation. But there was only himself. And he had no idea what he was doing. He remembered the session on giving birth that they'd attended. And he'd listened intently to the nurse going over the breathing and pushing process. But everything that came before that, he'd forgotten. It was the nurses' job to check when the woman was ready to push. But how did they check? In the obvious way? He knew she should be dilated to ten centimetres. Not from the sessions, but from a movie he'd directed once with a graphic birth scene.

"Don't look, don't look at me", Lola begged, and Ash stared only into her eyes, as he reached around and checked her body gently. "Well?" she asked, "what do you think?"

"I think it's not time yet. You need to keep breathing. In and out. In and out."

Ash pulled away from her body for just a moment, and unbuttoned his shirt, throwing it over her lower back. Then, he ripped off his t-shirt, and balled it up, placing it on the grass.

"Do you want to lie down? Use this as a pillow", he said, gently helping her down onto her knees.

She fell gently onto her back, propped up by her elbows. And he pulled her jeans over the bottoms of her feet, letting his shirt cover her dignity.

She reached her arm across to the pit, grappling his hand and pushing her forehead into his. They breathed together, in and out, in and out, and each time she winced in pain, she sent surges of fear through his hand, along his arm, and into his heart. But he remained calm, calm and strong. He kissed her forehead, and willed her to carry on.

"It's going to be okay", he said again, and again, until she actually believed it.

*

When Frankie flung the door of the garden open again, he was juggling a collection of items in his panic. He dashed towards them madly, but carefully stepped around Lola.

"The ambulance is going to come as quickly as they can, but there's been a fire in town so it could be some time", he panted, throwing a blanket down on the grass. He also had with him, a small pickaxe and a hammer, some painkillers, a water bottle, and some empty green industrial sacks, which he was laying down in a frenzy.

"I got these from my car. But I could drive her to the hospital still?" he suggested. "Only if you want me to."

"Of course we don't want you to!" Ash said, scornfully, running his hand over his face.

Lola squeezed at him, "Ash, I'm frightened, what if the ambulance takes too long? You have to let him take me. I want to be with you baby, only you, I do. But I'm scared for the baby."

Ash gulped, "I don't want him touching you. I've got you, I'm helping you. I'm here. Give us those painkillers", he ordered, glaring at Frankie.

Frankie brought them to Lola's head, but she batted them through the air.

"Unless it's an epidural, I don't want them! Ash, you

have to let him help me! Help *us*. It's the only way. None of us know what we're doing!"

"But I can remember what to do, I checked you, you're nearly ready to start pushing and the ambulance has to come, they have to. I don't want to leave you. I need to be with you."

"Ash, listen to me! You know this isn't about that! Ash, it hurts! Do you love *this* baby more than you hate *him*?" she breathed, pointing at Frankie.

"What?"

"Which is it Ash, which is bigger? Your love for me or your hate for him? Because your love could save me, but your hate could kill us."

Ash let out a groan of anguish, literally thinking through his worst nightmare, staring it in the face.

Frankie knelt awkwardly, shaking in discomfort, like a timid child.

"Owwwwww!" Lola screamed, and he watched her arms and legs shake in suffering. In that moment, he realised his answer.

"You. I love you more. Of course it's you", Ash breathed. "I'm sorry I don't know what I was thinking. Frankie, take her. Take her to the hospital. Please, take her for me. I'm begging you."

"Of course", Frankie said, taking hold of Lola's arms, and lifting her to her knees. Ash watched in agony, as she wrapped her hands around Frankie's strong biceps, hauling herself to her feet. Ash's shirt dropped from her waist, revealing her body, and the blood, and the water which trickled down.

Frankie held her steadily and grabbed a green sack. "Wrap this around you", he said, but Ash snatched at it, and strained to spin it around her waist.

She swung her arm over Frankie's shoulder, "I love you, Ash. It's always been you", she panted.

"I love you too. You're going to be okay. Go and have our baby!"

Frankie kicked the pickaxe and the hammer, down into the pit, and it landed on the dry cement with a thud.

"Dig yourself out, and we'll be at St. Margaret's Hospital", Frankie said, as he turned to Lola, and she waved Ash goodbye.

Ash grabbed the pickaxe desperately, and placed its pointed edge over his feet. He then snatched up the hammer, and without a single hesitation, fighting through the pain of the awkward angle and stretch of his back and leg muscles, began smashing the hammer down onto the pickaxe, penetrating the cement, trying to break himself free.

"Ahh! Ahh, I can't! Stop! Stop, it hurts!" Lola screamed, and Ash flew up to see that they had only stumbled a few yards away, and Lola was falling to her knees, on the wooden path. Frankie fell to his knees beside her.

"Ash, I think the baby is coming, like, right now", he said, horrified. "What do you want me to do?"

"Um... can you bring her back? Bring her to me... slowly, *gently*", he insisted. "It's okay, Lola, honey, you're doing great. I'm here. I'm coming", he called, throwing the hammer down harder into the cement. He watched the solid trapping slowly begin to chip away and crack beneath his force, sending shards of grey cement flying through the pit.

Frankie held the entirety of Lola's weight on his shoulders, and carefully, stepped her back over to the pit. The dusty bag trailed on the ground, falling from around her waist. They reached close to the edge of the pit, and Lola collapsed into Frankie's arms tiredly, and he lowered her onto the blanket. Ash strained to reach her, but she was a few inches too far.

She covered herself over with the other half of the blanket, and spread her legs wide, leaning back on her elbows.

"That's it, Lola. Well done, sweetie. Keep going."

In between her deep breaths, she occasionally let out a squeal.

"What now? What now, Ash?" Frankie panted, careful not to stare at the woman in labour, even though her sweating brow and screaming grimace was all he could see.

"Um, I need to check that she can push, I think. I need to check she's ready", Ash said uncomfortably.

Frankie cringed, "Really? I'm not sure I can do that."

"You won't be doing it!" Ash insisted. "Can you get her any closer? Closer to me?"

Frankie looked at the predicament, at the woman who was laid on her back, in a slump, ready to give birth.

"I don't think she can be moved", he concluded.

Ash panted, exhausted from his digging. He glanced up at Lola's frightened face, as she turned to face him in agony. Her body was turned from him, so he could only see her shoulders, neck and head, and two knees which rose up in the air.

"Well, well can you come and get me out then?" Ash asked, completely beside himself.

He winced as the willing man, leapt into the unrelenting pit, and fell at his feet. Frankie bowed his head at Ash's feet, and chipped away carefully at the cement. His hammering was far more precise and effective than Ash's mad and enraged digging had been. He focused on pinning into one section of cement, creating neat, deepened holes which in time, Ash could see would be joined to lift one huge chunk away. Ash wriggled and squirmed aggressively, though he fixed his eyes on Lola.

"Ahh! Ow!" she screamed, biting down on her lip.

"Are you pushing? Are you pushing, honey?"

"Yeeeeeess! I'm pushing! It's coming! It's coming!" she cried.

Ash glanced down at his feet, where Frankie was still chipping away at the ground vigorously, to the sound of Lola's screams. The determined man slammed the hammer down repeatedly, and Ash watched as he created a deep indent of holes, in a semi-circle around the tops of Ash's feet.

As time went on, the sky had now turned dark blue, revealing a full litter of shimmering white stars, which glinted down on the willow trees, outlining them in silver. Ash continued to encourage Lola over the top of the pit, longing to be beside her.

"Ash, I think it's coming out. Ash, help! Get over here!"

Ash wriggled his feet, but they were still trapped. Frankie had managed to break away half of the cement laying on top of them, but there was still a thick layer to cut through. He glanced at Frankie uncomfortably, knowing he wouldn't be freed in time, despite Frankie's efforts.

"Ash, I need someone here", Lola begged.

But it was only her next scream which caused Ash to surrender.

"Please, get my baby out", he asked, placing his hand

defeatedly on Frankie's shoulder.

Frankie handed Ash the hammer and pick-axe, and crawled out of the pit. He scurried over to Lola's head.

"Don't look below her waist", Ash commanded, frantically smashing the hammer down into the ground immersing him.

"Ash, I need him to", Lola panted, "I think the baby's head is coming out, aaahhh!"

Ash growled.

"Well?" Frankie asked.

"Get down there and get it out! Please, I'm begging you", Lola gasped, pushing at Frankie's shoulder.

But Frankie hesitated.

"Do as she says, please", Ash confirmed, before Frankie plunged down to take a look between Lola's legs.

Ash's whole body was overcome with a sickening discomfort, but it only forced his body into battering the cement harder.

"Keep pushing! Keep pushing, you're almost there", Frankie called, grimacing squeamishly at the sight before him, whilst trying to mask his repulsion. "I think it's the head! The top of its head is coming out!"

Ash looked at him worriedly, "Um…" he stammered, "… um, keep pushing."

"I am!"

"That's it, it's coming out, it's coming out!" Frankie yelped, screwing up his face in disgust. He reached for some more green sacks and bunched them up at the bottom of Lola's thighs.

"What are you doing?" Ash asked.

"There's so much blood!"

Ash pounded the ground harder and faster.

"The head's out", Frankie said grimly, but his face was troubled. "It's not crying. It's a bit purple, there's something wrapped around its neck."

"*What?*" cried Ash, "No!"

"The cord! It's the cord", Lola screamed. "Take it off, you have to take it off. Unhook it. Please!"

Frankie held his hand over his mouth. "Ash? Are you nearly out? I don't think I can", he quivered. "I can't. I can't do it."

"Do it! Please! Ash tell him, Ash the baby-"

"*Please, please,* Frankie, take the cord off." Ash asked, as he pulled a huge chunk of cement away from his feet, and stepped one foot out of the hole. The other one began to wriggle, but was still trapped.

"Please don't make me", Frankie sobbed, trying not to wretch.

Ash touched the man's hand.

"Do this for me, and your debt is repaid. I'll owe you everything."

Lola listened to his words.

"Okay, okay, I'll try." Frankie gasped, reaching his hands into the mess. He squirmed and squealed, as vomit crept up inside his throat, and Ash watched with desperate hope. His thoughts now were only for their baby.

"It's off." Frankie finally breathed, in another attempt not to spew. "It's off."

And then, the sound of a small cry filled the garden.

When Ash heard his baby call out to him, he yanked his remaining trapped foot free of the hole, scraping all the skin off his ankle. He then hauled himself out of the pit, and crawled desperately across to Lola.

He slipped his hands underneath Frankie's, which

were cupping the tiny round head, and together, they waited for the shoulders to slip out into their arms, the body, and the little feet.

Lola gave one final screech, and the baby lay in the men's arms.

Frankie stabilised the newborn in Ash's hands, and then let his own hands fall away, and rubbed Ash on the shoulder, collapsing on the grass, finding his breath.

It was a little girl.

Lola sat up, exhausted.

"It's a girl!" Ash elated.

"Bring her to me, bring her", Lola begged.

Ash cradled the tiny bundle adoringly, and brought her up to Lola's chest, where he rested her very gently.

He then wrapped his arms around Lola, kissing her head, and she leant on him, as they cuddled their little girl.

"Oh, *wow*", Lola expelled, feeling utter *joy* at the sight of the perfect gift.

Ash stroked the tiny button nose, and ran his hand over her soft head, slipping his finger into the squidgy small hand which clasped his. Her eyes opened for the first time; they were a deep blue, wide like her mother's.

Ash's heart felt like it was about to burst, the feeling consumed him from head to toe, and left space for absolutely nothing else. He was in pure love. And it was the best feeling in the entire world.

Lola laughed gently, letting a tear fall onto their daughter's cheek. Ash sobbed harder than the baby, overcome with adoration.

There was room for *nothing* else.

The lanterns shone down onto the baby's perfect face, and the family huddled together, lost in the love.

Ash looked up for just a moment, and caught a glimpse of Frankie, who was smiling gently from where he looked on. Then, he stood up. "I think that's the ambulance", he said softly, as they listened to the faint sirens outside. "I'll go and let them know where to come."

Ash nodded, as Frankie began walking away.

"Frankie?" Ash said.

"Yes?"

"Frankie - thank you."

Then, Ash returned to his loving embrace with his daughter, and Lola kissed him passionately.

23

THE TEST PAPER

Surrey, England, 2019

Ash opened the envelope carefully, as Lola's distant voice sung their infant to sleep in the nursery upstairs. As he brought it into his living room, which overlooked the Surrey hills, he read the letter that had slipped out of the envelope and onto the carpet.

Dear Asha,
I'm sorry I kept this for so long, but I'm glad I did keep it. This was our mock exam paper back at school. It was in Daruk's school bag the day he died. It turns out he did have a friend. The best friend of all, it would seem.
It was you.
In faith,

Frankie

UNDER THE BANYAN TREE

ENGLISH LANGUAGE PAPER
MOCK GCSE EXAM

DATE: 17th September 2001
NAME : Daruk Anjani Lakhanpal

Question: *In as much detail as you can, describe a memorable place which is of significant importance to you. You should explain what your choice symbolises and why it means so much to you, highlighting the emotions, connotations, and memories you associate with it.*

*A Banyan Is Forever
by Daruk Lakhanpal*

Most people in this country might have never seen or heard of a banyan tree before. Banyan trees grow in India and begin life as epiphytes; that means they grow from another plant. However, the banyan, once a small fig dependent on another living thing, after time, gains enough strength to generate a life of its own. And when it does, it is magnificent. Banyan trees can grow up to one hundred feet in height and their branches and roots are able to spread over several acres. They are the most spectacular, enticing, and inspirational tree of all.

A banyan tree is the symbol of immortality. I looked up immortality in the dictionary, in my father's mansion, when I was seven years old. Immortality is defined as:

"the ability to live forever; eternal life."

Therefore, I chose to use this tree as an analogy for explaining to my little brother how much I love him. He used to ask me all the time, "How much?", "For how long?", "How far?" The banyan tree which stood outside my home, in Kashmir, India, is of the greatest significance to me, because it reminds me of my brother, Asha. And Asha Anjani, is the single most important person to me in this world. He is my best friend.

My brother looks up to me. He believes that I am brave, strong and intelligent. I would agree with the intelligent part - most children don't know how to use a dictionary when they are only seven. And yes, I suppose the strong part is true as well; Ash has never been able to beat me in an arm wrestle. But what my brother does not realise is, he is so much braver than I am. You see, Ash lives in a world of fear. He suffers from anxiety and worries about all that is around him. But, my brother wakes up every day and faces all that frightens him. As a person who is unafraid, I am inspired by how brave he is. For without fear, there can be no bravery.

I watched Asha walk to school, when he knew there were snakes on the path.

I watched him set foot on an aeroplane, when he was frightened of the take off, and even more scared of the place we would land.

I watched him walk through the playground of a new school, in a new country. The new kid.

I watched him stand by my side when we were in trouble, when I knew all he wanted to do was run.

I am so proud of him.

It is Ash and I against the world. It has always been that way. I have loved Ash since the day my mother told me that I had a baby brother in her tummy. All I ever wanted was a brother. And Ash has been that, and so much more. I remember the day he was old enough to climb the banyan tree with me, for the first time. He was frightened initially, but after that, the banyan tree is the place we would always go to hide from the rest of the world. It kept all our secrets. It heard all our dreams. A banyan tree's arms are always inviting; they will hold you up whether you are black or white or brown.

So, I guess that brings me back to when Ash questioned how much I love him and I told him,

   "For as long as this tree is standing."

He wouldn't have been able to understand back then, but, it was because the banyan is a symbol of immortality. And I will love my brother for all time; through life, past death, and into eternity. If someone was to cut the banyan down or remove it, it wouldn't matter, because its roots run too deep. A Banyan Is Forever.

I feel like Ash depended on me as he started out in life. He learnt from me and needed me to protect him and encourage him and let him know everything would be okay. But Ash, once a small child dependant on his older brother, has become strong enough to generate a life of his own. And now that he has, he is magnificent. I know my brother will grow into the most spectacular, enticing and inspirational person of all, because to me, he already is.

24

THE BANYAN TREE

Kashmir, India, 2023

Ash stood on the widespread veranda, beneath the shade of the balcony, and leant against a pillar, looking out at the garden on the perfect summer's day. It was as wild and enticing as it had ever been when he was a child. The flowers were still abundant, and their sweet scents floated through the warm air. He listened to the sound of the crickets and kingfishers chirping, as they got lost in the vines and the trees.

He watched as a small Kashmiri boy who had been found begging on the streets of Srinagar, jumped over the crumbling walls of the garden, and hit the grass with a thud.

"*I'm late! I'm late for class!*" the child exclaimed, dusting off his knees and racing towards the mansion. He was so distracted by the beauty of the garden, and the expanse of the mansion, that in his fluster, he tripped and fell at Ash's feet.

"*Mister! Mister, please help me*", he gasped, "*I'm late for my first class here! I heard that Mr La-Pal, the Hollywood director, is here visiting and I don't want to walk in late to his school on my first day. Will you help me find the right room?*"

Ash grinned and crouched down in front of the small boy, until they were of equal height. He lifted his Ray-Bans, and giggled.

"*Calm down! It's okay. I'm sure Mr La-Pal will understand.*"

"*I don't know, Mister! He's the owner of this whole academy and he's opened it up to children like me, who can't afford to go to school. I'm so scared I've ruined my chances by being late. My mum is going to kill me. I'm the first one to go to school in our whole family!*"

Ash looked at the small boy with even greater fondness. He admired his honesty.

"*Haven't you got a watch?*"

"*No, Mister. None of my family do.*"

"*What's your name?*"

"*Aarush, Sir. I'm sorry, it's just there was a snake on the path this morning and I was-*"

Ash's smile grew.

"*Then you should take this one, Aarush, then you won't be late again*", he said, unclipping the golden Rolex from his own wrist. He held it out to the small child.

Aarush's eyes widened and he slowly accepted the gift, in wonder. He folded it and slipped it into his chest pocket.

"*You're him, aren't you? You're Mr La-Pal.*"

Ash winked at the boy.

"*I told you he wouldn't mind you being late. Now run on*

inside, and enjoy your first day of school. My mother will help you to your class."

It had been a joyous moment when Ash had held his hands over his mother's eyes, and lead her up to the gates of the mansion where they'd previously shared so many precious memories. He'd purchased his childhood home back in 2021 and converted it into an academy for the less fortunate. He knew it was what Daruk would have wanted. Roshni lived as the housemother of the academy, along with her longstanding friend and her cousin from the village. They took care of the children who boarded at the school. Though Roshni missed her own children dearly, Ash and Lola promised to bring their family to spend their summers in India, every year. Jayminee was also a frequent visitor during the holidays.

This year, Ash had been directing the first film he'd ever written by himself. He entitled it "Kaiya", after his daughter, meaning *forgiveness*.

*

Ash waited in anticipation, as the black car rolled through the front gates and pulled up to the mansion. It was late afternoon.

Frankie's face was smothered in a thick layer of shiny sun cream, and he had sweat patches all over his light pink shirt. He stepped out of the car, beaming.

"Ash, it's stunning! Just like you said", he laughed, running towards the house.

Ash jogged down the steps, and shook Frankie's hand, slapping him on the back, and then embracing him.

"Is it hot enough for you?" he chuckled.

Roshni appeared on the veranda, carrying a tray of hot chai teas. Jayminee followed, placing her slim hand on her mother's shoulder.

"He's here, that's him", she whispered.

Both the women waited on the steps, Roshni somewhat nervously. But she was ready, she'd been ready to meet him for a long time. Ever since she had found out what happened, she released all of the anger and torment she'd felt towards her eldest son. And like Ash, she'd found it in her heart to forgive. It was truly uplifting, although the sadness was still there, the hurt was less, and each hug with her two grandchildren, Kaiya and Daruk, felt even more precious.

"Welcome", she said warmly, as Frankie handed her flowers.

"Hello. It's very good to meet you", he replied nervously.

Jayminee shook his hand. "You must be thirsty", she exclaimed, beckoning him to a seat.

Roshni couldn't take her eyes off the pale stranger, although she gazed at him with a deep kindness and empathy.

"I'll get you some water, mate. Or would you like a lie down first?" Ash asked.

"Oh no, I'm feeling good thanks. I'm excited to be here!"

Ash danced off the balcony and into the house, leaving the three adults in intense silence.

"So, how was your flight, Frankie?" Jayminee's words broke through the awkwardness and immediately put Frankie and Roshni at ease.

"Yes, yes it was good thanks. I watched a few movies

and then I was here!" he laughed.

Ash appeared again on the veranda. "Here they are!" he exclaimed, beckoning his wife through the doorway. Lola looked more beautiful than ever, wearing a long black maxi dress. Her hair had grown down past her shoulders and her skin was fresh. She held Daruk on her hip, and his bright eyes stared at the stranger.

"Frankie", she said happily, reaching over to kiss him on the cheek.

Frankie gulped.

"And this is Kaiya. You've met before", Ash laughed, as his spirited, four-year-old danced towards Frankie. Her face was the spitting image of her mother's, with huge planet-like eyes, a smooth button nose and a dazzling smile. Her ringlets bounced in rhythm with her.

"Hello!" she sung excitedly.

"Hello."

Frankie couldn't believe how beautifully she had grown, from the little lump of flesh he had delivered some years before.

"Wow, this is quite surreal", he remarked.

Kaiya danced back over to Ash, and tugged at his hand.

"Daddy, Daddy, this is the man from the story!"

"That's right, Kaiya."

"From *my* story", she said proudly. "I want to sit next to him."

Ash giggled.

"Go on, I'm sure he won't mind", Lola said softly. Then Kaiya climbed up on the wicker seat next to Frankie, gawping at him.

Lola placed Daruk on Ash's lap, and he gently

rubbed his son's back.

The family asked Frankie about his plans for travelling round India, and he told them of how he'd always wanted to see the Taj Mahal, and the beaches of Goa. They told him about the beauty of Dal Lake, and said that he'd come at just the right time for them to show him the wild meadows and the deer. They sipped at their teas, and listened to Kaiya as she made them laugh with made up stories about how she'd seen and battled snakes at the lake.

"That never happened, sweetie", Lola laughed, and everyone else joined in.

*

Later, when the sun was sitting on the rooftop and setting the lawn on fire, Roshni took to her feet.

"Shall we do it now?" she asked.

Ash looked to his family and smiled. "Yes, now."

"I'll help you, Mum", Jayminee said, and the two women disappeared into the house. When they reappeared, Roshni was carrying the blue china urn, preciously.

The unlikely group made their way down through the beauty of the garden. Frankie admired the flowers, the old crumbling ruins, the waterfall, and the pond.

Ash held his son tightly, and followed after his daughter's enthusiastic dance, watching her adoringly as she spun, and skipped and hopped over the tall grass.

"It's this way to the tree, Frankie. It's my dad's favourite tree", she exclaimed. "What's your favourite tree?"

Frankie stopped to think, "Well, I like willow trees"

he explained kindly. "Have you seen a willow tree before?"

The little girl shook her head inquisitively. "Have I seen a willow tree, Mum?" she asked, and Lola glanced at Ash, winking at him.

"When you were very, *very* little, there were a lot of willow trees around."

They made a circle around *The Banyan Tree*, looking up at its twisted arms and obscure body, with hanging fluffy white vines. Its leaves were green and lush.

They stood beneath its shade, and a wave of peace flooded through Ash, as he kissed his son on his sweet temple, lovingly.

Daruk and Asha's Tree

The carving was still there.

Roshni kissed the urn.

"Why don't you say something, Ash?" Lola whispered.

Kaiya edged towards her father, and nestled her face into his leg, glancing up at the adults.

Ash gulped.

"Thank you all for being here. It means a lot to me", he said softly, squeezing his daughter's hand. "Daruk was an exceptional human, and I'm forever blessed to call him my brother. As long as the sun rises and sets in the sky, we will miss you Daruk, we will love you. I pray we make you proud."

Then, Ash went to pass his son to Lola, and take the urn. But when he saw Frankie's face, his eyes fixed on the tree, with floods of tears rolling down his cheeks, Ash stepped over to the man, feeling only love in his heart. He looked at his son's pure face, and held him out to Frankie, instead.

"Can you hold him, for me?"

Frankie nodded. "Yes", he wept, accepting Daruk into his arms, and holding the infant tightly.

Jayminee squeezed her brother's shoulder, and they all edged closer together. Ash took the urn out of his mother's hands, and opened the lid.

Then he stepped forwards to the base of the tree, and tipped the ashes into the hole which he had dug beneath its overarching branches. As the ashes blew through the wind, and were sprinkled into its deep roots, Ash felt, *free*.

A Banyan Is Forever. He remembered.

The sun's final streaks winked across the dusty garden, and Ash watched the people he loved most in all the world, walk back up towards the house, with Frankie.

He stayed for a moment, smiling up at the tree and feeling peace wash over him. Kaiya turned from her mother's grip, and ran back down to the tree, hugging her father's leg.

"I love you, Daddy", she whispered.

Ash picked her up zealously and placed her on his shoulders.

"And you love me, too" she continued affirmatively.

Ash grinned and placed his hand on the tree.

"That's right, Kaiya", he said, "*For as long as this tree is standing*".

ACKNOWLEDGEMENTS

There are so many people in my life that make me question, 'how did I get to be this lucky, to know someone like you?' Though too many to name, I hope you all know who you are. Maybe we don't even speak regularly anymore, but to the following, I want you to know you have inspired me. I will never forget how important you are to me and have been in my journey. I have some words left over, for you.

Thank you to my mum and dad, for loving me beyond words.

Thank you to my brother, Tom, for being there since the start of my story.

Thank you, Hannah, for no matter what the chapter, it is not *I* but *we*.

Thank you Catherine and Nick and family, for the room inside your hearts.

Thank you Helen, for your prayers, your faith and your smile.

Thank you, Harley, Lydia, Josh, Elsie-Joy, Kyle and Rio, for teaching me no mountain is too tall.

Thank you, Anna, for sharing your gift with me.

Thank you, Alex, for making a dream reality.

Thank you Kat, for your endless generosity and always speaking up for those who can't.

Thank you Ethan, David and Jordan, for a summer of memories and a lifetime of friendship.

Thank you to my shredders in Fernie 2019, for picking me up every time I fell.

Millie, Mollie, Phoebe, Alex, Steph, Rachel and Milo.

Thank you Rav, Jay, Nikita, Maria and Rosh, because every girl needs her *sisters*.

Thank you Bex H and Emily B, for your ever-inspiring work and lives. In the shape of Uganda.

Thank you little Rach, for the big love.

Thank you Denise and Chris, because I can't think of you without being thankful.

Thank you Em B, for living out what is within.

Thank you Martin, for the blessing you are to my life, and so many others.

Thank you Resty, for finding me where I was, as I was, and changing my life.

ABOUT THE AUTHOR

Anna, born in Southampton in 1991, has always loved to write. Stories, songs, spoken word and poetry have been a passion of hers from an early age. Publishing a book has been on her 'things I dream of doing before I turn 30' bucket list for a long time. However, in between working as a sign language interpreter, ski instructor, and travelling around the globe on various ventures, time has never been something she had to spare. That is until, the Covid19 national lockdown 2020 happened, whereby she was able to write and complete her debut novel, *Under the Banyan Tree*.

If you'd like to find out more about Anna please follow her on Social Media at:

Instagram: @AnnaElizabethHaig

Facebook: Facebook.com/aehaigwriter

Printed in Great Britain
by Amazon